BENEATH CORNISH SKIES

Also by KATE RYDER

Summer in a Cornish Cove
Cottage on a Cornish Cliff
Secrets of the Mist

BENEATH
CORNISH SKIES

Kate Ryder

An Aria Book

A CIP catalogue record for this book is available
from the British Library.

E ISBN 9781800243811
PB ISBN 9781800245983

Cover design © Charlotte Abrams Simpson

Typeset by Siliconchips Services Ltd UK

Aria
c/o Head of Zeus
First Floor East
5–8 Hardwick Street
London EC1R 4RG

www.ariafiction.com

Into the forest I go,
to lose my mind and
find my soul.

John Muir

Prologue

Before me lay a thick, impenetrable forest stretching as far as the eye could see. It was dark and foreboding and I shivered with apprehension. In the distance, a firefly darted towards me through the trees and, as the pinprick of light grew closer, it hovered at the edge of the woodland... beckoning. I knew I had no choice but to enter, and though fearful of the unknown I took a tentative step. Pushing aside the undergrowth, I followed the beacon of light and drifted through the foliage like a spirit, twisting and turning through the trees. As I glanced up at the dense canopy that inhibited any natural light, I found my body rising through the branches, without control over speed, until high above the forest I gazed down upon a wild, rugged landscape shrouded in darkness.

On the wind I detected a scent of the ocean. Raising my eyes to the heavens, I watched dark cirrus clouds scudding across the night sky to reveal a wash of twinkling stars and planets. A halo of light surrounded the moon, its inner edge tinged red; the outer an altogether bluer hue. Gazing earthwards again, I noticed the thick tree canopy stretched for miles – like a spill of ink across the landscape – and all at once I was descending. As I plunged through the roof of the forest I closed my eyes, bracing myself against the scratch and claw of twig and branch. But, unscathed, I floated gracefully to the forest floor.

The firefly had waited for me. Resuming my journey, I followed its beacon of light through the trees until we came upon a clearing. Ten brightly coloured gypsy caravans encircled a campfire around which sat a group of people warming themselves from the flames. An assortment of scrawny, raggedy dogs wandered the encampment or slumbered beneath the steps of the caravans, and somewhere close by I heard the comforting sound of horses grazing.

As I hesitated at the edge of the clearing, a sudden burst of laughter drew my attention to a small group of men sitting on the far side of the fire. A man plucked at the strings of a guitar and started to sing; his baritone voice pleasingly deep and smooth. Another cajoled a mandolin into life, while a third accompanied on an accordion. As the song gathered pace, increasing in intensity and tone, a young lad tucked a fiddle under his chin and enthusiastically joined in.

A number of children chased each other around the campfire until someone shouted and briefly halted their game, and swarthy, black-haired men danced with sultry, dark-eyed women – a twist of limbs and swirling colour, as their bodies responded ever more urgently to the primal beat.

Suddenly there was a roaring sound in my head, and as I became aware of the rush of blood pumping through my veins, I realised I wasn't a wraithlike apparition or some whimsical spirit, but that I, too, responded to that beat. For the first time in many years I felt alive.

And then, through the flickering firelight, I saw you sitting on a log on the far side of the camp, deep in conversation with the man beside you. No one had noticed me and, moving closer, I took the opportunity to gaze at your face in wonder. You were not like the others; you shared none of their darkness. Prone to curls, your dark blond hair framed a genuine, open face that was teasingly familiar, and yet not. As your lips formed silent words I studied you: the slant of your brow; the sharp angle of your cheekbones; the shape of your nose; the tight line of your jaw. And I noticed the way your eyes crinkled when you laughed. Suddenly you smiled and I gasped, as intense, stirring sensations took hold deep in my belly.

From out of the corner of my eye I saw a man approaching. He requested a dance but, impatiently, I brushed him away, and when I turned back you were looking directly at me. Your gaze asked a question, and for a heartbeat I stopped breathing. I no longer had the ability to drift and cautiously, as if in experiment, I placed one foot in front of the other and stepped uncertainly towards the fire. But the heat was too fierce and I glanced at you in confusion. Had I misunderstood?

In a voice soft and tender, you encouraged me. 'You can do it. Follow the path.'

A man threw more logs onto the fire and I watched the sparks fly as flames leapt into the cool night air. I bit my lip. How could I follow the path? It wasn't safe. I would burn. Anxiously, I looked across at you again. You were still there, holding out your arms to me with that look in your eyes, and as I made to circle the campfire you spoke again.

'Trust in the journey. Do not fear the process.'

Your words made me hesitate and, filled with trepidation,

I stepped into the fire. But I needn't have feared – there was no heat – and as the flames parted I left my world and crossed into yours.

'I know you,' I whispered, as I looked deep into your eyes.

'You do,' you replied, taking me in your arms.

And as you covered my mouth with a kiss of such sweet urgent tenderness, our passion took me far, far away...

Opening my eyes, the first thing I'm aware of is an unaccustomed easing to the ache that consumes my heart these days. The second is the realisation that I've had *the* dream again. As always, it feels vivid and real... but what does it mean? As the grey light of dawn seeps through a crack in the curtains, the harsh reality of my life swiftly replaces the earlier glow that so cruelly and fleetingly encompassed me.

Sussex

I

It's odd how a relationship can end on such a seemingly small, inconsequential incident. But that's what happened, and however many times I went over the minutiae of our life together there was never any satisfactory explanation as to how we had unravelled so spectacularly without my noticing.

At seventeen and a half I was plucked from a life of indescribable greyness when a tragic accident claimed my parents. They'd never bothered much about me but it wasn't that they didn't care; they were just too wrapped up in each other. They thought that providing me with a roof over my head and putting food on my plate was enough and, subsequently, I spent much of the time left to my own devices. Basically, I brought myself up. I was the unplanned, much younger 'mistake'. My brother was fifteen when I was born and used to having the monopoly on our parents. He showed no interest in this latest addition to the family, and by the time his baby sister was truly aware of him he was on the verge of leaving the family home and off to university; eager to embrace the wider world.

I was a solitary child and had few, if any, I could call true friends. Although, during early childhood there was Shannon, and we were inseparable. She lived three doors up with her family in a small, matching, red-brick, Victorian terraced house, originally built for the local farmworkers. We shared the same view and from our respective bedroom windows looked out across fields of ponies towards the South Downs. Neither of us came from horsey backgrounds but we'd spend every spare minute hanging over the field gate, dreaming of riding wild and free across the downland with the wind in our hair and the sun beating down upon our backs. At first the ponies were wary of us, but we sat quietly where they grazed, only moving when they wandered away. Over time they grew accustomed to our presence and we hopped on their backs while they meandered around the meadows, quietly grazing.

However, at the age of thirteen this idyll came to an abrupt end when Shannon's father accepted a job in Edinburgh and relocated the family to Scotland. What should have been the experimental teenage years – when I discovered what made me tick – were spent largely in my bedroom or wandering the South Downs; the ever-present backdrop to the family home. I often felt adrift and confused, but I found comfort in nature, observing the natural rhythm of the seasons and the way the animals, birds and insects responded to the changes in their habitat.

I could lose myself for hours out there on the Downs, and when the curtain of night fell I would lie in the grass and gaze up in wonder at the constellations. The skies in

Sussex seemed vast. I could recognise the Plough and knew how to locate the North Star, but that was about all. When I was feeling lost and acutely aware of my *aloneness*, it calmed me a little to know that I was but an infinitesimal piece of a much larger puzzle and that there were probably other worlds out there amongst the twinkling stars and planets, as yet undiscovered.

As time went by, the previously shy, wild animals grew ever braver and eventually accepted the girl who sat amidst their natural abodes. Rabbits and hares stood on their hind legs and curiously observed me, and mice and voles scurried around, their noses inquisitively twitching. On several occasions, a hunting kestrel hovering overhead landed beside me. It became quite a game and sometimes she would swoop low over my head, making me duck.

I often returned to the house long after dark, slipping in quietly through the back door. My parents rarely worried about my long absences and I wasn't reprimanded for staying out late. I wondered if they even noticed.

Shannon and I exchanged a few letters, but as she made new friends her correspondence eventually dried up. I drifted through school, daydreaming of the sun, the moon, the wind and the stars, with the intoxicating whisper of a different land and a distant shore forever teasing me, and barely participating in the school curriculum, I was fortunate to scrape through my exams. But always there were the ponies speaking to me of unconditional love and I watched the dynamics within the herd, fascinated by their interaction. I examined their pecking order – sometimes brutal, but always honest – whilst trying to make sense of my own family set-up. What role did I play in my parents' life?

One day, the ponies were loaded into lorries and taken away. I waited patiently for their return, pausing at the gate each time I passed on my way to and from school, but the fields remained stubbornly empty. When the planning notice went up everyone in the road was outraged, but despite the many objections and highly charged meetings, the views of those who lived in the neighbourhood went unheeded. The council approved the developer's planning application and within a few short weeks the builders moved in, and it wasn't long before that once-open landscape was indelibly altered and the fields became an estate of executive homes. Each property mirrored the other with only the subtlest difference, but all had the obligatory manicured patch of lawn and herringbone driveway, on which would sit the latest model of car. All too soon, a new breed of people moved in.

And then one rainy day, a few months after my seventeenth birthday, my life changed forever.

My parents had treated me to lunch at the local pub – an unusual occurrence in itself. The weather was awful and as my father drove home, I grew mesmerised by the momentum of the wipers gliding across the wet windscreen. My parents' banter faded into the background as I concentrated on the manic swish of the rubber blades valiantly attempting to combat the driving rain. A squeal of brakes was the only precursor to mayhem. Suddenly, we were propelled sideways and the car planed across the road, clipping the pavement before rolling over and over.

They say tragic accidents occur in slow motion and it

was certainly true of that day. As we somersaulted across the road and down the embankment, eventually coming to rest in the muddy field below, I had time to coolly reflect that this must be what it's like trapped inside a washing machine. All at once the shocking commotion was replaced by an unsettling stillness. Thick, penetrating quiet filled the air and even the rain was horrified into momentarily abating.

I tried to move my head, but a searing pain shot through my neck and shoulders. Uncomprehendingly, I watched banks of dark clouds scud across the grey sky through an opening where the windscreen should have been. I tried calling out to my parents but I couldn't find my voice, and I noticed how the now-motionless wipers protruded at an odd angle, like broken limbs. And then suddenly he was there, peering in over the smashed bonnet through the open windscreen, and I watched as his stunningly handsome face registered shock and then horror, swiftly followed by anguish. I will never forget that look.

'Shit!' He ran a hand across his forehead, sweeping a long, wet fringe out of his eyes.

My eyes followed him as he moved around the car, and when he looked in through my shattered window his face was ashen.

'Can you move?'

I tried but pain flooded my body. 'No,' I mouthed.

'OK, stay put.'

As if I could have gone anywhere anyway...

He called the emergency services on his mobile phone and I was impressed by the way he effortlessly took control and provided precise directions.

We were only a few hundred yards from our house and I realised the car had come to rest in the last of the pony fields the developers had yet to obliterate. The good-looking young man turned back to the car and peered in at me again.

'Hold on. The ambulance will be here shortly. Be brave.' Inserting his arm through the smashed window, he caught hold of my cold hand.

I gazed at the gold signet ring on his little finger. No one I knew wore such an accessory. This hand belonged to a man of money, someone outside my orbit, and I wondered if he lived in one of the executive homes on the newly built estate.

And then I heard the screaming. It went on and on...

Why didn't the stupid woman stop?

'Shhh, honey. Hold on. Everything will be OK.'

I blinked in surprise. Why was he talking to me like that? But as the screaming subsided I realised the dreadful noise was coming from me.

I tried not to move my neck and shoulders, but as shock set in the spasms became ever more violent and the screaming started up again. The young man with the movie-star looks suddenly withdrew his hand from mine. It had started raining again, coming down in unyielding ramrods but, despite this, he removed his jacket and draped it over my upper body. My eyes widened in surprise and I watched in fascination as his expensive white shirt became saturated and turned translucent, revealing dark nipples that sprang to attention under the onslaught of the cold, unforgiving rain.

In the distance I heard a siren grow steadily louder.

'Not long now.' Movie-star looks glanced up the embankment. 'The ambulance is almost here.'

All at once there was a surge of people and a flurry of activity, and he moved away.

'How are you doing?' A middle-aged man with a kindly face took his place at the broken window.

'I can't move my head or left arm,' I croaked. 'And I can't feel my legs.'

'Don't try to move. I'll brace your neck and then we'll get you out in a jiffy.' He smiled reassuringly.

But they didn't get me out in a *jiffy*. Cutting equipment had to be used to remove the buckled doors. It seemed like hours, but eventually I was carefully eased from the back seat, placed on a spinal stretcher and carried up the muddy slope to the waiting ambulance.

Movie-star looks was still there. He watched over proceedings, wearing a troubled expression, and the paramedics asked who he was.

'David Ashcroft. I was driving by and witnessed the accident. I'd like to accompany her to hospital.'

He was told he would have to follow separately in his car as he wasn't family. When the stretcher was carefully lifted into the ambulance, he stood back and smiled sheepishly at me.

During the journey to hospital, I drifted in and out of consciousness and wasn't aware of much, apart from the sound of torrential rain beating down on the metal roof. However, I was cognisant of the concerned looks on the paramedics' faces as they fussed over me, and when I was eventually told my parents hadn't survived the accident, in my heart I already knew.

David visited every day, each time presenting me with a fresh bouquet of flowers and it wasn't long before my corner of the ward overflowed with various blooms and heady scents. I shared his flowers with the other patients to brighten their day. Everyone loved David; it was easy. Not only was he extremely pleasing to the eye, he was also concerned, charming and witty, and as the weeks passed by I became ever more dependent on his daily visits. If he ever missed one, I grew fretful and my thoughts turned inward as I contemplated my uncertain future.

I had not recovered sufficiently to arrange my parents' funeral – my now married brother did that – but David accompanied me to the crematorium and took control, manoeuvring my wheelchair and staying by my side throughout the ordeal. My family is not large and only a dozen people attended the service, but each remarked how lovely and considerate my partner was and how fortunate I was to have him at this difficult time.

David and I talked about what I would do once my injuries healed and, thinking back, it's hard to recall the precise moment when I made the decision to move in with him. It just happened. I'd received a nasty break to my right leg, which required two operations to re-pin the bones. My broken left arm was less of a problem and the collarbone healed in time. It took a while to find my feet – literally – and when I emerged from hospital into the world once again, there was never any thought of returning to the family home; the only house I had ever known. Everyone assumed David and I were together. My fellow patients and the nurses, *especially*, often remarked how lucky I was to have such an attentive boyfriend. Neither of us was in a hurry to correct them.

One sunny morning, exactly three months to the day from being first admitted to hospital, David collected me. With fond farewells ringing in my ears, I made my way unsteadily on crutches across the reception area and out through the entrance doors towards his waiting car – a shiny, brand new Aston Martin.

And so, halfway into my eighteenth year, I entered David Ashcroft's world.

And that's where I stayed for the next ten.

2

'Steady, Caspian.' His ear twitches at the sound of my voice and I stroke the gelding's silky neck.

The path leads tantalisingly into the distance towards a copse of beech trees on top of the hill. Knowing that, if given his head, my horse will increase his pace and this steady canter will develop into a full-pelt gallop, I apply subtle pressure to the reins. Immediately, he softens to my hands. A warm breeze drifts across the South Downs and wispy clouds dot a sky the colour of forget-me-nots. High above, a skylark sings. I love days like this; riding the open downland. The views span across the coastal plain to the English Channel – azure today – and inland, across a lowland landscape to Surrey and beyond. I check Caspian again. Attentive to the softest of aids, he slows to a comfortable trot.

'Good boy.'

David has bestowed a great many gifts on me over the years – jewellery, designer clothes, exotic holidays, cars – but none means as much to me as this magnificent horse. Caspian is the best. The buckskin Arab cross Warmblood gelding is always there for me, regardless of what mood I'm in, how I look, if I have make-up on, or whether I wear dirty clothes or bang-on-trend riding gear. It doesn't matter. He is my *constant*, and I'm often reminded of those ponies from my childhood that lived in the fields at the back of my parents' house with their unwavering promise of unconditional love. It has something to do with the frequency of a horse's heartbeat matching the rhythm of a human's. Whatever... Caspian is my conspirator, my soulmate, and the one with whom I share my deepest desires and concerns. He knows I imagine riding across the open terrain with David's and my future children on their ponies, each confident and at ease with their charges whilst enjoying being out in nature, safe in the knowledge that their mum and her horse won't let anything untoward happen to them.

Caspian slows to a walk across the closely cropped turf that is often meticulously attended to by an army of sheep and rabbits, although none are present today. Briefly, I wonder why. They must be on another part of the Downs. Approaching the summit, I check if I can detect anything odd in the air, as sometimes there is, but all is well. I bring Caspian to a halt and quickly dismount. Slipping the reins over his head, I lead him into the ring of beech trees and across the quiet interior that whispers of magical and mysterious forces, before emerging from the circle of trees on the opposite side.

'We'll stop for a while,' I say quietly.

From this elevated position the view is intoxicating. One can look down upon the scattering of houses and outlying farms nestled at the base of the South Downs and watch the comings and goings, unseen. Fanciful, I know, but whenever I rest here, I have the impression I've stepped straight into the pages of *Gulliver's Travels* and am gazing upon the small world of Lilliput.

I loosen Caspian's girth a couple of holes and sit on a log. Instantly, he lowers his head and begins to graze alongside me. As I watch the traffic make its way silently along the A283, the cars and lorries appear as small toys come to life; an occasional blast from a horn carrying up the escarpment. Before long, other sounds come to me. Rustling in the undergrowth, perhaps a mouse or a shrew going about its daily business, and Caspian munching grass. It's such a contented sound.

Suddenly, a highly flirtatious giggle carries on the breeze, slicing through the peace, and as I scan the lower slopes I see two people emerge from the newly painted back door onto the terrace at Stone Farm. The reason I know the door is newly painted is because I only settled the invoice the previous week. My left eyebrow twitches involuntarily as I watch David carry a mug in each hand, as he follows Melanie out to the table and chairs. Their figures are no more than two inches high, but as Melanie sits in one of the wicker chairs I can't ignore the dazzling smile she bestows on David as he places the mugs on the table. I frown. Why is my partner – *the serial workaholic* – taking time out to have coffee with our cleaner?

Caspian crosses in front of me, searching for tastier grass and blocking my view. I shift along the log. David Ashcroft – mastermind behind a hugely money-making invention whilst still at university and now the owner of a successful and profitable business – *never* takes time out from his precious working hours. It's taken me years to understand the balance of work-versus-play. It's as if I live with two different people. Once the businessman comes to the fore, *playful* David is cast aside for as long as *driven*

David dictates. But, mid-morning, when he's normally on the phone negotiating the latest deal, here he is, gaily abandoning his desk for a pleasant coffee break… with Melanie, for God's sake! I snarl and Caspian throws up his head in alarm.

'Sorry, boy. I'm just being a jerk.'

He blows warm air onto my cheek and I stroke his soft nose. Satisfied there's no immediate danger or any reason to take flight, Caspian returns to foraging amongst the undergrowth for the sweeter blades of grass.

My gaze swivels back to the farmhouse below.

Despite attempts at blocking it out, as I watch my partner and our cleaner enjoying a cosy drink together, their body language screams at me. Again, Melanie's flirtatious laugh carries on the wind. David can be fun – I've been on the receiving end of his mischievous playfulness many times, especially in the early years – but he isn't *that* funny. And then my jaw drops as she stretches out her hand across the table to cover his. However much my mind tries to find excuses for what I'm witnessing there is nothing to explain why our cleaner believes she can do that with her employer. Narrowing my eyes, I focus on David's face, but at this distance it's hard to make out any nuance of expression. Melanie's high, girly laugh trills out again. As David swiftly removes his hand from beneath hers and glances around nervously, I snort with contempt.

My mind races. I should be happy that *everyone* loves David, but I've always found it hard to accept. Once again, guilt engulfs me. Thinking back to the previous evening's dinner party, I relive my feelings of exclusion when I'd opened the front door to find not only David's Managing

Director and Head of Finance standing on the doorstep
– *expected* guests – but also Denise 'bloody' Phillips;
newly appointed Sales Manager and previously David's
personal assistant. I must have looked shocked – whilst at
the same time frantically working out how to stretch the
food to cater for an extra mouth – because when David
initially discussed his plans for the latest dinner party
he'd conveniently omitted to mention her.

'Oh, didn't David tell you he'd invited me?' Denise had
commented in a sickeningly coy voice. 'Naughty boy!'

All evening she'd watched me like a bird of prey waiting
to attack, and it had reminded me of how unwelcome
she'd made me feel when David and I first got together. We'd
been introduced at a fund-raising event that his company
was sponsoring, and as his personal assistant Denise was
responsible for overseeing the arrangements. She'd made
sure I was seated further along from him, on the opposite
side of the dinner table, while she sat at his side, and when
I'd gone to freshen up she'd followed me into the ladies'.
All evening she'd been nauseatingly sweet to me, but once
out of earshot of anyone she wanted to impress she didn't
hold back.

'Don't get too comfortable – you won't be around for
long. David only goes out with girls for a few weeks before
he gets bored.'

I was in the first throes of love and her words had hit
their mark. Naïvely, I couldn't believe anyone could be such
a bitch, but I'd been plucked from a life of limited worldly
experience and placed in the centre of one full of jealousy
and subterfuge without any training whatsoever! David's
so-called, well-meaning friends quickly filled me in. Denise

and he were once a couple, albeit briefly, and she'd never fully recovered from being dropped as swiftly as he'd swept her off her feet. However, instead of resigning and having nothing more to do with him, she'd continued as his PA, cleverly securing a presence in his life and masterminding her way to Sales Manager.

But, as my relationship with David developed – the weeks turning into months – she'd altered tack and acknowledged I was now a definite fixture in his life. Even so, at every given opportunity she delighted in reminding me that although I may have David *at home* it was she who had him *at work*. Once, after a particularly trying day, I mentioned this to David but he'd simply laughed.

'Silly girl, don't worry about Denise.' He'd pulled me into his lap. 'You're being far too sensitive. She's not a threat. You're far better looking! And, anyway, I'd much rather have you at home than at work.'

He'd kissed me lightly on the tip of my nose, as if the matter was now resolved. But it wasn't. Why should better looks make for a more secure relationship? His words offered no reassurance.

'But, David—'

'Shhh, love.' He'd raised a finger to my lips.

I'd grappled with the feeling that the subject had not been dealt with and, as always when I was anxious, my mind cast back to the day of the accident.

'That day you found me in the car…'

Interrupting me with a groan, David had removed me from his lap. 'Not *that* again, Sandie. I've told you already, I happened to be in the vicinity.'

He always said that, but I was never comforted.

'Why do you want to revisit that time, love?' Turning towards me, he'd placed his index finger under my chin and raised my face so that I looked into his eyes. 'You know it only upsets you.'

Obediently, I'd nodded. We never discussed the accident. Whenever I brought it up he immediately closed down the conversation, telling me we should never look back... only forward. I knew he did it with my best interests at heart, sparing me further anguish, but I wanted to discuss it. I needed closure.

'Come here.' He'd put his arm around my shoulders. 'No more of this nonsense, Sands, please. I have enough problems to contend with at work.'

He'd drawn me into a deep kiss and I was soon lost in the moment. However, despite the ensuing and enthusiastic lovemaking, I was left with a niggle that refused to go away. Not only did he deny me the opportunity to discuss my parents' death, but also he'd given Denise even more reason to crow over me having now promoted her.

I sigh deeply as I watch David drain his mug and say something to Melanie. Rising to her feet, she picks up the mugs and walks towards the farmhouse. He remains seated for a moment longer and glances around again before following her inside.

Why do I have the impression he looks around *guiltily*? Am I being oversensitive, as he so often tells me I am? Intuition tells me I'm not. Something about this little scene reminds me of Denise 'bloody' Phillips and her insidiousness, but Melanie is nothing like David's scheming Sales Manager. Our cleaner is an uncomplicated, pretty, young mum who's been in our employ for the past seven months. But the way

David has made himself available to her today reminds me of how he was when he'd first wooed me – charmingly attentive and with nothing too much trouble. I imagine that's how he'd seduced Denise.

All my instincts tell me to watch out, but surely there's nothing to worry about? We've been together for a decade and although marriage is never discussed, we are very much a couple. Everyone knows that!

I rise to my feet. Tightening Caspian's girth, I slip the reins over his head and, placing my left foot in the stirrup, quickly mount. We ride along a path leading off the South Downs Way and carefully navigate the steep, chalky escarpment until reaching a small wooden gate that gives access to Stone Farm's land.

3

David is on the phone when I pass by his home office and acknowledges me with a brief nod through the open doorway. I continue on to the kitchen where Melanie is stacking dirty plates in the dishwasher. She stiffens as I enter the room... or is it my imagination?

'This is the last load.' She inserts a tablet and closes the door.

I glance across the hallway into the dining room. When I'd eventually staggered to bed early this morning, leaving David still the 'life and soul', the room had looked like a war zone. Now there is nothing to suggest a full-on dinner party has taken place. Melanie is good at what she does.

What exactly is that? I stop my overactive imagination from running amok.

'Thanks, Melanie. You've done a great job. Sorry it was such a mess. When David's employees come to dinner at the boss's house they believe anything goes.'

I laugh but I'm not sure why, because there was nothing particularly funny about the previous evening. It was a trial for me – as these occasions always are – but it hadn't helped that Denise had sneered down her nose and tried to catch me out whenever possible. Also, and I didn't like to admit this, it's mainly because of David. He has such a *natural* bonhomie. I, on the other hand, have had to learn the art of being the hostess, unguided. It still doesn't come naturally; I hate being 'on show'. All eyes judge me – the girl who came from nowhere, plucked from obscurity and chosen to be the lucky partner of their beloved and oh so generous boss.

I turn as David enters the kitchen.

'You went out early this morning. I didn't hear you leave.'

Did a look just pass between him and Melanie, or is this also imagined?

'I wanted to take Caspian out before the Downs got too crowded. I'm glad I didn't disturb you.' Crossing the room, I kiss him lightly on the lips. 'What are your plans for today?'

'I've a mountain of work and a conference call with the Americans at two.'

'That's a shame. I hoped we could have lunch at the pub.'

'Sorry, love.' He pulls an apologetic face. 'Can't afford to let the grass grow under our feet.'

I swallow my disappointment. Even though I'm David's partner I rarely merit his undivided attention. I've had to get used to sharing him with the thirty-four staff he employs at Ashworth Enterprises' Brighton office always demanding his attention over one thing or another. But – and it bothers me more than I care to admit – whenever we are alone together, even though he engages in conversation I get the impression his mind is elsewhere. I put it down to his entrepreneurial mindset, always considering the next innovative product. However, sometimes, I wonder if there's something more ominous going on. I realise I can't expect the 'honeymoon' period to last forever. Those early days following the car accident, when he'd expressed deep concern for my welfare, are far behind us.

Our first year together was a particularly difficult one for me, and not just because my body had to heal. I had to adjust to a new way of being. Orphaned and with a brother who rarely made contact, especially once the sale of the family home went through, I found myself thrust into the limelight as partner to a high-flying, high-profile businessman.

But it wasn't just that. David took out a lawsuit against a rival firm, accusing it of stealing one of his designs and it had left him severely stressed. The charming, affable man took off for the hills. With no business experience to fall back on, I'd felt useless and unable to offer any meaningful support. All I could do was be there for him. Eventually he'd won the case and Ashcroft Enterprises grew ever more profitable due to all the press coverage surrounding the incident. We'd celebrated that win – and our first anniversary – at a charming hotel in the New Forest and on the surface all appeared well. The perfect, privileged life still intact...

As I look at David now, from out of the corner of my eye I see Melanie gathering her long hair into a ponytail. She appears startled. Letting her hair fall, she starts fussing with both earlobes.

'Oh well.' I keep my tone casual. 'Your loss.'

He throws me a small smile before walking back to his office.

'Have you much more to do, Melanie?'

She doesn't answer immediately. 'Melanie?'

'Sorry,' she says in a flustered voice. 'Yes, no. I mean, I've still got the bathrooms to do and the living room to hoover.'

She gives me a furtive glance and two red spots appear on her cheeks.

'Are you feeling OK?'

'Yes, I'm fine.' Turning away, she hurries from the kitchen.

As I watch her rapidly disappearing figure, I frown. I can't put my finger on it but something isn't right. I make a cup of coffee and carry it through to the garden room. When he first purchased Stone Farm, some thirteen years ago, David employed architects to come up with a bespoke design that complemented the farmhouse. Now, there is a large and impressive oak-framed, glass-roofed extension.

Selecting a magazine from the side table, I curl up in one of the large comfortable armchairs and glance out of the windows. The view is as immaculate as the house. David makes sure of that. Our two gardeners are instructed to maintain pristinely mown lawns, ensure borders are weed-free at all times and hedges neatly trimmed. I look out over the decked area immediately adjoining the garden room, which leads down by half a dozen steps to a stone terrace and the swimming pool. To my right, peeping above a sharply edged mature hedge – surely trimmed by guidance of a spirit level – a mesh fence discloses the location of the tennis court. Beyond that, approximately one hundred yards away, a clock tower graces the entrance to an impressive stone and flint stable yard. Adjacent to this is David's twenty-first birthday present to me, six years previously – a floodlit, all-weather outdoor arena. Thirty acres of level pastureland surround the house, divided into paddocks neatly bounded by post and rail fences.

The final icing on the cake is the private gate from the

property, which gives direct access to the South Downs by foot or horse. Stone Farm is a property to aspire to. Little wonder, then, that the county magazine insisted on featuring it heavily in their recent interview with David for the article, 'Sussex people of influence'. Even I'd been commandeered for a couple of photographs.

'We want to give our readers a flavour of the personal life behind the "man of the moment",' the journalist had eagerly explained.

Young, glamorous and obviously impressed by David's wealth, despite my presence she'd flattered him to the point of nausea, praising him for the beautiful eighteenth-century stone and flint farmhouse nestling at the base of the Downs; commented enthusiastically, if not knowledgably, about the original paintings adorning the walls; cooed over his expensive and stylish taste in furniture; almost expired at his impressive collection of cars; turned gooey over the horses and sheep in the paddocks, the stable yard and equestrian facilities; the grounds; the swimming pool; and the tennis court... Need I go on?

I sigh deeply.

Half an hour later, replacing the magazine on the side table, I carry the empty coffee cup back into the kitchen and stack it in the dishwasher. As I leave the room Melanie emerges from David's office. Spotting me, she instantly colours.

'I've finished for the day so I'll be off,' she says in a rush. 'I've put fresh towels in the bathrooms and placed the dirty ones in the laundry. See you next Wednesday.'

'Thanks. See you next week.' I watch as she scurries along the hallway towards the front door.

I pause at David's open door and glance in curiously. He stands at the filing cabinet, rifling through a pile of papers.

'Is everything OK?'

He looks up briefly but immediately returns to the papers. 'Yes. Why?'

'Oh, I don't know… Melanie seemed in hurry to get away.'

He hesitates momentarily. 'Probably in a rush for her next appointment.'

I watch him a moment longer.

'Is there anything else?' he asks, glancing at me again. Irritation flickers in his eyes.

I shake my head. 'I'll leave you in peace.'

Leaving the papers on top of the filing cabinet, he walks towards me. 'Sorry, love, but I've got a ton of work to do before this meeting. I tell you what, I'll take you out to dinner tonight. What do you say to that?' Putting his arms around my waist, he pulls me into him.

Gazing up into his clear, dark brown eyes, I banish my insecurities and smile.

'That would be good.'

'It's a date then.' He plants a kiss on my mouth. 'Now, I must concentrate…'

Returning to the filing cabinet, he opens the middle drawer, pulls out a folder and then walks to his desk without a further glance in my direction.

I turn away from his office. As I ascend the stairs I berate myself for my suspicions. What's so wrong with David having coffee with Melanie? It's nice that he takes the time with his employees. I open the door to the master suite. It's as stylishly decorated and furnished as the rest of the house but it suddenly strikes me as a showroom, giving away very little about the personalities that inhabit its space.

As I observe the room I have the strongest sense that something isn't quite right, but everything seems as it should. Nothing is out of place. Taking the time, I look slowly around. Why did the little scene I'd witnessed from the Ring this morning unsettle me so much? Unable to stop myself, I walk to the bed and throw back the covers. Newly made, the sheets are freshly laundered and pressed. I shake my head, embarrassed by my suspicions. But why do I feel so violated, as if a burglar has rummaged through my belongings?

Pulling the duvet up neatly to the pillows, I re-straighten the cover and am just about to turn away when I notice something glinting on the carpet, caught in a shaft of sunlight. Tucked in close to the bed, it winks teasingly.

Bending down, I pick up the pretty object and place it in the palm of my hand.

4

'So tell me, Sandie. Where are you and David going on holiday this year?'

The question is innocent enough.

'Not sure, Denise.' I take a sip of champagne. 'It all depends how the American deal turns out.'

'Ah yes, but I hear it's shaping up well.' She glances at me slyly. 'It's so good of David to ask me to accompany him to Detroit for the full ten days. I must say, I was rather surprised.'

Champagne bubbles hit the back of my throat and I try not to gag. I refuse to give her the satisfaction of knowing this is the first I've heard of it.

Her hawk-like gaze never wavers. 'I thought he might take you as well and extend his stay after the deal is done so that you two could holiday in the US of A.'

She says it lightly, but as she knocks back her drink I catch the glint in her eyes.

I fight to keep my composure. 'Oh, you know David. He's so focused and likes to keep things compartmentalised. I doubt mixing business with pleasure appealed.'

I smile inwardly as I see her flinch, knowing she's perfectly understood that I refer to *her* as business and *me* as pleasure. But she has a point. Why hasn't he asked me? A relaxing holiday in The States is the perfect antidote to intense business dealings. I glance around the room and wonder where he's got to. He said he'd only be gone a minute.

John Price, Ashcroft Enterprises' managing director, and his wife, Veronica, are hosting a 'white party' in celebration of their fifteenth wedding anniversary. The guests include business colleagues and extended family as well as friends, and I know quite a few. John and David go way back to university days where both had studied for a business degree. In fact, John was the sounding board for the first invention that ultimately paved the way to David's phenomenal success. As soon as the company was formed, David employed John as sales director. Together, they'd shaped the direction of the business, and six years ago John was appointed managing director. He's a nice guy, balanced and fair, and I like Veronica and their three delightful children.

As I scan the room for David, I acknowledge a couple of the girls from my Pilates class standing by the windows overlooking the garden.

'Well, I don't know about you but I'm getting rather peckish,' Denise says. 'Shall we see what's cooking?'

I follow her into the crowd.

'Sandie!'

A high-pitched voice carries above the general buzz of conversation and, turning, I see John and Veronica's eldest daughter making her way towards us through the sea of people.

'I'm so pleased you're here.'

'Hello, Rachel,' says Denise pointedly.

'Hi.' Linking her arm through mine, Rachel briefly acknowledges Denise. She's pretty, like her mother, with the easy nature of her father. 'I've got a favour to ask you.'

'Go on. Ask away.'

'It's my thirteenth birthday in a couple of weeks and Mum and Dad asked what I'd like. The pony I ride at Welltown Manor Stables is for sale and I said I'd like him.' She beams up at me.

Keenly recalling that desire, I smile down at the girl.

'Trouble is,' she continues with a small frown, 'Mum and Dad don't know anything about horses and they said I could only have him if I kept him at the riding school, but I don't want to do that. Shadow doesn't want to stay there either.'

'So what's the favour?'

She tightens her grip on my arm and looks up at me beseechingly. 'I wondered if Shadow could come and live with you. That way, you can show me how to look after him properly.'

I consider her request. It's not as if we don't have enough land and there are a number of empty stables.

'I'd come up every day after school,' she continues in a rush. 'We'd be no trouble.'

All at once I become aware of Denise's intense scrutiny and, glancing at her, I'm shocked by the look in her eyes. It turns my insides to ice. Overtly interested in this exchange, I can tell she's itching to see if I have the power to make a decision without referring to David.

'I don't see why not. There's plenty of room for one more.'

Surprise registers on Denise's face. Privately, I revel.

'Oh, that's fantastic!' squeals Rachel. 'I'll go and tell Mum the good news.' Extracting herself from my arm, the girl takes off across the room at a gallop, only to turn and rush back and give me a big hug. 'Thank you, Sandie.'

I laugh. 'I wonder if you'll be thanking me when you have to break ice on water troughs in winter.'

'I will. Promise!' Once again, she sets off across the room in search of her mother.

Turning to Denise, I catch a brief look of begrudging respect before she's had the chance to disguise it. She always point-scores when she has the chance, but this time it is definitely one to me.

'Let's find that food.' I turn towards the open French doors that lead out onto a paved patio. Obediently, Denise trots behind.

Despite being early summer, there's a definite nip to the early evening air and I readjust my white tasselled Pashmina as I glance around for David. Where *has* he disappeared to?

Veronica approaches, holding the corner of her white kimono with one hand and stretching out the other to me. 'Come, Sandie, dear.'

She leads me across the patio to a line of giant shallow pans filled with simmering paella, behind which John and a couple of other Ashcroft Enterprises' staff members masquerade as chefs for the evening.

'This smells good.' I sniff the fragrant air.

Veronica lowers her voice confidingly. 'When John offers to do the cooking I never say no.'

'Help yourself to a bowl,' instructs her husband. 'There are French sticks on the tables.'

A table groans under the weight of fine white porcelain

bowls, and laid alongside, in military fashion, are sets of silver cutlery sheathed in white linen napkins. Helping myself to a bowl, I pass it to John.

'We have two types of paella on the go tonight – seafood or chicken. Which would you like?'

'Seafood sounds wonderful.'

'Tell me when to stop.' He ladles a generous portion into my bowl. 'I must say, Sandie, you look lovely tonight.'

I smile. He is always so charming. 'Thank you, John.'

'Where's that man of yours? Don't know why he's left you on your own.'

I look around again. Still no sign. 'Oh, I expect he's in deep discussion with someone about the latest project.'

'I expect so.' John smiles kindly. 'Sit anywhere you like.' He nods at the three white marquees erected in the large garden. 'I'll send him over once he decides to join the party.'

My fellow Pilates girls are sitting at a table in the centre marquee and I step down from the terrace to join them. Barbara and Susan, mums from the village, are good fun. We have a hoot every Wednesday morning at the local memorial hall, and often finish with coffee and cake at the village tea rooms following the class.

'Hi, Babs and Sue.' Pulling out a chair, I sit at a table covered in pristinely laundered white linen. In the centre is a large basket of French breadsticks.

'Love your outfit,' says Sue. 'Where did you get it?'

I glance down at the white wrap dress with its flattering ruffles laced in silver thread. It's pretty and feminine, confirmed earlier this evening by the way David looked at me when I gave him a fashion show. The dress hadn't stayed on for long...

'From that new dress shop in Brighton. Number Seventeen; the one in the Arcade.'

'Oh yes,' says Babs, 'I was there last week. They've got some fab designs. I treated myself to a couple of things.'

We look up as two men approach.

'Hi, Sandie. David not here?' asks Babs' husband, Terry.

'He's somewhere around.' Helping myself to a chunk of bread, I dip it into the bowl of paella and take a bite, making sure not to spill any juices on my white dress.

'I saw him earlier chatting to Graham and Melanie,' Sue's husband says.

The bread sticks in my throat and I swallow hard. I didn't know Melanie was here! But, then again, why wouldn't she be? We don't have the monopoly on her; she also cleans for John and Veronica.

'I think they've got troubles.' Sue toys with her food.

'You don't know that for a fact, Sue.' Her husband's voice holds a warning. 'You don't want to start spreading rumours.'

Sue blinks at her husband. 'I'm not spreading rumours. She told me only last week they argued a lot these days. It's such a shame. Their kids are so sweet. But it must be hard raising two under the age of four and making ends meet when Graham only brings in a mechanic's wage. She said she finds it difficult juggling being a mum and topping up his wages with cleaning jobs.'

Babs agrees.

'She looks good on it though,' Terry comments through a mouthful of bread, as Babs hits him playfully on the arm.

'Terence Marshall, what are you doing noticing other women when you have this beauty at home?' She outlines her body with her hands. 'I'll have you know, it costs me a fortune to maintain this physique!'

'I think you'll find it costs me a fortune,' says Terry with a straight face.

Babs punches him again.

He grins at his wife. 'Anyway, there's no harm in window shopping occasionally.'

'Terry!' she wails.

'You must admit she *is* pretty.' But seeing the look on his wife's face, he quickly adds, 'Of course, not a patch on you, Babs.'

It's true. Melanie is pretty, in a doll-like way. Small and pert with long blonde hair, a button nose, blue eyes and kissable lips... I glance around for David again.

In the neighbouring marquee, Denise is seated at a table with other members of Ashcroft Enterprises. As she entertains them with what must be an amusing story, judging by the fits of giggles around the table, she glances over at me. I wonder if the laughter is at my expense.

There you go again, oversensitive and taking everything to heart, David's voice resounds in my head. *Why do you have so little self-confidence?*

I watch Denise a moment longer. She doesn't stop talking but her eyes open wide as she looks at something over my right shoulder. Swivelling in my seat, I see David and Melanie emerging from the summerhouse at the far end of the garden and, before I can stop myself, I look back at Denise and catch the smirk of satisfaction on her face. The woman is barely able to resist rubbing her hands together. I look down the garden again.

As David steps onto the grass, Melanie smooths down her

short white skirt and glances towards the party now in full swing on the lawn. It wouldn't surprise me if they walked up the garden hand in hand, they look so cosy together! I narrow my eyes. Why does he always abandon me at parties and expect me to fend for myself? And what possible explanation can he have for being in the summerhouse with our cleaner?

'Oh there he is,' points out Terry, 'your errant partner!'

He says it in jest, but I don't appreciate the humour.

Without any further interaction with Melanie, David approaches our table; all smiles and friendly geniality.

'So you decided to join us then?' says Sue, throwing me a look.

'Couldn't stay away from you for too long, Sue.' David gives her a wicked grin.

'We were just talking about window shopping,' says Terry. 'I see you enjoy it too.'

David's face momentarily freezes, but it's only me who notices. I know him too well. The next minute he springs into cheeky fella mode, slaps Terry on the back and sidles into the chair next to me.

'You're getting slapped about quite a bit this evening, Terry,' Sue's husband comments drily.

Across the table, Babs pulls a face.

I lower my voice and turn to David. 'Where have you been?'

I really want to demand what the hell he's been doing.

He doesn't reply immediately and it occurs to me he's deliberately stalling.

David tears off a chunk of French stick.

'Chatting to Graham about doing some work for me.'

'Oh, what work is that?'

David bites into the bread and glances at me. Placing a hand on my knee, he slides his cool fingers under the ruffles of my dress and up the inside of my thigh. 'This and that. Come on, Sands, we don't want to ruin the party talking about boring things like work. I'm off to get a plate of that delicious-looking paella while there's still some left.' He squeezes my thigh and rises from his chair.

I watch as he strides across the lawn, stopping to speak to several people before making his way up onto the stone patio and the simmering pans. This is David's life. He can't go anywhere swiftly. He knows too many people for that. Everyone wants to rub shoulders with him in the hope that some small portion of his magical life may transfer and bestow them a fraction of his success.

Once again, I glance across at Denise's table. She's laughing hard at the conversation circulating around her table but, ever aware of me, unwaveringly she returns my gaze. I swear there's a look of triumph in the flinty eyes that hold mine. Turning back to my table, I force myself to eat but with each mouthful I feel I'm about to choke.

5

The following morning I awake sometime around ten with a thumping headache. Champagne doesn't suit me at all these days. Turning over, I find the bed empty beside me. Slivers of sunlight steal through the slats of the closed blinds, creating a series of railway tracks across the thick pile carpet.

Climbing out of bed, I pad across to the en-suite and blink rapidly in the glare of the down lights. As I approach the double basins I gaze at my reflection in the mirror. Pale and drawn, like a shadow... and it isn't just due to the amount of alcohol I'd consumed the previous evening.

Throughout the party, David maintained his affable 'good chum to everyone' routine, never missing a beat. The occasion was a complete success and we didn't leave until well after two in the morning, but as we drove home I'd remarked again on his absence earlier that evening. He'd silenced me with an uncharacteristically cutting remark, accusing me of having a suspicious mind and being oversensitive. When I mentioned his forthcoming sales trip to Detroit and suggested it would be a good excuse for us to have a break in The States, he'd laughed.

'I don't have time to take a holiday. Besides, ten days

away with Denise is enough to bring any man rushing home.'

His response didn't pacify me at all, and when I had the temerity to comment that I hadn't known Denise would be accompanying him, he'd cut me off with a curt answer.

'Wasn't aware I had to run every business decision by you.'

His sharp response put paid to any further communication. Even though it's only four miles between John and Veronica's house and Stone Farm, the ensuing silence had stretched uncomfortably. Once we'd arrived home things hadn't improved. David headed straight for his office and closed the door firmly behind him. I didn't even have a chance to mention Rachel's request for livery. Like a naughty child, well and truly chastised, I'd retreated upstairs to bed.

Now, I open the bathroom cabinet and take out a box of paracetamol. Popping two capsules into my mouth, I throw back my head and swallow.

What is happening to us? We used to be so happy.

'So, what are you going to do?' I ask my reflection.

It doesn't respond.

Am I over-reacting, as David so often insists I do? The events of the previous evening could all be so innocent. Maybe he and Melanie had been discussing the work he had in mind for her partner, but why talk about it squirrelled away in the summerhouse? Why not out in the open? And what about that object I found in our bedroom? I shake my head. It may have simply fallen off when she changed the sheets, but if it was innocent why didn't she tell us she'd lost it and ask us to keep a lookout for it? I stare deep into

my pupils. Despite my strong gut instincts, I dare not voice
what's inside my head.

If I'm honest, in all the years I've lived with David I've
never felt truly comfortable at Stone Farm. I cast my mind
back to that first day when I was still learning to walk with
crutches. He'd helped me over the threshold and welcomed
me into his house, pronouncing it was now my home too.
He was as excited as a kid with a new toy, showing off
his property with such passion, and I'd melted completely.
I couldn't believe this gorgeous man with the movie-star
looks, who had so unexpectedly come into my life under
such tragic circumstances, was offering me a shiny new
life to replace my smashed and destroyed, previously grey
existence.

As one door closes another opens, I'd thought.

But now – with the dubious benefit of hindsight – I
realise that, although used to having anyone he wanted, for
whatever reason David had been motivated to install me in
his life as his most recent *acquisition*.

Even to this day, everything in the house reflects his
personality and taste; decorated in his style and filled with
his possessions. Whenever I propose a change he indulges
me by listening politely but rarely acts upon my suggestions.
I walk back into the bedroom and look around with
fresh eyes. Apart from the rumpled bed linen, this room
is immaculate. With sudden clarity, I realise that David's
obsessive behaviour concerning neatness and tidiness is
something far more complex than I'd previously considered.
If he ever comes across a discarded piece of my clothing,
with an irritated tut he instantly picks it up, neatly folds it
and puts it away in my drawer or hangs it in my wardrobe.

As I open the blinds, sunshine streams in through the windows and captured dust motes dance in the shafts of light. I grimace as a vision comes to me of David vacuuming the specks of dust away before they can further pollute the room. My heart aches. I don't want to view him like this. I want to believe in the happy, gregarious, fun-loving man I've always perceived him to be.

From somewhere deep in the house a telephone rings, jolting me from my depressing thoughts. Quickly, I dress and face the day.

6

'If you're making coffee I'll have one,' David calls from his office.

'OK.'

Taking a jar from the shelf, I'm so engrossed with the task in hand that I don't hear him enter the kitchen. I jump when I see him.

'Oh God, David.' My hand flies to my chest.

'You're jumpy today.' He strides to the sink and turns on the cold tap. Selecting a glass from a cabinet, he holds it under the stream of water.

'And you're obviously hungover!' I say, as I spoon ground coffee into the filter. I switch on the machine and after a few clicks and wheezes, brown liquid starts trickling into the glass jug.

'What are your plans today, Sands?' He downs the glass of water in one.

'I've a training session with Justin in thirty minutes.' I check the kitchen clock. 'What about you?'

'Holed up in my office for most of the day. I've called a board meeting first thing tomorrow and there's a mountain of preparation to do before then.'

Ever the workaholic.

'You know, it would be good if you gave yourself an occasional Sunday off.'

'I know, love, but it is what it is. We can't expect to live like this without my continuing input.' His hand sweeps around the expensively sleek kitchen with its top-of-the-range, bespoke units and sparkling marble worktops.

With a loud hiss the coffee machine ends its cycle. Opening a glass-fronted kitchen cabinet, I select two delicate white porcelain art deco mugs from the shelf.

'I'll have it black.'

I raise an eyebrow. 'That bad?'

He grimaces. 'If there's one thing the Prices know how to do well it's throw a memorable party.'

'Talking of which…' I pour coffee into the elegant mugs and pass one to him, '…did you know Rachel's getting a pony for her birthday? She asked if she could keep it with us. I said yes.'

Steady brown eyes observe me.

'It's one from her riding school, but she doesn't want to keep him there. I thought I'd move Harvey into the larger box, one down from Caspian, and put him in the stable between.'

'Is this a DIY arrangement or full livery?'

'I'll help out, but Rachel wants to do as much as she can.'

'Whatever, Sandie.' He takes a large mouthful of coffee. 'It's your call. One more won't make a difference.'

'Thanks. I know what it's like to long for a pony of one's own.' I smile at him. 'You will definitely be Rachel's favourite uncle.'

A small smile pulls at the corners of his mouth.

'And, besides, it will be good practice.' I gaze at him beneath uncertain lashes.

'What for? Are you planning to run a livery yard at Stone Farm?'

I frown. Is he being deliberately obtuse?

'No, not a livery yard, David. Having a child about the place.'

He stares at me for what seems an eternity and I feel the heat rise in my face.

'Not that old chestnut, Sandie. You know my thoughts on the subject.'

'Of course… not now.' Suddenly I'm embarrassed.

'Not ever.'

'You don't mean that.'

He looks me squarely in the face. 'I do. I can't be doing with all the mess associated with kids.'

Panic grips me. I hadn't realised his thoughts on children were cast in stone. I'd believed that at some point he'd mellow.

'Don't go getting any ideas, Sandra.' I flinch at the hard edge to his voice. 'I don't want you suddenly announcing one day you've messed up taking your contraceptives and you're pregnant.'

I will myself to breathe.

'Because if you are thinking along those lines you should know now that it won't force me into a U-turn. Kids are *not* on the agenda… End of!' His nostrils flare as he steadies his breathing. 'Besides, why would you want to mess up that beautiful figure of yours? A woman's body is never the same after having a child.'

Well, of course, with the variety of girlfriends you had before I came on the scene, you'd know all about that...

I stare unhappily at David. Although we've skirted around the subject several times before, never has he laid out his thoughts so clearly. He's always hinted that his reluctance for fatherhood is because he's too young, but he's in his mid-thirties now. Grabbed by paralysis, my mind attempts to assimilate the deeper implications of what his view on our future life means for me. I've imagined our children so many times it's as if they already exist.

'Don't worry about lunch for me. I'll grab something while you're with Justin.'

He says it as if we've just had a casual conversation about the weather!

Gulping down the remaining coffee, he abandons the mug on the counter and strides towards the door. At six feet two inches, muscular and trim, David's presence fills a room, but now the kitchen feels empty. It's simply another beautifully staged showroom.

Reeling from our discussion – or, more accurately, his declaration – I place my mug carefully on the counter, surprised that it hasn't shattered into a thousand pieces as I've been gripping it so tightly. Wildly, I look around and catch sight of my reflection in the window. It's totally in keeping with its surroundings – slim, attractive, long shiny black hair, and dressed in the latest must-have designer riding clothes. I *get* why people like Denise are jealous. It appears to be the perfect life. If only they knew. Stirring myself into action, I stack the mugs in the dishwasher, place the coffee filter in the compost bin, wash the spoon, dry it and put it back in its drawer, before taking one last look around, ensuring the kitchen is spotless... just as David likes it. The flawless impression intact.

Then, silently I slip from the room.

Two hours later, as I ride Caspian out of the arena and into the stable yard, Harvey puts his head over the top of his stable door and watches our approach with interest.

'You did well today,' says Justin, walking at Caspian's shoulder.

'Yes, I'm pleased. He tries so hard, and flying changes are new for the both of us.' I stroke the buckskin's neck. 'Good boy.'

'You've got off to a good start. You'll probably have nailed it by the time I come next week. You should think about entering a few dressage competitions.'

I shake my head.

'Why not?' Justin gives me a quizzical look.

'That's not for me. I'm happy that Caspian and I have a connection and knowing I'm doing the best for him.' Taking my feet out of the stirrups, I dismount. 'I don't have to announce it to the world.'

'You're so different to my other clients.' Justin gives me a smile. 'It's all I can do to stop them competing before they're properly prepared.'

'You don't think I'm wasting Caspian's talents, do you?' I glance anxiously at my trainer.

'On the contrary, Sandie. It's a refreshing attitude... putting the horse first.'

I pull back the bolt to Caspian's stable door. 'By the way, there will be a new pony here next month.'

'Oh?'

Undoing buckles, I slip the bridle over Caspian's ears.

'David's managing director and his wife are giving their daughter a pony for her thirteenth birthday. Lucky girl! She's keeping him at livery with us and may want lessons. Are you interested?'

'Could be. What experience does she have?'

Undoing the girth, I lay it over the seat of the saddle. 'I believe she's had lessons for a year or so. Basically, she's a blank canvas.'

Grasping the pommel and cantle, in one easy movement I remove the saddle from Caspian's back.

'That's good. Less to unlearn. Here, let me.'

'Thanks.' I pass Justin the saddle. Bolting the stable door, I drape the bridle over my shoulder and walk with him to the tack room. 'Do you want a cup of tea?'

Justin eases the saddle on to its rack and checks his watch. 'Unfortunately, I haven't time. I have a new client in Forest Row and I should make tracks if I'm to arrive on time. Don't want to be late for the first training session!' He pulls a wry face.

'OK. See you same time next Sunday.'

'Just keep doing what you're doing with young Caspian and you'll soon master the canter pirouette.'

I laugh. 'Thanks for your confidence in me.'

'I have every confidence in you, Sandie. It's you who has to believe in yourself.'

My laugh stalls to an uncertain smile.

As Justin exits the tack room, my brow furrows. Why did he say that? I watch as he crosses the courtyard and disappears through the archway beneath the clock tower. Perhaps David is right; I don't possess any self-confidence. Perhaps that's why Melanie – always so bright and engagingly sweet – has caught his attention. Sighing deeply, I pick up a sponge and start cleaning the tack.

After turning Caspian and Harvey out in the paddocks, I walk back to the house deep in thought. It's a beautiful day and the Sussex countryside shimmers in the surprising warmth of the afternoon sun. I stop and take in the view. The two-hundred-year-old farmhouse looks comfortable and at ease, set in the centre of its own acreage. It's easy to understand why David was so taken with the original run-down, tenanted property. He always sees potential. He's thrown a considerable amount of money at it over the years, remodelling and bringing it up to today's standard of luxurious accommodation.

As I appraise our home, imagining it as depicted in the photos David took when he first purchased the property, the colours suddenly intensify. The mellow stone elevations gain an extra depth of honey and cream; the water in the swimming pool appears impossibly azure; the grass gleams emerald green; and the sky takes on a deep cerulean hue. Even the white cotton wool clouds are tinged with pink. It's like an airbrushed version and I wonder if this is how Denise and the others see David's empire? No wonder she hates me. In her eyes, I've swooped in and snapped up the prize from under her very nose.

I carry on across the lawn towards the house and step onto the terrace. Turning, I observe the backdrop of hills.

These, too, appear changed; their outline softer and more Disneyesque. Shielding my eyes, I raise my gaze to the circle of beech trees dominating the summit: the ancient hill fort of Chanctonbury Ring. All my life I've lived in the shadow of the Downs. Littered with ancient flint mines, barrows and hill forts, they inspire a rich folklore. Many myths and legends surround the Ring, which is reputed to be one of the most haunted locations on the South Downs. From a very early age I was aware of the numerous reports of ghosts, paranormal activity, levitation, UFOs and witchcraft because my brother had a keen interest and had collected many books on the subject, only abandoning them when he went off to university. Subsequently, I'd had an extensive library at my disposal.

One such book was an account of twenty-year-old Charles Goring, of nearby Wiston House, who, in 1760 – against public opposition – planted beech trees on top of the hill fort in order to improve his view. I'd spent many hours wandering amongst those trees after school and at weekends, considering that privileged young man. Not only did he have the means to consider the view from his estate but also he possessed the foresight to create a landscape that future generations could enjoy. I marvelled that people were able to think outside themselves and look at the bigger picture, because my life was so small and shrouded in greyness.

According to local stories, walking widdershins (anti-clockwise) seven times around the Ring would call up the Devil, who then offered the summoner a bowl of milk, soup or porridge in exchange for his or her soul. Shannon and I were both intrigued and terrified by this tale in equal measure, but it didn't stop us from trying to summon him and see if the legend was true. Thankfully, the Devil never appeared.

Over the years, I've visited the Ring many times. For some unknown reason I'm drawn to it, and only occasionally do I find it spooky. Sometimes I sense *oddness* in the air, and on those occasions I avoid the circle of trees. It's a strange feeling and hard to explain. It's as if someone... or something... observes me. I feel exposed to my core and however hard I try to hide, I cannot.

Charles Goring reached the grand old age of eighty-five, and during his lifetime many of the trees fulfilled his vision by achieving maturity. At school, I learnt that the Great Storm of 1987 brought tragedy to the Ring when over seventy-five per cent of the trees were destroyed, but, fortunately, the Goring family rose to the challenge and undertook a schedule of replanting. Today, the new trees are only just approaching maturity and restoring the Ring to what I imagine was its former glory.

But long before Charles Goring left his mark on the majestic landscape it was the site of Bronze and Iron Age forts, and a Roman temple. The hill fort commanded a strategic position from both a military and historical perspective and over the years it had many uses, both religious and sacrificial. As Charles Goring's beech trees grew, their roots disturbed a previously undiscovered ruin. It wasn't until the early nineteen hundreds that the site was excavated, and its results showed a Romano-British temple with a court that had sunken into the soil. Further excavations revealed several finds dating back to the Nero period (54–68 AD) and the Gratian era (375–383 AD). In addition to the Roman offerings, Anglo-Saxon coins were also discovered, suggesting that both the early Romans and Saxons regarded the temple as significantly important and of great spiritual value.

Maybe this deeply ingrained history reaching back centuries explains why I'm aware of a strange silence to the Ring. It hints at something magical, mysterious and just beyond reach; perhaps this is what I'm conscious of when the wind is in the wrong direction and I have nowhere to hide. However, on this beautiful early summer's day there is nothing sinister or otherworldly about the copse of beech trees.

It's not the only spot on the Downs that gives me cause to pause and consider. A half-day circuitous ride I like to do encompasses the ocean-facing side of the Downs and passes an intriguing tunnel of trees stretching for some five hundred yards. Each time I approach it from over the brow of the hill I'm aware of whispers on the breeze. I put this down to the stunning views of the English Channel and the wind holding sounds of the sea, but I can't deny its beckoning call. It's as if something tries to connect. I'm not particularly spooked by the experience, just aware.

There's a strange, ancient resonance to this place. The horses pick up on it too. Both Caspian and Harvey tend to play up whenever we near the entrance and I've never ridden through the tunnel. The interior is murky and its shadows are long – even on the brightest day – with branches stretching out and twisting eerily to create the thick canopy. It's only my imagination, as I've seen walkers emerge unperturbed. Nevertheless, I stick to riding in the bright daylight along its outer edge.

Rubbing goose bumps that have suddenly sprung up on my arms, I take one last look at the circle of trees dominating the skyline before following the terrace around the side of the house.

7

D avid's raised voice carries along the hallway.
'You can't expect me to do *everything, Jason.* Why do you think I employ you? Sort it out! And I want you in the office tomorrow morning, eight sharp.'

I frown. It's unlike David to be so dictatorial with his staff. Removing my riding boots, I place them on the rack and glance around – all is neat and tidy. Quietly, I step into the hallway and pull the door to behind me.

'No excuses, Jason.' David's voice is impatient. 'Just do it.'

I wince as he slams down the phone and swears loudly. Cautiously, I approach the open door and peer in. He sits with his back to the door, staring out of the window with fingers interlocked behind his head.

'Everything OK?'

He doesn't turn immediately. When he does, his expression is strained.

'I pay decent money to my employees and I expect good results and loyalty in return. He will learn.'

'No doubt.' I nod supportively, although I have no idea what Jason has done to incur his wrath. 'I'm just popping out to Waitrose to get something for supper. Do you want anything in particular or are you happy for me to make that decision?'

He doesn't answer.

'David?'

'What?' His furious eyes suddenly clear. 'Oh, I'm easy. Buy what you want.'

'OK. I'll be off then.' I give him a small smile and turn to go.

'Do me a favour, love. I'm leaving early tomorrow.' Opening the top drawer of his desk, he takes out a key on a leather fob and throws it across to me. 'Take the BMW and fill her up.'

Deftly, I catch the key. 'Sure. Anything else?'

'No need to take that tone, Sandra.'

'There isn't a tone.' I bristle with indignation. 'I'm simply asking if there's anything else you want.'

He looks at me through cool eyes. 'Sorry.'

'Why are you so uptight, David? Is it anything you want to share?' I walk around the desk and attempt to hug him, but he holds me at arm's length.

'Not now, Sandie. Cut me some slack. I'm up to here with problems. Just give me space and let me work through them.'

I stare at him. Exactly what problems is he referring to? Business... or personal? And what does he mean by giving him space? It isn't as if I'm on his back. Far from it! I put little pressure on David; his life with me is *extremely* free and easy.

'Do you mean Jason?'

He grimaces. Taking a deep breath, with some effort, he

rearranges his face into a semblance of a smile. 'Just fill up the car, love.'

When had I slipped into being simply another of his employees... just someone to do his bidding? I assess him for a long moment.

'OK, David.' I turn away, but at the door glance back. 'See you later.'

He's studying the papers on his desk and raises a hand without looking up.

I rush upstairs, change out of my riding clothes and into a pair of skinny jeans and a clean T-shirt before grabbing my handbag. Descending the stairs, I pass by David's office and am surprised to find the door closed. It's unlike him. Normally he doesn't like to be shut away, even when in work mode. I frown. What work problems does he have, and why doesn't he want to discuss them with me?

Exiting the house, I walk across the gravelled drive towards the six-bay timber carriage house. This is where David garages his impressive collection of cars. In one of the open bays is the BMW. Finished in pretty, metallic Mediterranean Blue, the convertible is his newest toy and a real head-turner. Repositioning the driver's seat, I adjust the rear-view mirror, flick a switch and watch as the soft-top retracts neatly into a compartment behind the rear seats. As the engine roars into life, I nose the sports car out of the bay and glance at the house. No sign of David. I turn onto the parish road, which serves only two further properties nestling in the lee of this particular stretch of the Downs, and after a quarter of a mile I join the main road.

An hour later, having made my purchases at the supermarket, I head for home via the petrol station, as instructed. There are three other cars at the pumps and I pull up behind a battered old Land Rover. Switching off the engine, I get out, and as I start to fill the tank I can't help but notice the customer at the far pump casting envious looks at the convertible. I catch the man's eye and smile, but he quickly averts his gaze. Replacing the petrol nozzle in its cradle, I grab my handbag and walk across the forecourt towards the shop.

The queue is two deep when I enter, and while waiting for the customers to be served I check out the magazine rack. There are the usual women's titles sitting alongside television guides and a variety of car magazines, but it's the front cover of *The Lady* magazine that catches my eye. An arresting photo of a tunnel of trees with a man at the far end, standing with legs apart and arms folded, appearing through swirling mist. Something about the accompanying headline captures my imagination: *'Investigating Britain's Ancient Holloways with Hunter Harcourt'*. Immediately, I think of the tunnel of trees on the Downs overlooking the coastline. Maybe that's what it is – an ancient holloway. Behind me, someone clears their throat and I glance over my shoulder.

The man who covets the BMW raises his eyebrows at me. 'Your turn.'

I look in the direction of the sales counter. The queue has disappeared.

'Thanks.' I give him a fleeting smile.

His expression is impassive.

'Pump four,' I say, approaching the counter.

'That's fifty-four fifty,' the shop assistant responds in a bored voice. 'Anything else?'

'No, that's all.'

Sliding David's credit card into the reader, I punch in the PIN and wait for the receipt. Transaction concluded, I walk towards the door. But, as I pass by the magazine rack, once again I'm drawn to the image on the cover of *The Lady*. Extracting a copy, I rejoin the queue behind 'covetous man' and gaze at the headline.

Having paid for his fuel, the man turns and blatantly trails his eyes across my body. Raising an amused eyebrow, I step into his vacated space.

'I'll take this.'

The shop assistant rings up the purchase. Again, I present David's card. As I exit the shop and return to the car, 'covetous man' drives slowly out of the forecourt, unashamedly checking me out.

8

David enjoys the meal I prepare that evening and we share a bottle of Californian Zinfandel before adjourning to the living room to watch television. The hours pass pleasantly enough, although I'm aware we don't communicate on any great level. He seems distracted, but this is nothing new, and I put this down to the board meeting the following morning. At around nine he rises from the couch.

'I'm off to bed.'

I look up in amazement. By David's standards, this is early. As he walks from the room my forehead creases into a small frown. What *are* the problems he keeps from me? I try to concentrate on the television programme but my mind races. Suddenly the phone rings and, instantly, I snatch it from its cradle on the side table. If David is trying to get an early night I don't want anything to disturb him.

'Hello, Sandie.'

'Hello, Melanie!' My voice registers surprise. She doesn't usually phone between cleaning visits. 'Is everything OK?'

'Sorry to phone you on a Sunday evening, but I've been offered another job and it clashes with my Wednesday slot with you. Would it be possible to change our day?'

'I don't see why not. What day were you thinking?'

'Um… Monday or Friday mornings.'

I consider the options. David likes to host social events at the weekend and it takes me a good day to clear up after them.

'Monday suits us better. As usual this week?'

'Yes. I'll start Monday week…'

She falls silent.

'Is there anything else, Melanie?'

Nervously, she clears her throat. 'Can I speak to David?'

My eyebrows scoot into my hairline. 'I think he's busy. Let me find out.' I put the call on hold and buzz through to the bedroom. David answers immediately. 'It's Melanie. She wants a word with you but I can make an excuse.'

'Put her through.'

My eyebrows rise even higher. *Not too tired to take a call from Melanie!*

As I put the call through I wonder what they could possibly have to discuss. Maybe something to do with the work David wants Graham to undertake, but as soon as the thought occurs I know it's not that. I'm clutching at straws.

I expect the call to end quickly but it goes on for ages, and I sit on the couch chewing over what's playing out upstairs. Eventually the light on the phone goes out.

Five minutes later, David appears in the doorway. 'Just popping out.'

'I thought you'd gone to bed!'

'Something's come up that needs sorting.' He avoids making eye-contact.

'I'll come with you.' I rise from the couch.

'No.' It's almost a shout. 'Melanie has a problem with Graham and I don't want you getting involved,' he says, softening his tone.

I sit down slowly. He still can't look me in the eye. What possible reason can there be for me not to be involved? Surely a woman's take on things would far outweigh a man's, in the circumstances.

'I won't be long.' David turns away.

I listen as he walks down the hallway and opens the front door, and a couple of minutes later a car sweeps out of the gravelled driveway. It sounds in a hurry. Switching off the television, I sit for several minutes before rising to my feet. As I walk through the house I dispassionately observe each room. It's an empty film set with everything in place, but the cast has yet to appear and 'Action' yet to be called. I consider the life David and I share in this beautiful farmhouse with its luxurious accommodation and extensive playground, and despite trying to block out the unwelcome thoughts, I face up to reality. This lifestyle is no longer enough to sustain me.

Entering David's office, I sit at his chair in the hope that some of his lingering charisma will shake me out of my melancholic musings. Unsure of what I'm looking for, I move a couple of papers on the desk and then open the drawers. Feeling guilty, I rifle through their contents, but there's nothing incriminating. I glance at my watch. Ten-forty. Surely, the problem won't take long to sort out. Exiting his office, I walk upstairs to our bedroom, hating myself for what I'm about to do. Methodically, I go through all his clothes, searching the pockets for anything to corroborate my growing suspicions. But there's nothing. Either I'm being oversensitive – as so often accused – or he's clever at this game. I gaze around the room. I *so* want to believe in our life together.

Slowly, I undress and climb into bed. I try to sleep, but the minutes tick by and my mind refuses to stop conjuring up various scenarios. Sighing deeply, I sit up, switch on the reading light and check the alarm clock on David's bedside table. Twelve-thirty. Where *is* he? And what is he doing? He has an early start! I wonder if by some cruel twist of fate he's had an accident. I'll never forgive myself if he's lying in a ditch somewhere and I've spent the night going through his things, trying to catch him out. Picking up the mobile from my bedside table, I phone his number. Instantly, it goes to voicemail.

'I hope everything's OK. Please phone me when you get this message.'

Replacing the mobile on the table, I gaze around the room. Sleep is far away... *The Lady* magazine lies on the dressing table where I'd left it earlier. Retrieving it now, I stare at the front cover. What is it about that image that draws me? The photographer has captured a wonderfully atmospheric shot, but it's more than that. I study the figure in the distance dressed in wet-weather gear and walking boots, surrounded by mist. His features are indistinct but there's something about his stance that speaks to me. Despite the photograph being otherworldly, the man seems grounded and real. Hunter Harcourt... I flick through to the article about Britain's holloways, and suddenly it's as if I've stepped through a portal into another world.

'Holloway – a hollow way, a deep and shady sunken path, greenway, droveway, cartway, corpseway, coffin-path, ghostway – routes harrowed deep into the land by centuries of feet, hooves, wheels and rain. Worn down by the fretting of water and the traffic of ages, it's not uncommon to find these tracks some eighteen feet beneath field levels. Hunter Harcourt explores the many holloways of Britain and finds his way into a shadowy landscape of strangeness and spectres.'

Immediately I think of Chanctonbury Ring and the unusual activity that reputedly surrounds it, and I wonder if Hunter Harcourt has ever visited.

'Nowadays, holloways exist only indistinctly. Few are in use, being too narrow and slow for modern-day travel. They are too deep to be filled in and farmed over, and over the centuries they have created their own disguises and defences. Today, nettles and briars guard their entrances whilst, on either side, trees bend over to lace their topmost branches and form a protective tunnel or roof. Growing between their wild, grotesquely snaking tree roots one can find moschatel, the lover of shade; hart's tongue fern; shining cranesbill; and ivy.'

I devour the article and all too soon it's come to an end. I stare, unseeing, into the room. Hunter Harcourt's words have spoken directly to me, wrapping me in the comfort of a rich and diverse language and opening up a new world. I consider my life. Have I, too, created disguises and defences to cope with what has happened to me in my own relatively short existence? I glance at the bedside clock – one-fifteen. Whatever David is up to he will surely suffer later this morning. Chairing a board meeting on less than a full night's sleep will not be an easy task, especially if there's trouble brewing within the company.

I skim through the rest of the magazine and arrive at the 'Situations Vacant' page. Glancing casually at the various jobs available and exclaiming at the low pay most positions offer, I toy with the idea of a housekeeper's role requiring the successful applicant to live six months in Antigua and six months in Putney. And then I see it...

DESPERATELY SEEKING SUPERHUMAN!

Frazzled mum of three, having failed miserably to clone herself, seeks urgent HELP. Children, dogs, cats, horses, housekeeping, PA duties, caring for an old country pile, holiday let, and anything else life throws our way! In return, we offer a realistic salary and accommodation (en-suite) in a fabulous setting on the North Cornish Coast. Use of car. Well-behaved pets by consideration.

Below is a name and telephone number. I stare at the advert for some time, sympathising with *frazzled mum* Ginny, and the ongoing struggle to achieve balance in her full but messy life. In contrast, I consider my own sterile existence, and with sudden, shocking clarity realise how empty it is. Taking a pen from the bedside table drawer, I circle the advert and re-read it. It shouts of such a different way of life to my own. I glance at the digital clock again.

Seeing red, I decide I'm not prepared to accept David's version of our future. I will get him to discuss it properly.

By the time he returns home it's way after two. I'm awake, stewing, but when I hear the crunch of tyres across gravel, I switch off the light, roll over and face away from the door. Several minutes later he silently slips into the room. As he tiptoes across the carpet and undresses, I hear the imperceptible click of his wardrobe doors opening. All the while I feign sleep and when he carefully raises the duvet and slides into bed, I pretend to come to.

'What time is it?' I ask in a sleepy voice.

'Late.'

Propping myself up on one elbow, I make much of glancing at the alarm clock on his side of the bed. 'It must be some problem to take all this time. Did you resolve it?'

He doesn't reply.

As the moment lengthens my indignation and anger rise. 'Exactly what problem does Melanie have that takes you so long to put right, David?'

'Not now, Sands. I've got to be up in four hours.'

In the dark I glare at his supine form. Taking a deep breath to steady my emotions, slowly I reach out and place my hand on his stomach. Immediately, he grabs my fingers and shoves me away.

'Four hours,' he growls.

Dredging up a seductive voice, I move closer and place my hand on his thigh. 'But I want you.'

'For God's sake, Sandie!' Throwing back the duvet, he gets out of bed and strides to the door.

'Where are you going?'

'The guest room.'

As the enormity of what has most likely occurred between David and Melanie settles heavily on my soul, I stare into the darkness. Life feels bleak, but I try to consider my options objectively.

9

The following day I'm on autopilot. I hear David take a shower and leave the house at just before seven. He doesn't bother to look in on me and I rise soon after. It's only when I interact with the horses that I feel any spark of life and I spend an hour exercising Caspian in the outdoor arena. Once again he is a complete star, sensitive and attentive, and I'm elated when we manage flying changes with ease. It's another glorious day and I take Harvey for a blast along the ridgeway. At 16.2 hands high, David's Irish Hunter can be strong, but I don't care. Recklessly, I urge him on into a gallop along the South Downs Way. Briefly, the hurt shifts.

Once back at the stables, I start preparing for the imminent arrival of Rachel's pony, sweeping away cobwebs and laying a new bed of shavings in the large loose box that Harvey will be moved into. However, despite the work, my mind insists on examining my growing suspicions about David and Melanie. I can't shake off the feeling of being trapped and I find myself contemplating the advert in *The Lady* and wondering about *frazzled mum* Ginny, desperately attempting to be all things to all people. What exactly does 'caring for an old country pile' incur? I'm no slouch and well used to meeting David's exacting standards with Stone Farm. It occurs to me that apart from the children angle, I have experience enough to fulfil all Ginny's other requirements.

In the afternoon I swim and as I power from one end of the pool to the other, the water silkily caresses my skin. After eight lengths I stop and sit on the tiled edge, luxuriating in the warmth of the afternoon sun. I close my eyes. It is *so* tranquil... Suddenly, a buzzing sound breaks the silence and, shielding my eyes, I gaze skywards. A microlight follows the course of the ridgeway, its vibrant red paintwork standing out sharply against the infinite blue. I wonder what the landscape looks like from the air. With the horses and sheep grazing peacefully in the paddocks, it must surely paint an idyllic picture of early summer in the Sussex Weald. But that's all it is – *a picture* of a perfect scene.

Rising to my feet, I grab the towel I'd previously draped over one of the perfectly positioned recliners lined up alongside the pool and rub my hair. The paving stones feel hot to the soles of my feet and I step up smartly onto the wooden decking before entering through the French doors into the quiet of the garden room.

At five I phone David.

'What time do you expect to be back?'

'Not early. There's a crisis at work.'

Not half as bad as the crisis looming at home.

'Do you want me to do supper or shall we eat out?'

'No. I'll grab something here. If I'm not back by ten, don't wait up.'

'Not another late night!' The words slip out before I can prevent them.

He doesn't comment, but the weight of his silence speaks volumes.

'I'll see you when I see you,' he says eventually.

In fact, David arrives home at nine-thirty. I'm half-heartedly watching a film when I hear the front door open. Turning down the volume, I listen attentively as he enters his office and pulls open a drawer of the filing cabinet. A few minutes later he crosses the hallway into the kitchen and opens a cupboard door. Then silence. I wait a couple more minutes before rising and walking to the kitchen door. He sits at the island unit with head in hands, a large tumbler of whisky on the worktop in front of him. Approaching, I pull out a bar stool and sit down on the opposite side of the island. I don't say a word. After a while he glances up. He looks pale, but the eyes that survey me are trademark strong and confident.

'What a day.' He picks up the tumbler and raises it to his mouth.

'Did you sort out your problem with Jason?'

'What? Oh yes. I've issued a written warning.'

What has his employee done?

Pursing my lips, I decide there's no point in asking. He's unlikely to tell me. Instead, I change the subject. 'I rode Harvey on the Downs today. He was well behaved and not too strong, so I gave him a good gallop.'

David stares at me but makes no comment.

'I also started to sort out the stables. Rachel's pony should settle quickly, sandwiched between Caspian and Harvey.'

Still David says nothing, although I can see his mind is in overdrive.

Annoyed at his lack of response, I climb off the stool

and switch on the kettle. It doesn't take long for the water to reach boiling point and I make myself a strong cup of coffee. I need it to steady my nerves for what I'm about to do. Returning to the island, I try again.

'You must be exhausted with so little sleep.'

He pulls a dismissive face.

'So, what happened with Melanie?' Nonchalantly, I blow on the hot coffee whilst watching him carefully.

He almost jumps out of his skin.

'Nothing!'

His answer is way too quick and defensive. I would have laughed if I wasn't so upset by this obvious admission of guilt.

'I mean, did you sort out her problem with Graham?'

Colour floods into his face. 'No. It's ongoing. He's treating her badly, the little shit.'

I'm so tempted to clout him. How does he think he's treating me? I know that now is probably not the best time to tackle the discussion that needs to take place, but how much longer can I continue as the docile, pliant person David expects me to be? My heart leaps wildly in my chest.

'You know, David, what we need is a change of scene.'

He blinks in surprise. 'What do you mean *a change of scene*? Where did you have in mind?'

'I don't mean a change of location. I mean a different situation.'

He frowns.

I've come this far... I might as well say it all.

'You have a successful career and the business is thriving. We've been together for a decade and I'll be thirty in a couple of years...' I let the sentence hang.

He can't mask the anger – or terror – in his eyes.

I do my best to ignore his expression and smile sweetly. My nerves are in shreds, but I plough on. 'It's all very well looking after the horses and keeping things ticking over here, but I'd like to start a family one day.'

'Fuck it, Sandie. I can't believe you're bringing this up again!'

'Why?' My foot nervously taps the bottom strut of the bar stool; waist up, I make sure I appear perfectly assured.

He swallows hard. 'I told you yesterday. I don't want children.'

'But I do.'

He doesn't comment. Stalemate.

'I assume it's because you think you're too young, but you're nearly thirty-six, David.'

'Age doesn't come into it. I told you, children are messy. They clutter up life.'

And what's so wrong with that?

'You won't have to see any clutter because I'll clear it up. I promise.'

He runs a hand through his hair, his gaze anywhere but directed at me.

I decide to appeal to his vanity. 'Don't you think we'd make beautiful children, David?'

'That's as may be, but as I've already stated I'm not about to embark on that particular journey. Get your head around that.'

His determined voice stuns me into silence. As quickly as it had appeared, anger and fear leave his eyes and, once again, David is composed; oozing his usual self-confidence.

I try not to panic at having reached a dead end. My throat

constricts and I want to cry, but I'm not going to give him the satisfaction of witnessing that. I have a shocking vision of my future self, perfectly coiffed and dressed, living in the lap of luxury, entertaining his guests and constantly working out to maintain the 'sexy' figure he expects me to have, whilst endlessly waiting for him to return from his latest pursuit... or conquest. The person I'd always viewed as a handsome man, full of charm and charisma, is rapidly morphing into a two-dimensional cardboard cut-out that perfectly reflects this imagery. Every which way I turn I can't envisage myself in that future. I need *more*, and I realise I want the loving mayhem of Ginny's life.

My heart aches as the imagined future I'd hoped for with David slips through my fingers and turns to dust. The growing lump in my throat makes it almost impossible to speak, but I force myself to. In a brutally honest way, I lay my cards on the table.

'I love you, David, but I don't think I can have a life without children. The thought of years of constant socialising and always being abandoned at parties, with you only seeking me out at the end of the evening, makes me ever more world-weary. I crave more.'

David makes a dismissive noise at the back of his throat. 'I don't know what more you could want, Sandra. Just look around. Most women would give their eye teeth to have what you've got. And as for abandoning you at parties... why the hell would I waste precious time with my partner when I can do that whenever I want? Social time is for networking and making new contacts. Anyway, I don't know what you're complaining about. It's not as if I don't always go home with you.'

After messing around with the cleaner in the summerhouse...

When I speak, my voice is horribly small. 'I'm sorry, David, but I need more.'

A heavy silence descends. Knocking back the remains of his whisky, he rises to his feet, crosses the room to the dishwasher and places the empty glass on the top rack before standing with his back to me, gazing out of the window into the dark night. A few minutes later he turns and my poor battered heart cowers under the steely eyes that coldly survey me.

'You know, Sandra, it's not me who has the problem. You need to sort yourself out.'

I shudder at the harshness in his voice. But as the final bolts slide into place on my life as I know it, I refuse to crumple before him. I'll have plenty of time to do that in private.

10

David and I don't share a bed again. After a night spent in tears, during which I almost weaken my resolve and seek him out to explain it was all a silly mistake, I lie in bed listening to him getting ready for work. I hope he will come in and say something before he leaves, but he doesn't and my pride refuses to let me run after him.

When I finally climb out of bed, it's as if the weight of the world rests upon my shoulders. My limbs are unaccountably heavy and each step takes an inordinate amount of effort as I stumble across the room to draw back the curtains. Fog creeps across the escarpment, softly draping the Downs and the surrounding countryside, and giving the landscape an ethereal feel. Treetops loom out of the grey swirling mist, like ships' masts momentarily lulled in unnatural quiet before an approaching storm.

A heavy silence settles over the land, mirroring my sombre mood. All too keenly I realise what I've done. Forcing David's hand hasn't worked. He refuses to budge. I hold back yet another sob. *He* may be happy to continue on his chosen trajectory, but I can't shake off the feeling there should be more to my life. If I don't act now, I run the risk of sacrificing any potential future happiness for a life only half lived. Hunter Harcourt's fertile, rich words have opened up a magical door through which I'm willing to step. They whisper a promise of an alternative life; one that I can't now abandon.

Dressing quickly, I snatch up *The Lady* magazine and make my way downstairs to the kitchen. As usual, it's immaculate. Not a single stray dirty spoon or overlooked glass litters the worktops. In contemplative mood, I switch on the kettle, throw a teabag into a mug and take a carton of milk out of the fridge. Having made the tea, I take it through to the garden room and stand at the French doors staring out at the misty vista. Nothing is clearly defined… just like my future. A deep sigh escapes from my lips, but I've made up my mind. There is no turning back.

Opening the magazine to the 'Situations Vacant' page, I pick up the phone and make the call.

It takes a further three weeks to organise everything and it's unbearable going through the motions of living with David until my departure, but I have little choice. There is nowhere else to go. My brother and his wife, and their ever-increasing family, don't have the room; anyway, we're estranged. And there's no one locally I can turn to. Besides, I don't want anyone knowing what's happening to us. The last thing I want is to be the subject of gossip and speculation. But, as it turns out, I hardly see David. He is either hard at work, or equally hard at play. I don't question which. We speak very little, and when I tell him I've found a job and will be working away he offers no opinion. As hard as this is to accept, it only confirms he no longer truly cares. Otherwise, surely he wouldn't let me go through with my plan?

One fine morning in late June, having heard David depart for the office at some ungodly hour, I pack my few belongings into two suitcases and load them into the Range Rover. As if to deny the reality of my situation, I waste no time in walking around the house and sentimentally saying 'goodbye'; I simply work through the necessary tasks before closing the door on my life at Stone Farm. Driving the short distance to the stables, I hook the horse trailer to the Range Rover and load Caspian's tack, rugs and equipment into the travelling compartment. Aware something's up, my horse looks over his stable door and quietly observes. I stuff a couple of nets with hay, hang them in the trailer and fill a carrier with cold water. Finally, fetching a halter and travel boots from the tack room, I approach Caspian's box and slide back the bolts.

'You and me, young Caspian, we're setting out on an adventure.'

He nuzzles my hand and I feel his velvety softness on my skin. Without fuss, I wrap the boots around his legs.

Suddenly a shadow falls across the doorway.

'Morning, Sandie. Everything OK?' asks Richard, David's farm manager.

I glance over my shoulder. 'Yes, thanks.'

'Are you using the trailer today?'

'I am.' I keep my voice breezy.

He scratches his head. 'David didn't mention it.'

'No. It was a last-minute decision.' I glance down at my watch. 'Sorry, I must be on my way or I'll be late.'

'Is Harvey to be kept in until you get back?'

'No, I'll turn him out in the paddock before I leave.'

'Don't worry, I'll do that,' Richard says.

'Thank you.'

He holds open the stable door and I lead my horse out into the bright sunshine. I'm jittery and nervous. Will Caspian pick up on my heightened emotions and make a fuss loading? Thankfully, he steps confidently onto the ramp and follows me into the trailer.

'Good boy,' I whisper, as I tie his lead rope to the travelling ring. Immediately, he pulls a mouthful of hay from the net. 'We've a bit of a journey ahead of us. Sorry.' I stroke his silky neck.

His soft, liquid eye observes me wisely.

As I climb down from the side door, Richard joins me. I can tell he's itching to quiz me further, but he remains silent and, together, we lift the ramp and bolt it securely in place.

'Thanks, Richard.' I walk quickly around to the driver's door and climb in. I don't want to give him the chance to ask any more questions.

As I drive out of the stable yard beneath the clock tower, I glance in the side mirror. David's farm manager watches my departure wearing a puzzled expression, so I put my hand out of the open window and give him a cheery wave. However, it's with a heavy heart that I drive by the farmhouse, and I force myself to look straight ahead and not at what has been my home for the past ten years. Otherwise, it will be my undoing. As I cross the gravelled driveway, I glance at the line of pristine cars parked in the open-fronted bays of the coach house and smile sadly. So many toys to distract a man. Halting briefly at the entrance gates, I look right and then pull out into the parish lane.

The A283 is busy with commuter traffic and I have to wait several minutes before a large enough gap presents itself to pull out safely. Fighting back tears, I set out on the journey away from my Sussex life... but there's just one more thing I have to do before putting it all behind me.

Like a snake, the heavy traffic wends its way slowly towards Storrington. Indicating right at the roundabout, I feel Caspian shift his weight as we head north towards one of the many modern estates that have sprung up in recent years and now extend the village boundary. I find the address easily enough and I recognise the car parked on the driveway of No. 5. It's a neat box of a house, the mirror image of its neighbours, apart from the mauve paintwork on the doors and the swing in the ragged front garden.

After pulling over to the kerb on the opposite side of the road, I cut the engine and stare, unseeing, through the windscreen as I clutch the steering wheel. My knuckles turn white. I peer in the rear-view mirror and the eyes that gaze back at me are bright with unshed tears. Taking a deep breath, I will myself to find the strength to carry this off. Then, reaching over to the glove compartment, I extract the envelope and open the car door. I have to wait for a passing car before crossing the road. Again, as if denying the reality of what I'm doing, I walk purposefully up the path, noticing several of the paving stones need replacing, past the motionless swing drowning in the long grass and up to the mauve front door. Before I have a chance to turn tail, I press the doorbell. After what seems ages, I hear footsteps on the stairs and, suddenly, a shadow falls behind the opaque glass. As the front door opens, shock registers on her face.

I stretch my mouth into a smile.

'I have something for you, Melanie.' I hold out the envelope.

She frowns.

'Here.' I shake it at her.

Hesitatingly, she takes it from me.

'Open it.'

She glances anxiously down the street both ways.

'Go on.'

Tearing open the top of the envelope, she extracts the small package, which I've carefully wrapped in tissue paper; like a present. Her fingers fumble as she opens it. A pretty silver earring glints in the morning sunlight. Her sharp intake of breath and flushed face are enough to confirm my suspicions.

'Thought you'd like to have it back,' I say without emotion.

'Where did you find it?'

'Somewhere it shouldn't have been.'

I walk away, but after a few steps turn back. She still stands in the doorway, staring at me like a rabbit caught in headlights.

'Melanie.' I take a step towards her and she shrinks back. 'I'm sorry if things are not so good between you and Graham, but I wouldn't go looking elsewhere for solutions.'

I glance over her shoulder down the hallway. Through the open kitchen door I see a toddler sitting in a high chair.

'Don't expect David to be the answer, because a knight in shining armour he's not. Far from it!' I give a hollow laugh.

She opens her mouth but just gapes, reminding me of one of those fish at the aquatics centre gasping for air at the water's surface.

'Do you still want me to clean for you?' she manages. 'I *so* need the job.'

I gaze at her dispassionately. 'Should have thought of that before bedding the boss.'

Guilt sweeps across her face as her hand flies to her throat. 'I – I'm sorry. It just happened.'

'Save it, Melanie,' I say fiercely. 'I'm not interested in your excuses. Anyway, what you do now is not my business.'

I turn and walk down the path, feeling as if I've been punched in the stomach. Up until now, some small part of me had hoped I was overreacting, as David always insinuates. I'd mistrusted my suspicions and gut instincts, but this brief exchange has removed any uncertainty.

Angry tears prick my eyes as I cross the road and climb into the Range Rover, and I pull away from the kerb refusing to glance back to see if Melanie is still standing at her door. I drive through the sprawling modern estate and out onto the main road, but at the roundabout I hesitate. This is my last chance. I could turn left and return to Stone Farm, unload Caspian and park up the trailer and David would be none the wiser. But what's the point? In that direction lies a childless future and a world of discontent. A hard lump forms in my throat. I turn my head in the opposite direction. I have no idea what the future will bring, but at least I will have some control over my destiny. Indicating right, I ease the trailer out into the mid-morning traffic and head west.

Cornwall

11

The journey from Sussex is long but uneventful, and eventually I turn onto the driveway leading to Foxcombe Manor. As the late medieval house comes into view I'm powerless to prevent a gasp escaping my lips and, slowing to a stop, I gaze in awe. Before me is a perfect Tudor manor, not of any great size, with a picturesque cluster of low roofs, gables and chimneys. Externally, it appears mostly unchanged over the centuries. Quickly assembling my thoughts, I ease the Range Rover into gear and pass between a pair of massive entrance pillars under the watchful eyes of two stone eagles; their wings outstretched. Coming to a halt, I pull on the handbrake and switch off the engine, and as soon as I step out onto the stone-chipped driveway I'm aware of an old-world air; as if I've been transported from the twenty-first century to the Middle Ages.

Ginny must have been watching for me as she immediately appears at the heavy studded, oak front door, a springer spaniel and Jack Russell at her heels. She's a flurry of energy and her smile is filled with such warmth that the tension and doubt, which has been steadily building during the journey, lift from my shoulders.

'Cassandra, I am *so* pleased you are here!' She approaches and wraps me in a hug, while the dogs sniff inquisitively at my ankles.

I look into an arresting face framed by a shock of curly auburn hair falling over her shoulders in an unruly mess. I like the clear brown eyes that gaze back at me. They hold no guile.

'I hope the journey wasn't too trying.'

'It was fine, thank you, Ginny. Caspian travelled well but I expect he'll appreciate escaping the trailer.' I stroke the dogs' heads as they bounce up at my legs.

'Of course! We must unload him immediately. Zac has made up a stable for him. Roly, Pumpkin, get down. Leave Cassandra alone.'

I notice that although she scolds the dogs, she doesn't do anything to stop them from checking me out.

'Is it OK to unload here?' I glance around.

'Yes. We'll walk Caspian through to the yard and then you can drive around and park the vehicles in the open-fronted barn.'

Following me to the rear of the trailer, Ginny helps to release the catches, and as we lower the ramp, Caspian turns his head and thoughtfully observes us. The dogs peer in with interest and, momentarily, their tails stop wagging.

'What a handsome horse.'

'He's an Arab cross Warmblood. Ginny, meet Caspian.' I enter the trailer and walk to the front.

'We've arrived. This is our new home,' I whisper, as I untie

Caspian's lead rope from the ring and guide him backwards down the ramp.

As my horse stands patiently in front of the manor house, his buckskin coat gleams in the early evening light. Suddenly, three children – a boy and two girls – appear in the entrance porch and rush towards us. It's mayhem, just as I knew it would be, and the dogs take this as an excuse to jump up at us all.

'Steady,' warns Ginny. 'We don't want to frighten Cassandra and Caspian the minute they've arrived.'

I struggle to hold my emotions together as she introduces me to the family that will welcome me so readily as one of their own.

'He's gorgeous.' The eldest girl, Rhea, strokes my gelding's neck. 'What's he called?'

'Caspian.'

On cue, he drops his head and blows warm air onto her face.

'Oh, I love him,' she cries.

'I love him too!' says a small voice behind me.

I turn.

Four-year-old Tegan, who I'm informed is known as Tiggy, has the biggest blue eyes and wayward, corkscrew blonde hair that sticks out at crazy angles. She gazes up at Caspian in wonder.

'I think we all do, Tiggy,' says Ginny.

'I've made up the stable next to Dylan's... my pony,' Zac says, with pride.

'That's kind of you.'

'Come on, kids. Let's show Caspian his new home.' Ginny catches hold of Tegan's hand.

As I lead my horse behind Ginny and her youngest

daughter, the older children fall into step beside me. The springer and Jack Russell scamper excitedly ahead.

'This is the old Porter's Lodge.' Ginny indicates a building to our left with a door and portcullis. 'See the arrow slits in the thick walls? It was built during times when Foxcombe had to be wary of armed attacks.'

'I'm sure the manor house has an interesting past.'

Ginny shoots me a look, which I find hard to interpret. 'Yes, it does.'

I expect her to say more, but she doesn't elaborate.

'We rent out the lodge to PGs.'

'PGs?'

'Paying guests. We have a couple in at the moment.'

'I expect it's a great place to stay.'

'People seem to enjoy it, judging by the number of positive comments left in the visitors' book. Changeover day is Saturday but these people have only just arrived. They've booked two weeks, so you'll have a chance to settle in before we have to roll up our sleeves.' Ginny glances at me apologetically. 'I'm afraid it takes a few hours to prepare.'

'I'm not shy of hard work and I'm used to fulfilling exacting requirements.' I give a wry smile.

'I knew you were the one for us!' Ginny chuckles. 'I have to warn you, though, however much you scrub and clean there will always be more dust and cobwebs around the next corner. But don't worry, Cassandra...'

'Cassie, please.'

She smiles. 'As I explained on our Zoom call, *Cassie*, it's a varied role and we don't expect you to be our full-time housekeeper. We do, however, want you to take over responsibility for equine management, which will effectively free up some time for me. I'd also like you to give the children riding lessons and generally assist in ferrying them between various commitments. That way, we will at least attempt to get the right child to the correct activity on time!' Again, she looks apologetic. 'There's a fair amount of farm admin too. I make a stab at it when I have a moment to spare, but I know Gyles would be hugely grateful for any help in that direction.'

When I'd first contacted Ginny – and during our subsequent 'official' online interview – she'd explained she was looking for someone to shadow her. Now, however, overwhelm threatens. Perhaps it's due to the long journey from Sussex, but for one awful moment I wonder what I've done. Nervously, I push aside my doubts.

Walking at Caspian's head, Rhea glances at me. 'How old is your horse?'

'He's eight.'

'Same age as me,' she says with a smile.

'What do you do with him?' Zac asks enthusiastically.

'Does he like carrots?' Tegan says in a high-pitched, squeaky voice.

As I answer the children's barrage of questions we enter a quadrangle of barns, each befitting the manor house in style and preservation. Once again I have the impression of stepping back in time. In fact, it wouldn't surprise me if a man of good yeoman stock suddenly appeared around the corner of the open-fronted barn, coming in from a long, hard day in the fields. I notice a number of black and white cats mooching around while a couple of kittens play with a blade of straw. On the far side of the yard, four handsome

Labradors peer eagerly through the wire mesh fencing of an outside kennel.

'My husband's gun dogs. These two are house dogs.' Ginny indicates the springer and terrier.

'Like Marmaduke,' says Tegan.

'Marmaduke's not a dog, silly.' Her older sister pulls a face. 'He's a cat.'

'House cat.' Tegan regards me solemnly.

I smile.

'We use this yard for the horses, gun dogs and our personal vehicles; the farm cats live in the barns. The working side of the farm is a short distance away.' Ginny motions vaguely over the roofs to our right. 'We run a herd of Friesians for organic milk and a flock of Poll Dorset sheep. We have free-range chickens, too. They often find their way over to this yard.'

As Ginny, Tegan and the dogs enter the nearest barn, Caspian surveys the yard with a calm inquisitiveness. My heart swells. Whatever I ask of this horse he always accepts without fuss. Feeling more emotional than I care to admit, with difficulty I swallow the lump forming in my throat. I follow Zac and Rhea into the barn's cool interior. Immediately, a cacophony of excited whinnies fills the air and four faces suddenly appear over the stable doors. As Caspian snorts and visibly grows in stature, I smile to myself.

'That's Dylan.' Zac points to a grey pony with a pretty head; typically Welsh.

'And that's Biscuit.' Rhea indicates an Exmoor pony in the stable beyond Dylan's.

True to its name, the pony is biscuit-coloured and displays the breed's distinctive mealy eyes and muzzle.

'This is my pony,' Tegan cries excitedly.

A black Shetland pony peers over a half-height door and she rushes towards it. Stretching up, she places her hands on either side of its face and plonks a kiss on its nose. Graciously, the pony doesn't flinch.

'What's its name?'

'Inky.' Tegan squeezes her pony tightly. 'She's a girl.'

I look along the row of stable doors. In the furthest box, an elegant bay thoroughbred watches us through soulful, expressive eyes.

'And that's my mare.' Ginny's voice is as proud as her children's. 'Fairweather Indiana.'

'Well, Caspian, aren't you one lucky fella to share a barn with such a fine collection of stablemates?'

I lead him into the empty box next to Dylan's, which has been prepared with a deep straw bed. A full hay net hangs from a ring on the wall and in one corner is a full bucket of clean water. As soon as I remove his halter, Caspian is at the door gazing inquisitively at his new companions.

'Let's leave the horses to get acquainted. We'll check on them later,' Ginny says. 'However fine a journey you've had, Cassie, you must be exhausted and I'm sure you could do with a cup of tea.'

'Thank you. I wouldn't say no.'

'Roly, Pumpkin, come,' Ginny calls to the dogs.

Sniffing amongst the chests and buckets lining one side of the walkway, the dogs look up at the sound of her voice. Obediently, they trot after her.

Before exiting the barn, I glance back at Caspian. He doesn't appear too exhausted by the journey. As I walk with the Kinsman family towards the manor house I have the strongest feeling that life, as I know it, is about to be reshaped out of all recognition.

12

Three days later I'm introduced to Gyles Kinsman's filing system... or rather the lack of one.

Having already experienced forty-eight hours of life at Foxcombe, I set my alarm for 6am; thirty minutes earlier than the previous two mornings. I'm determined not to be caught out again and have to spend my day playing catch-up. Since first coming across Ginny's advert I'd felt sympathy for her frantic lifestyle, but now I have first-hand experience and it's full-on. I'm shattered! It doesn't help that I'm not sleeping well, partly due to the unfamiliar bed and new surroundings, but also because I miss David... despite his faults.

Rubbing sleep from my eyes, I drag a brush through my hair and throw on a pair of jeans and a shirt. In the compact en-suite shower room, I turn on the hot tap only to find the water cold. Ginny warned me the plumbing at Foxcombe Manor was geriatric and highly temperamental, but now I add *choosy* to those descriptions, drawing the conclusion that there's only a small window during which the household has the luxury of hot water... and this is obviously not the allotted time. I walk to the kitchen and quickly lay the table for breakfast and then rush upstairs to wake the children and help Tegan get washed and dressed. By the time Zac and his sisters are seated at the kitchen table eating cereal I am about ready for bed. Placing a full rack of toast in the middle next to the jams, I stifle a yawn. Rhea notices and grins.

So far, all three children have displayed happy dispositions and a great sense of fun, but I must keep my wits about me as I know they'll be testing me during the early days. Whatever impression I make now will set the tone of our relationship. Fortunately, Zac and Rhea are in awe of my experience with horses, listening attentively and willingly following instructions. However, there's not much organisation to the days and we lurch from one 'almost missed' moment to another. Also, Ginny makes few demands on the children to help out around the house. Although I'm new to the household, I intend to introduce a rota where each child will be responsible for keeping their own room tidy and making their bed, and also to help set and clear the kitchen table at mealtimes. I doubt I'll be popular and Tegan won't be able to do much, but Zac and Rhea are old enough to take on responsibility.

From the open hall, the grandfather clock strikes the hour. Moments later, Ginny appears in the kitchen doorway.

'Good morning, Cassie. Hello, children.' She ruffles Zac's hair and squeezes Rhea's shoulder as she passes behind her daughter. Coming around the table, she gives Tegan an affectionate kiss on the cheek.

The little girl raises her shoulder and scrunches up her nose. 'Mummy, that tickles!'

'Would you like a cup of tea?' I ask.

'Please.' Ginny pulls out a seat and sits down. 'What a treat it is to have breakfast ready and waiting.'

Zac eyes his mother across the table. 'Who's taking us to school today?'

'I am. Your father wants Cassie to make a start on the farm admin.' Ginny helps herself to a slice of toast.

This is news to me! My left eyebrow twitches as I pour Ginny's tea.

'I'm afraid I haven't kept on top of it.' She gives me a rueful smile. 'But, hopefully, you'll make sense of it. If not, shout.'

'Don't forget I've got netball club after school,' Rhea says through a mouthful of Cornflakes.

'Oh, I had forgotten.' Ginny pulls a face. 'Is your kit clean?'

Rhea nods.

'Good. I've got to go into Bude this afternoon so I'll collect Tiggy at lunchtime and take her in with me, and then I can fetch you on my way back through. Cassie, you should have made headway with the admin by the time school finishes, so please collect Zac.' She frowns, and then smiles. 'Yes, that should work.'

'Of course.' I place a cup of tea on the table in front of her.

How did she manage to juggle the children's timetable before appointing me? A rota is a good idea, if only to act as a reminder to Ginny of the various extracurricular activities her children have.

'Morning, all.' Gyles appears in the kitchen doorway.

With a grin, Zac mimics his father's voice. 'Morning.'

'Hi, Dad,' Rhea says.

Tegan waves her spoon at him.

'Do you want a cooked breakfast, darling?' Ginny smiles at her husband.

'No thanks. I'll just a grab a coffee and take it through to the study.'

Turning on the cold water tap, I refill the kettle and place it on the hob.

'That's kind of you, Cassie, but there's no need to take care of me.' He grabs a mug from the counter. 'Will you be ready to start on the admin at, say, nine?'

I make a quick calculation. After the children have finished their breakfasts, I have the table to clear and the washing-up to do. Then the horses and ponies have to be brought in from the fields, but as long as none of them play up I should be ready.

'Don't see why not.'

'Good. It'll be a case of finding your way around the system today and acquainting yourself with what's required.' Gyles spoons coffee into his mug. 'I'll be around for most of the morning but I've a meeting with my farm manager at eleven, although that shouldn't take long.'

I smile at the large, genial man.

'Don't frighten her off, Gyles,' warns Ginny.

'Of course not. I'll go gentle on her.' He gives me a wink as he stirs his coffee. Then, with steaming mug in hand, he walks towards the door. 'Enjoy your day, children. Learn lots.'

Once the Kinsman family has vacated the kitchen, I clear away the breakfast table and wash the dishes and cups, leaving them to dry on the draining board... what a novelty! A smile tugs at the corners of my mouth as I think back to my first evening at Foxcombe when I'd offered to help clear up after supper. Ginny was doing the washing up and I'd picked up a cloth to dry the dishes, but she'd quickly instructed me otherwise.

'Goodness, Cassie, leave the plates to drip-dry. If we spend our days trying to keep this house clean and tidy we'll have no life at all. We've far better things to do with our time.'

Now, as I cross the yard and head towards the barn, I gaze up at a leaden sky. It's cool today. Racing clouds chase each other and it feels like rain. But there's something else, and I sniff the air – the ocean – and I make a promise to myself that I'll walk to the sea once I have time. Entering the barn, I take down five halters from their hooks and make my way towards the fields. As soon as I round the corner of the barns, Caspian looks up and whickers a welcome. He sets off at a trot towards me. Dylan brings his head up sharply, whinnying loudly as he follows in hot pursuit. Ginny's thoroughbred mare gracefully raises her head and watches, but the other two ponies ignore the distractions and continue to graze.

'Hello, my boy.' Caspian lowers his head into the halter and his soft lips nuzzle my hand. 'Looks like you're settling in nicely.'

Dylan comes to a flying stop. Cheekily, he nudges my elbow with his nose.

'Young man, you may get away with that sort of behaviour with your young owner but you do not beg for treats from me. Understand?' I look the Welsh pony straight in the eye.

I'd intended to bring in the two larger horses first.

However, as Caspian and Dylan have come up, I lead them along the track to their stables and then return to the field for the others. Indiana is now at the gate and Rhea's Exmoor pony slowly makes its way over, in no particular hurry. The little Shetland pony hasn't moved. I take Indiana out of the field and walk her to the barn and, by the time I return, the two remaining ponies are hanging around the gate wondering where the rest of their herd has gone.

'You two... I see I'm going to have fun and games with you,' I chide softly.

Both ponies lead well and it's obvious they're used to doing things together. I wonder if they've ever worked *at liberty* in the sand school. It will be fun finding out.

After checking that the horses and ponies have full hay nets and clean water, I walk back to my rooms. Glancing at my watch, I see that it's five to nine. Quickly, I wash my hands and make my way along the corridor to the study. The door is ajar. Beneath a single window overlooking the yard is a large wooden desk on which is an early model computer. Gyles sits with his back to the door and, unobserved, I take the opportunity to check out the space. It's the antithesis of David's neat, organised home office with its state-of-the-art technology.

As with my rooms, the study has white-washed stone walls without the wood panelling prevalent throughout the rest of the house. On one wall is a whiteboard, divided into three columns by a black marker pen and filled with what looks like field names, figures and percentages in blue and red. Alongside this are two tall, grey filing cabinets; no doubt stuffed full of documents and papers. Lining the opposite wall is a bookcase, stacked high with farming newspapers, magazines, heavy ledgers and a selection of other weighty tomes. Every available surface is buried beneath papers and journals. Even the chair in the corner of the room is piled high. Inwardly, I groan. I don't flinch from a challenge, but...

'Ah, there you are.' Gyles glances over his shoulder. 'I thought I sensed a presence.'

I give a brief smile, but his choice of words and strange expression give me pause to consider.

'Don't be shy, Cassie. Come on in.'

Something tells me I've got my work cut out and it's going to be a very long day.

13

That first Saturday at Foxcombe Manor, as I stand at the kitchen sink washing the last of the breakfast dishes, Ginny and Tegan appear in the doorway. I smile at the little girl. She looks so cute with her pink ballet tutu peeping out from beneath the hem of her older sister's oversized, hand-me-down cardigan.

'I'll take Rhea and Tiggy to their gym and ballet classes and perhaps you'd take Zac and Dylan for a ride around the farm. Zac knows the tracks. He'll show you the way.'

'Sure. It's a perfect morning for it.' My eyes slide to the oblong of pale blue visible through the window.

'We should be back by one.' Ginny glances up at the kitchen clock. 'If not, you and Zac help yourselves to lunch. Don't worry about Gyles – he'll sort himself out.'

'Mum, we're late!' Rhea bellows from the open hall.

'I know. Come on, Tiggy, we'd better not keep Miss Bunting waiting. Come, Roly, Pumpkin.'

Lying comfortably in their baskets in the corner of the room, the dogs raise their heads.

'Come now… or not at all.'

As if deciding whether to do as instructed, both dogs look at each other before rising to their feet. I stifle a laugh.

Firmly settled on the pew on the far side of the room, the family's ginger cat, Marmaduke, studiously washes itself.

Ginny ushers Tegan out of the door, but the little girl turns back to me. 'Can I give Caspian a carrot later?'

'Of course! We'll give one to all the ponies.'

She beams.

Once Ginny, her daughters and the dogs have vacated the house peace descends again. Ginny is *exactly* as her advert suggested – a whirlwind of chaotic energy and always in a rush. Possessing a heart of gold, she is *friend* to everyone and I realise how fortunate I am to have stumbled across the Kinsmans, who have welcomed me into their home with open arms. Already I'm beginning to feel part of the family and neither Ginny nor Gyles have enquired about my previous life. I am so grateful for that. Deeply hurt and – if I'm truthful – shocked at my sudden change in circumstance, I welcome the opportunity to nurse my broken heart and wounded pride in private. I still expect David to contact me; at the very least to make sure I'd arrived safely. But, so far, he's made no attempt. My mobile remains silent. Neither has he emailed.

Probably enjoying his newfound freedom with Melanie, or perhaps Denise has grabbed the opportunity to try her luck again.

Dragging my bitter thoughts away from David, I rinse the last piece of crockery and leave it to dry on the drainer with the rest of the breakfast dishes. As I walk from the kitchen into the open hall, Zac's face appears over the minstrels' gallery. Aged eleven, he is going through the gangly stage; his body unsure of its sudden, newfound spurt of growth. Like his mother, he has an arresting face, clear brown eyes and a shock of auburn hair that curls beautifully at his temples and onto his collar.

'Fancy a ride around the farm? It will do Caspian and Dylan good to stretch their legs.'

The boy grins. 'I'll get changed.' He turns, on the point of rushing away.

'Zac, will we pass a post box?'

'Yes.'

'Good. See you in the stables.'

As I walk across the open hall's massive flagstones, I marvel that despite the chaotic noise created by the family currently residing at Foxcombe Manor, deep peace and tranquillity pervades the air. It struck me the moment I'd arrived.

Ten minutes later, I'm doing up the buckle to Dylan's throatlatch when Zac appears at the stable door, dressed in breeches, sweatshirt and boots. In his hand is a riding helmet.

'Thanks for putting Dylan's bridle on but I'll saddle him.' He places the helmet on the floor.

I leave him to finish off and quickly tack up Caspian before following Zac and Dylan out into the yard. The sun is surprisingly warm and there's not a cloud in the sky. It's different air to Sussex. Breathing in deeply, I detect a strong hint of salt in the breeze. As Zac leads the Welsh pony to the mounting block, a sudden clucking makes me glance towards the entrance where half a dozen chickens, investigating the grassy embankment on the other side of the farm track, stand alert as a couple of farm cats saunter by.

'Your mum says you know all the tracks around here.' I check Caspian's girth.

Zac nods. Putting his foot on the first stone step, which has been smoothed into a shallow pit from centuries of footfall, he gathers up the reins and leaps onto his pony's back.

I raise an eyebrow. 'Well, that's an interesting way to mount!'

The boy grins and urges Dylan away from the block.

'Is there a circuitous route that takes about an hour?'

I position Caspian alongside the block and mount, settling quietly in the saddle. Checking the girth again, I raise my knee, lift the saddle flap and take it up another hole.

'Yes, up the lane, through the village, down to the church, across the stream and along by the woods. There's a good blast back up the hill to the house.'

I encourage Caspian forward to catch up with Zac and Dylan, already eagerly heading off. From their outside kennel on the far side of the yard, all four gun dogs watch as we exit the quadrangle of barns.

Zac is a good rider. He needs to be. Dylan is cheeky, with a habit of snatching at the long grasses growing in the hedgerows and breaking into a jog without warning. The boy handles the pony's mischievous traits with ease and isn't unseated when Dylan suddenly whips round, although Zac's expression is of one of embarrassment when he comes face-to-face with Caspian and me.

I'll have to keep an eye on that pony. These habits could develop into something a bit more challenging.

Even though I'd lunged Dylan the day before while Zac was at school, it's obvious the pony needs regular exercise to keep his exuberant character in check.

'You're lucky to have such quiet lanes around here.'

Zac glances across at me. 'Don't you have good riding where you live?'

Where I live... Where exactly is that? I check myself.

'There's great riding on the South Downs but there's also a lot of traffic on the roads. You have to keep your eyes peeled for lorries and motorbikes.'

As we ride up Foxcombe Manor's drive and join the parish lane, I gaze across fields of cows and sheep stretching away into the distance. I don't know the area at all, and since my arrival I haven't had the chance to explore. We trot for a while, passing a couple of farm entrances, and soon come to the outskirts of a village, which mainly comprises picture-postcard cottages, some thatched, with a smattering of grander stone houses and a number of new-builds. Presently, we reach the post box. Halting Caspian alongside, I take the envelope from my pocket, lean down and insert the letter addressed to Rachel Price. The girl deserves an explanation as to why I won't be around to help with her pony.

In the centre of the village Zac turns left and, once again, we urge Caspian and Dylan into a trot. We don't talk and I'm happy to simply enjoy the passing scenery, which is both beautiful and unspoilt. Soon, we arrive at a pub – The Bush Inn – the sign informing passers-by of its thirteenth-century origin. Bringing the horses back to walk, we continue for a short way and pass an obviously popular tea rooms, judging by the number of parked cars outside.

It is *so* quiet. So far, we have seen only one tractor and two cars, and I revel in hacking through the ruggedly attractive, remote countryside with its glorious backdrop of cliffs set against a deep blue sea. Suddenly, a square tower comes into view. According to the board at the entrance, it is the Church of St Morwenna and St John the Baptist.

'Do you know about our famous vicar?'

'No.'

Zac stares at me in astonishment. Straightening up in the saddle, the boy puffs out his chest and prepares to enlighten this ill-informed southerner.

'His name is the Reverend Robert Stephen Hawker and he lived here in the eighteen hundreds. He invented the Harvest Festival.' Zac checks to make sure I'm paying attention.

I encourage him to continue.

'He was the vicar for nearly forty years and he built that vicarage over there.' Standing in his stirrups, he points beyond the church.

Turning to my right, through the trees I see a substantial house with a number of unusual chimneys.

'He also gave drowned sailors proper burials in the churchyard.'

'He sounds a remarkable man.'

'And he built a hut in the cliffs where he did drugs. It's still there.'

I pull a disbelieving face.

'It's true! There *is* a hut in the cliffs.'

'I believe you. But are you sure he *did drugs*?' My right eyebrow twitches.

'Yes. Ask anyone.'

I glance at my watch. 'Where do we go from here?'

'There's a track back there.' He points behind him. 'It goes across the fields down to the stream. It's not a bridle path but we're allowed to use it.'

'OK, Zac. Lead the way.'

In the middle of the lane the boy turns his pony on a sixpence.

The track crosses open fields stretching down to the edge of the cliffs, with the sea beyond sparkling under a strengthening sun. The countryside is stunning and as Caspian and I follow the boy and his pony, my spirits lift. Although emotionally raw, I'm never happier than when out in nature; *at one* with my horse. As I think about all the recent changes in my life, I know that being so readily accepted by the Kinsman family is helping to fill the void brought about by my abrupt departure from David and Stone Farm. As I relax, Caspian grows soft beneath me. He is so tuned to my emotions, and I'm thankful I have my loyal ally with me. Life without him would be too awful.

The track leads downhill to a dense area of woodland that follows the fold of the land. I ride alongside Zac in silence and listen to him chatting to his pony, now settled and no longer showing signs of wanting to break into a jog. Still, I make a mental note to give the intelligent Dylan more challenging schooling in future.

'It's quite steep going down to the stream.' Zac glances across at me. 'Will Caspian be OK?'

'I think so. He's very sure-footed.'

'The trees are low in places. You'll probably have to duck.'

'Thanks for the warning.'

On reaching the woods Zac turns left, and for a short distance we ride along the edge of the field, following the treeline.

'This is the track.' Suddenly turning his pony, Zac disappears through a well-camouflaged opening.

I urge Caspian to follow. As soon as we enter I'm struck by not only the chill but also an eerie stillness. There's something ancient to this place. The hillside is covered with gnarled and twisted trees fighting the prevailing wind, their lichen-draped branches interlacing. Suddenly alert, Caspian twitches his ears as he evaluates the new terrain. In front, Zac and Dylan confidently navigate a narrow path leading steeply downhill and further into the gloom. I shiver. Although we're out of the mid-morning sun, I have the feeling the chill is caused by something other than that.

The path is little more than an animal track and tree roots criss-cross our way, making the going precarious. Carefully, we progress downhill until reaching a wider path that runs alongside a fast-flowing stream, which tumbles over moss-covered boulders as it seeks out hidden corners.

'Good. It's not too high.' Zac glances back at me. 'The crossing's just ahead.'

As I follow the boy and his pony, I take in my surroundings. The land on the opposite bank rises steeply and the grotesquely shaped trees continue up the hillside. They look like witch trees. Despite my relatively down-to-earth nature, I find myself considering goblins and fairies,

Cornish piskies and things that go bump in the night. Swallowing hard, I concentrate on the path ahead.

'Here we are,' Zac suddenly announces.

The stream at this point is less deep and a cutting in the riverbank allows us to access a pebbled crossing with a number of stepping stones. As Dylan steps confidently off the track into the water, I encourage Caspian to follow. It takes a couple of attempts but eventually he leaps into the centre of the stream before rushing across to the other side and coming up fast behind the Welsh pony.

'Not much water on the South Downs, then?' Zac gives me a cheeky grin.

That boy! Much older than his eleven years.

'Not in such a rugged setting.'

'See that track over there?' He points into the thicket. 'That takes us up to the bottom of Stream Field. Then, it's just two fields to home.'

Without warning, Caspian snorts and shoots forward. I check him and speak soothingly. This is odd behaviour for my horse – he usually has a steady disposition – and I peer deeper into the trees. What has spooked him? Is it my imagination or is something moving higher up on the hillside? I can't be sure what I'm looking at. It isn't solid or a shape I can put a name to; it appears to be mist circling amongst the trees, rather than something substantial. But when I blink it's gone. I urge Caspian forward. He's reluctant, but trusting me, he makes his way up the steep hillside keeping close to Dylan. In several places I'm forced to lie along his neck, and as low-hanging branches scrape across my back I firmly banish any thoughts of fingers grabbing at my shirt. Suddenly, glancing to my right, I spy a thatched roof away through the trees and immediately think of *Hansel and Gretel*. I shiver again.

For pity's sake, Cassandra, grow a backbone!

Five minutes later, we emerge from the eerie woodland into a field; its long grass shimmering under the midday sun. All at once, the spooky feelings are gone. We are simply a couple of horse riders enjoying a quiet hack in this peaceful corner of the Cornish countryside.

14

From out of nowhere, a large tan-coloured animal springs from the thicket. Dylan puts in an explosive buck, his hind hooves missing my knee by a matter of inches.

'Whoa!' shouts Zac, as his pony takes off.

I can't do anything to help, as Caspian leaps into the air, twists sideways and the next minute I'm unceremoniously dumped on the ground. Badly winded, I lie on my back fighting for breath. The sun is unseasonably strong on my face and, suddenly, a wet nose snuffles my cheek. Once able to draw air into my lungs, with superhuman effort I roll over onto all fours and scan the empty field. Zac and the pony are nowhere in sight.

'Shit!'

What will Gyles and Ginny say if their beloved son has a serious accident on the very first day he rides out with me?

'Are you all right?'

I turn in the direction of the voice. A pleasant-looking, open-faced man with kind, hazel eyes gazes at me with concern. At his side is the largest Great Dane I've ever seen. Ignoring his question, I look towards Foxcombe Manor again, frantically searching for Zac and Dylan. As I struggle to my feet, a warm, steadying hand takes hold of my elbow.

'Let me help you.'

I shake him off and glare at the man, my face reddening in anger. 'You stupid oaf! Can't you control your dog?'

He stands back smartly, the concern rapidly diminishing in his eyes.

Checking my riding hat is still intact, I stride towards Caspian, who has taken this unexpected opportunity to graze. I gather up the reins, throw myself into the saddle and, not bothering with stirrups, encourage my horse straight into canter. As I urge him to go faster, I can't help but think how ironic it is that David judges his cars by their ability to go from nought to sixty in the least possible time, and here was I giving a good impression of that on my four-legged companion.

Where is Zac? I have visions of him lying in a ditch, broken and in pain... or worse.

A couple of minutes later I gallop from the field into the quadrangle of barns, only slowing slightly at the entrance. Stirred up by all the commotion, the gun dogs bark excitedly. As Caspian clatters into the yard and comes to a flying stop, I call out for Zac. There's no response and I leap from the saddle. Leaving my horse standing in the centre of the yard, blowing hard, I run into the barn with my heart hammering painfully against my ribcage.

'Zac, are you here?'

His innocent face appears over the door to Dylan's stable.

'Oh, thank God!' Relief floods through me and I rush forward. 'Are you OK?'

'Wasn't that cool?'

I stop, as if slammed into a wall. 'What...?'

'I didn't know Dylan could go that fast!'

'I thought you might have fallen off.'

I feel weak at the knees. Approaching the stable, I look over the door at the pony now contentedly munching hay.

'No, he's easy to sit. Anyway, we liked it.'

I clutch at my chest. If this is the level of fear when the boy isn't even mine, what on earth would I be like with children of my own? A vision of David swims into my head.

'Is Dylan OK?' Opening the door, I walk to the pony and check him over.

'Where's Caspian?'

'Oh crikey, I've abandoned him in the yard!'

'I'll get him.'

Once Zac is out of earshot, I quietly scold Dylan. 'You naughty pony. You have to look after that boy.'

Unconcerned, the Welsh pony pulls hay from the net, but an ear twitches in response.

'Did you know you've got grass stains on your breeches?' Zac comments, as he leads Caspian into the barn.

'That's not surprising. When Dylan took off, I hit the ground.'

'Caspian dumped you!' Zac's eyes open wide and a delighted grin spreads from ear to ear.

'Err… yes.'

I hear him chuckle. Exiting Dylan's stable, I walk to Caspian's door and peer over.

As Zac removes the saddle, he turns to me and pulls a small, insecure face. 'You won't say anything to Mum and Dad about this, will you?'

I hesitate. As the responsible 'Superhuman' I should report the incident to his parents, but I must admit to feeling relieved by this request.

'If that's what you want.'

He nods. 'I don't want them banning us riding together.' Suddenly he looks sheepish. 'I enjoyed it.'

'I enjoyed it too, Zac.' I quash the memory of the eeriness in the woods. 'I hope you'll show me many more tracks in the area.'

'I will. I know them all. Even some Mum doesn't know!'

As I take Caspian's saddle from him, my mobile alerts me to an incoming call. I grab the phone off the ledge where I'd left it.

Must remember to take it with me on future hacks... just in case!

I glance at the screen and pause. David. A cocktail of emotions flood though me, and even though I've wanted him to phone I consider letting it go to voicemail.

'Hello.'

'Sandie, what are you playing at?' His voice is trademark strong.

'What do you mean?' Wedging the mobile between my shoulder and chin, I place Caspian's saddle on its rack. 'I'm not *playing* at anything.'

'Oh, come on...' He sounds exasperated. 'You know exactly what you're doing.'

Did I?

'David, I told you this was my plan.' Aware that Zac can hear the call, I smile at the boy. 'It's OK, Zac, I'll finish up here.'

He nods and walks towards the entrance of the barn.

I turn my attention back to David. 'I haven't hidden anything from you.'

Unlike he has from me.

'What does that mean?'

'Just that.' Sitting on the wooden chest containing horse blankets not in use, I resign myself to a difficult conversation.

'You said you thought we needed some distance, but I didn't expect you to take off to the other end of the country! Come home, Sandra. Give up this nonsense and get back here where you belong. You're a hired hand to these people, not part of their family. There's no future for you there.'

I sigh. What he says is true. However welcoming the Kinsmans are, I am simply someone who answered their advert. But what would I be returning to? A dull ache settles in the pit of my stomach as every fibre in my body fights against returning to that gilded cage.

'Are you still there?'

'Yes.'

'Stop procrastinating, load up that horse of yours and come back.'

'I can't leave Gyles and Ginny in the lurch.' It sounds so feeble.

David snorts. 'For God's sake, the country is awash with people looking for jobs. There are plenty to employ.'

I hear the irritated tapping of fingers.

'Are you sleeping with Melanie?' I'm amazed I ask the question; I must be emboldened by the miles between us.

Caught off guard, David splutters before quickly turning it into a cough. 'Don't be ridiculous. Where on earth did you get that notion?'

'Oh, various things…'

'You are always *so* fanciful, Sandie. Start behaving like an adult and get on with your life. Stop wasting time.'

'Do you love me, David?'

Bristling impatience crackles across the ether.

'Of course. What is wrong with you? Stop this nonsense now and get back here.'

I think of the endless, unfulfilled days and the feeling of having my wings clipped, and then I consider my life here on the north coast of Cornwall, still in its infancy but full of unknown promise.

'I don't think I can. I've only just arrived.'

As the expletives resound, my eyes open wide. David has never shouted at me with such venom. As he spews his tirade, highlighting all my shortcomings, I hold the mobile away from my ear. I consider ending the call but a part of me responds to him, believing that some of what he says is true. Ten minutes later he falls silent.

'Have you finished?'

'Yes.' He sounds depleted.

I breathe in deeply, gathering strength and calm I didn't think I possessed. 'Unless you agree to children in our future I don't see how I can return.'

He doesn't respond and I feel his disquiet. After several minutes listening to his laboured breathing, I switch off.

Gazing around the beautiful barn with its intricate rafters reaching high into the roof space, I attempt to absorb some of its serene atmosphere and still my rapidly beating heart. There's no denying it; it's too soon following my departure from Sussex. David has stirred up strong emotions. Even at this distance he still has a hold over me. Squeezing my eyes shut, I curb the unshed tears that threaten to fall, because once I start, I'll be unable to stop.

After a while, having harnessed my tattered feelings, I grab a couple of halters and lead Caspian and Dylan out to the paddock where Inky, Biscuit and Indiana peacefully graze. It's therapeutic doing familiar things and as Caspian and Dylan join the rest of the herd, I stay and watch, breathing in the tranquillity and appreciating the pastoral scene.

Before returning to the barn and tack-cleaning duties, I pause at the top of Foxcombe Manor's land and gaze across the landscape of open fields and woodland down to the craggy cliffs and the sea. Diverting my gaze to the bottom field, I search for the man and the huge dog but they are nowhere to be seen... and somewhere deep in those woods is a thatched cottage.

I can't help but wonder what other secrets are hidden from sight.

15

Two days later, having completed the morning stable duties, I enter the back porch and pull off my boots. As I open the door to the kitchen, Ginny glances up from her seat at the table and quickly clears her expression.

'Is everything OK?' I ask, walking to the Aga and intending to boil the kettle, but it's already hot.

'Cassie.' Ginny rises to her feet, her chair legs scraping jarringly across the slate flagstone floor. 'The police are here to see you.'

I turn and face her. 'About what?'

She shakes her head. 'I don't know. They didn't say. They've only been here a few minutes. I put them in the drawing room and gave them coffee.'

I frown. Why would the police want to see me? Has something happened to my brother and his family... or David? Anxiety swiftly replaces my confusion.

'I'd best go and find out what they have to say.'

'Do you want me to come with you?'

I gaze at my employer. Her face shows genuine concern. 'Please. That's really thoughtful.'

She squeezes my arm, and we make our way across the open hall to the drawing room where a middle-aged male officer and a young policewoman sit in two large armchairs. Both get to their feet as we enter.

'I'm Cassandra Shaw. I understand you're here to see me.' I will my voice not to quaver.

The policeman shows no emotion. 'Miss Shaw, we are here on David Ashcroft's instructions to retrieve property that belongs to him.'

Property that belongs to him?

Blood drains from my face and my stomach cramps. 'What property?'

'Shall we all sit?' suggests Ginny.

Before my legs give way, I perch on the edge of the couch. Ginny sits down next to me.

Producing a small notepad from his pocket, the male officer flips open the cover and reads through his notes. He regards me with expressionless eyes. 'I believe you are in possession of a Range Rover and horse trailer.'

'Yes.'

He clears his throat. 'Apparently they do not belong to you.'

Deep inside a small ball of anger forms. 'They were gifted to me.'

The policeman glances down at his notes again. 'A gift, you say?'

'Yes. David gave them to me for my last birthday.'

'Not according to Mr Ashcroft.' He looks up, his eyes boring into mine.

My jaw drops.

'He says the car and trailer belong to Ashcroft Enterprises and that you have no right to take them without his permission. Both are listed on a company insurance policy.'

How dare David?

'That's not true. He gave them to me as a present.' Hearing my voice, I know I sound like a whining, lost soul.

'Unless you can produce paperwork that proves otherwise, we will have to impound the vehicles.'

What a fool... why didn't I look for the insurance policies before I left Stone Farm?

But I knew why I hadn't. In emotional turmoil during all the arrangements leading up to my departure, I'd simply forgotten to consider any legal documentation.

I stare at the policeman in disbelief. I can't prove otherwise, and now that I think about it I have never seen any policies. David always takes care of that side of things. For all I know, the bastard may well have insured them in the company name, conveniently omitting to tell me when he *oh so generously* gifted me the Range Rover and matching two-horse trailer for my twenty-seventh birthday. Recalling how overwhelmed I'd been by his generosity, I cringe. We'd celebrated in style and he'd certainly benefitted from my gratitude that night. My face colours with emotion – I feel *so* used and manipulated.

The young policewoman casts me a sympathetic look.

'I can't prove anything.' I get to my feet. 'It's his word against mine. I'll get the keys.'

As I walk from the room and cross the open hall, I'm distracted by a movement up on the minstrels' gallery. But that can't be. There's no one else in the house, apart from those in the drawing room. The children are at school and Gyles went to his office in Bude earlier this morning. Just shadows... tricks of the light. I continue to my rooms and, closing the door firmly, I lean back against the solid wood and squeeze my eyes tight shut. I'm livid, but also so sad that it has come to this. I know it's David's way of punishing me. Having demanded I return to him, in his eyes I should have done so by now. I'm lucky he hasn't ordered Caspian to be confiscated because he, too, was a present. I begin to shake.

How dare he do this, after what he's already done to me!

Taking a deep, steadying breath, I open my eyes. The keys to the car and trailer are in the chest of drawers by the window overlooking the yard. Crossing the room, I pull open the top drawer and pick them up. What does David expect to achieve by this? Is he trying to force my hand, thinking I will simply acquiesce and return to Sussex? I love him, but I can't return to the life I had with him. A soft knock at the door draws me from my musings.

'Miss Shaw?' The policewoman's voice is apologetic.

'Just coming.'

Balling my hand into a fist around the keys, I look out into the yard. On the opposite side, under cover of the open-fronted barn, is the trailer. I was so happy when David gave it to me. It opened up the rest of the country to me and I was no longer limited to the lanes and bridlepaths around the South Downs. Now, I'll be confined to this corner of Cornwall. But is that such a bad thing? I'm determined to forge a new life... somewhere.

Hearing the door opening, I turn. The policewoman peers uncertainly into the room.

'Did you think I was about to do a runner?' My voice sounds harsher than intended.

'No.'

But I can tell by the look in her eyes this is exactly why she was sent to find me.

'Here.' I stride across the room and thrust the keyring into her hand. 'The keys to my birthday presents.'

She looks embarrassed. 'I'm sorry. It's just my job.'

'I know. I'm sorry too… for having wasted so much time on that absolute bastard.'

The policewoman's mouth twitches into a small smile. 'It's hard knowing which ones are and which ones aren't.'

Despite my sadness and anger, I pause. If I'd met this woman in the pub we may have been friends.

'So it would seem.'

She turns from the room and I follow, closing the door quietly behind me.

Several minutes later, as I stand in the yard watching the policeman hook the trailer onto the Range Rover, I make no attempt to help. Ginny is with me and I'm grateful for her presence. David has completely and successfully humiliated me. I am *not* a common thief. I accepted his presents in good faith. How naïve…

As the Range Rover and trailer are driven out of the yard, the gun dogs peer through the wire mesh of their cage and start frenziedly barking. Ginny and I walk along the passageway between the barns and past the old Porter's Lodge, and as we approach the front door I see the young policewoman standing in the driveway by a marked car. Suddenly, the Range Rover and trailer appear alongside on the parallel farm track and she throws me an apologetic smile before climbing into the police car and following her colleague towards the parish lane.

'Oh Lord! That's bad timing.'

I watch as a silver car pulls over to allow the convoy to pass; Ginny's PGs staying in the Porter's Lodge.

'I'll make up some plausible story if they question why the police were here.' She holds out two keys to me. 'Cassie, here are the keys to the Peugeot. I told you at the interview a car came with the job. I know it's not as grand as the Range Rover, but it's yours to use as you wish.'

I swallow hard, unable to stem the stream of big fat tears. It's as if a tap has been turned on.

She draws me into a hug. 'Men! They can be tricky at the best of times.'

Seeing the curious looks on her guests' faces as their car passes by on the farm track, Ginny gives a friendly wave while quickly steering me into the house.

'But, there's nothing that a fresh pot of coffee and a slice of homemade cake won't put right.'

Oh, how I wish it were that simple.

16

Following the shock visit from the police, Ginny gives me the afternoon off. I decide to walk down to the sea and set off along the farm track at the edge of the fields. I stop to say 'hello' to Caspian who trots over as I pass by the horses' paddocks. Fishing out a packet of Polos from my pocket, I place one on my open palm and offer it to him. His lips delicately graze my skin.

It's one of those beautiful summer days that hold a promise of softer times to come. I so hope this is true. It's not getting any easier, and the ache in my heart and the dread in the pit of my stomach at having left all that I've known grow as each day passes. What if I've made the wrong decision? Caspian gently nudges my hand. What if David *is* the only one for me? I stroke the buckskin gelding's neck and whisper sweet nothings in his ear. As I resume my walk along the fence line, he accompanies me on the opposite side of the post and rails. I smile.

'Don't worry about me, young man. Go back and join the others.'

He watches me with a wisdom born of generations before him; my wise and loyal friend.

'Go on.'

He turns away and, with a flick of the neck, breaks into canter. Effortlessly, he covers the ground, mischievously scattering the peacefully grazing ponies as he makes a beeline for the beautiful Fairweather Indiana. I grin to myself as I continue walking down the track towards the woodland. Removing my sweatshirt, I wrap it around my waist and roll up the sleeves of my shirt, comforted by the warmth of sun on bare skin. Perhaps the heat will penetrate through to my heart and warm that too.

As I approach the outer reaches of the woods, I hesitate. Do I want to enter that dark, sinister environment? It spooked me more than I care to admit when Zac and I had ridden through it. I search for a field crossing to the other side of the valley, but the trees stretch for miles. Nearing the well-camouflaged opening from which we'd emerged a few days before, again I falter. Shall I just walk around the perimeter of the fields and return to the farm? I sigh in exasperation. For goodness' sake! When had I turned into such a wimp?

Steeling myself, I step through the opening into the woods.

The sudden coolness makes the heat of the day seem but a distant memory, and I tell myself it's the leafy canopy that has lowered the temperature and nothing else. I follow the track through the trees towards the stream down in the valley and feel a rush of relief when I realise that the further I go, the more easily I breathe. There is nothing sinister in the woods today. As I relax, I start to notice my surroundings and am surprised to find the lichen-covered trees have a beauty of their own. I'd considered them grotesque, but their gnarled and twisted shapes are beautiful today, like a work or art adorning the hillside in intricate patterns. And it is *so* peaceful. The atmosphere washes over me as I catch an occasional snatch of birdsong.

Suddenly, unexpectedly, as I plunge ever deeper into the interior I'm filled with contentment. I glance to my left, hoping to catch sight of the mysterious cottage in the trees but, curiously, there's no sign of a thatched roof – not even a glimpse. However, once I've dropped down to the stream I realise my mistake. I must be on a different path. The watercourse here is much wider and deeper than where Zac and I had crossed. I continue to follow the track. The stream twists and turns through the rugged landscape and a number of small rapids percolate the brown water to a frothy white, before suddenly rounding a corner and slowing to a deep, dark, silent pool. I stop and stand on a large, flat rock protruding out over the stream, and then crouch down to dip my fingers into the water. Too cold for a swim but, maybe, if this weather continues I'll be tempted.

As I make my way further into the valley the stream gathers pace and turns into a small river. I wonder if I'll have to retrace my steps but, eventually, I find a potential crossing. On a particularly sharp bend of the river, the water funnels into a fast-flowing force between two rocky embankments. I examine the ground; it seems firm. Calculating it to be little more than an extended jump, I take a few steps back and, setting off at a run, with a leap of faith I launch into the air. But, as I land on the opposite side, my feet slip and I throw myself forward, slamming down hard on my knees. Grabbing wildly at anything that offers the slightest purchase, my fingers close around an exposed root. My breathing is ragged and my heart pumps at an alarming rate. How idiotic! What if I'd twisted an ankle, or worse? It's doubtful there's a mobile signal here, deep in the woods. I have to be more careful. Too much depends on my fitness and health.

Half-crawling, I scramble up the steep slope to the track on the opposite bank. The woodland is thinner here and shafts of sunlight filter their way through the canopy, and there's something else… a tantalising hint of ocean on the breeze. I continue on and within no more than a hundred yards I emerge from the woods. I stop and stare in wonder. Dramatic cliffs dip to a 'V' and, hugging one side of the valley, the path leads out onto a high promontory that juts out into the ocean. Way below, the river continues undisturbed on its course to the sea. From the peace and quiet of the woodland suddenly all is energy and noise. Seagulls wheel in the air and a charcoal smudge hovers above the cliffs. Shielding my eyes, I see it's a peregrine falcon. Like a drowning person, I draw the salt air deep into my lungs and, closing my eyes, I luxuriate in the warmth of the sun as a gentle breeze caresses.

After a while, I continue on towards the beckoning deep, blue sea. The nearer I get to the cliffs, the stronger the breeze. Halting to get my bearings, I turn and inhale sharply. In the distance, at the head of the valley, is the thatched cottage in the woods… but it's far from a *cottage*. Hidden from view, only seen from this particular stretch of the coast path, a substantial stone-built house sits above an open-terraced lawn. Behind it are Foxcombe Manor's fields, dotted with Friesian cows. As I study the house I break into a smile. It's not at all like the *Hansel and Gretel* witch's house I'd imagined. It looks homely and welcoming and I can easily imagine a weary traveller drawn to the smoke that would undoubtedly rise from its three chimneys in winter. Today, however, there is no smoke. Basking in the early afternoon sun, the thatched roof glows burnished gold and beneath two gabled first-floor windows, a reed-covered veranda spans the full width of the house.

I wonder who lives there? Whoever it is must enjoy solitude.

The uninterrupted views down the valley to the sea must be stunning, and how wonderful to sit on that veranda at the end of a long day, enjoying a glass of wine whilst watching the sun slip slowly into the ocean.

A sudden gust of wind causes goose bumps to appear on my arms. I untie the sweatshirt from around my waist and put it on.

I continue on towards the headland. Spectacular cliffs stretch for miles in both directions. The closely cropped, open grassland gives a false impression of softness; this is a rugged, unyielding landscape. The sound of waves fills the air and seagulls screech into the wind as I step out onto a narrow path traversing the ridge of the promontory. Dramatic granite escarpments drop away steeply to either side. It's just as well I have a head for heights; this is no place for someone afflicted with vertigo.

Reaching the end of the path, I stand in awe and gaze out over the vast expanse of ocean and sky. It's good being out here, at one with the elements, and my spirits lift as I listen to the sound of the surf and feel the strength of the sun and wind on my face. Stretching my arms wide and inhaling deeply, for a brief, fanciful moment I imagine I'm Kate Winslet's aristocratic character, Rose Dewitt Bukater, standing above the bowsprit of the ill-fated *HMS Titanic* with Leonardo di Caprio's kind but penniless artist, Jack Dawson, lovingly holding on to her. But immediately I feel foolish; there is no champion in my life. Crossing my arms, I continue to gaze at the ocean. On the horizon is the hazy outline of an island and, suddenly humbled, I realise that however small I may feel, I am still a part of this magnificent world.

Several yards out, a cormorant skims across the water, unconcerned by the gulls swooping in the air above it. Shielding my eyes, I shift my gaze and look left. The coastline stretches away into the distance with dramatic cliffs falling almost vertically to the sea. Astonishingly, amongst all this natural beauty, on a nearby headland several antennae give away the location of a satellite station.

Turning one hundred and eighty degrees, with hands on hips I gaze northwards. Here, the high cliffs tower above a series of shingled coves with menacing fingers of rocks clawing their way out to sea, eager to catch any unsuspecting seafarer. A flash of colour catches my eye. Walking the shoreline of the nearest bay is a man carrying a bright red cool box that stands out sharply against the predominantly grey landscape. Instantly, I recognise the tan-coloured dog gambolling after the obligingly thrown ball – a very large, young Great Dane. What's the man doing? I squint to gain sharper focus. Moving from one rocky outcrop to another, he examines the seaweed before cutting several fronds and placing them in the cool box. Is he a marine biologist?

I'm on the point of retracing my steps when something delays me and I continue to watch. Although absorbed in his task, the man throws the ball for the dog, which obediently brings it back to him each time. Suddenly he glances up and even though he's at the furthest end of the cove, our eyes meet. For several increasingly awkward moments he holds my gaze. Foolishly, I blush.

How stupid! So what if some random walker casually observes him on the beach below? It's not *his* beach.

Growing increasingly hot under his scrutiny, I turn away and hurry along the ridge towards the safety of the valley.

17

As I enter the kitchen, Ginny opens the Aga door and takes out a tray of cupcakes. The table is set for five.

'Would you mind calling the *little darlings* down for tea?'

'On it straight away.' I turn to go in search of the children.

'And, Cassie…' I look back. 'Whatever's going on in your life, please know that we're very happy having you here with us.'

'Thanks,' I say in a strangled voice.

She bestows a warm smile on me before turning back to the task in hand.

Exiting the kitchen, I make my way across the open hall and welcome the illusion of the clock having turned back several hundred years. If only I could be miraculously transported to a previous century there would be no David constantly gnawing away at me with memories of happier times, and the ache in my heart would simply disappear. I pause at the foot of the stairs and gaze around. Ginny and Gyles, both aware of the importance of preserving history, have kept the interior just as it was when they inherited the property from his parents fifteen years previously. With very few nods to the twenty-first century, it's easy to banish the present at Foxcombe.

I examine the dark oak wall panelling that, in part, dates to the sixteenth century, on which are displayed portraits of several beloved, ancestral family heroes, antlered heads, rusty weapons, tattered banners and ancient coats of arms. I consider the great beams and trusses rising high above me and the flagged and sanded floor beneath my feet. The grandfather clock stands against one wall and an impressive stone fireplace houses a huge open hearth, which Ginny says is piled high with blazing logs in winter. I raise my eyes to the minstrels' gallery with its panelled screen of armorial figures, and to the upper-storey stone-mullioned windows that remind me of tall oriels in a dimly lit chapel.

As I step onto the first tread and slide my hand over the banister, I feel the wear of generations before me. This manor house has surely experienced so much history, witnessing both joy and sorrow, whilst sheltering its inhabitants from the vagaries of the wider Cornish countryside and, yet, somehow it has survived almost unaltered into the twenty-first century. I breathe in the solid, comforting atmosphere, and with each step I take a sense of tranquillity calms my unsettled heart. However much I may want to, I cannot force anything; what will be, will be. I just have to trust that my current, diminished circumstances are but a small part of a bigger picture and that things *will* work out for the best. Like a pack of cards thrown into the air, eventually all will settle and fall into place.

'Damn you, David,' I mutter under my breath.

As I step onto the galleried landing I become aware of a gentle sensation across my body. It's like the soft touch of silk on my skin, as if someone has just brushed past me.

How odd!

I continue along the passageway to the children's playroom. Rhea sits on a padded seat in the bay window, her forehead creased in concentration as she studies the open book on her lap. Marmaduke stretches out beside her, basking in a patch of late afternoon sun. Tegan, with her mad, corkscrew hair in bunches, sits on the carpet in the centre of the room colouring in a large book of fairies, a fair-haired rag doll suspended limply over the crook of her left arm.

This room, too, is panelled and enjoys the same timeless atmosphere that permeates the rest of the house. A number of granite mullioned windows overlook a delightful, enclosed part of the larger garden, and a narrow vertical slit gives a view of the hall below. When Ginny first gave me a tour of the house she'd explained that in years gone by, the mistress of the house would use the loophole, unseen, to enjoy scenes of revelry in the hall below, in which her gender denied her to participate. How times have changed.

'Tea's ready, girls. Where's Zac?'

'In his room,' Rhea says without looking up from her book.

Turning in my direction, Tegan points with her rag doll. 'Pretty girl.'

'Yes, your dolly is.' I smile at the little girl.

'No, pretty girl,' she repeats, shaking her doll at me.

My eyebrows draw together. I've been at Foxcombe for a week now and she's never referred to me in this way before.

'Come on, Tiggy, let's go downstairs. Mummy has tea ready.' I enter the room and hold out my hand.

'Pretty,' she says firmly, still pointing her dolly in my direction.

But as I walk towards her I realise she's not looking at me. She's looking beyond me and I glance over my shoulder. There's no one there. I turn back to the little girl who is, once again, colouring in her book. Returning to the doorway I peer out into the hallway. It's empty. With its old-fashioned air, odd flights of stairs, winding corridors and unexpected rooms, sometimes leading from one into another and all panelled in dark oak, I have to admit the house is the perfect setting for a ghost story. However, it doesn't feel unsettling. I'm not uncomfortable or afraid. I turn back to the playroom. The scene before me is one of domestic bliss – two sisters sharing time together.

As Tegan puts down her crayoning pencils and clambers to her feet, Rhea closes her book and looks over at me. 'She's talking about Mary.'

'Who's Mary?'

'A maid. Mummy says she lived here in 1602.'

Hairs prickle on the back of my neck. It's the way she says it – so matter-of-fact – as if Mary is simply another member of the family.

Tegan walks towards me and curls her soft, warm fingers around mine.

'Mary's pretty.' She looks up at me with innocent, big blue eyes.

'Is she?' I can't believe I'm discussing a ghost.

The little girl nods.

'What colour hair does she have?'

'Like Daisy's.' She holds up her rag doll.

'She's not very old,' Rhea says, rising from the window seat and crossing the room. Marmaduke doesn't stir.

'Mummy says girls of Zac's age had to work in the olden days.'

'That's right. Sometimes younger.'

As we step into the passageway I call out to Zac. Moments later his door opens and Roly and Pumpkin bound out into the corridor, closely followed by the boy.

'Tea's on the table.'

'Be down in a minute.' He shoots back into the room and the dogs do an immediate about-turn.

'Do you see Mary a lot, Tiggy?' I hold firmly on to the little girl's hand as she navigates the stairs.

She nods.

'I do as well, sometimes,' adds Rhea.

'What about Zac?'

'He used to, but not so much now.'

The first evening I'd arrived at Foxcombe Manor, Ginny was surprisingly evasive when I commented that the house must have an interesting history. Now, recalling the inscrutable look on her face, all is becoming clear.

As we enter the kitchen, Ginny is pouring tea from a large teapot into mugs.

'Sit!' she instructs.

Tegan clambers onto a chair, and I push it in closer to the table before sitting down next to her.

'I'm famished!' announces Zac, appearing in the doorway with the dogs.

Roly and Pumpkin make a beeline for their baskets in the corner of the room.

'Just as well I've made extra portions then. Tuck in. You as well, Cassie.'

'Thanks.' I help myself to a slice of homemade fruit cake.

'Tiggy saw Mary again.' Rhea bites into a cheese and tomato sandwich.

Ginny freezes.

'Wish I had. I haven't seen her for ages,' says Zac.

I notice Ginny give me a sideways look.

'So, there's more than just the Kinsmans residing at Foxcombe Manor,' I say, keeping my voice casual. Taking a sip of tea, I look across the table at my employer.

She avoids my eyes.

'There are loads here,' Zac says, reaching for a sandwich.

'No, Zac. That's not true!' Ginny turns pale.

'It is.' Zac stares at his mother in surprise.

At last, she looks at me. 'Cassie, I must explain.'

Please do!

I raise an eyebrow.

She takes a deep breath. 'There are several spirits here... but they're all friendly.'

'Several?' Carefully, I place my mug on the table.

'Three, possibly four.'

'Well, that makes it OK then,' I say unsteadily.

'It's only the children who see them.' Ginny's face is etched in worry. 'Gyles used to when he was a child, but I've never witnessed anything. However, it's a well-known fact locally and I should have told you. It's very remiss of me.'

How had I gone from the lap of luxury, albeit unfulfilled and unhappy, to living and working in a haunted house? I gaze down at my hands. They're surprisingly steady.

'Cassandra.'

I start at the urgency in Ginny's voice.

'I will understand if you want to leave, but I really hope you don't.'

'Oh don't leave,' cries Rhea.

'Don't go,' says Zac. 'Dylan likes his rides out with Caspian.'

'We've only just found you, our "Superhuman",' says Ginny sadly. 'We'd be lost without you.'

Three anxious faces peer at me. Everyone has stopped eating, apart from Tegan. Standing in her chair, the little girl reaches out to the plate of cupcakes in the centre of the table and selects one with a cherry on top. We all watch in silence as she puts the cake on her plate, carefully picks off the cherry and pops it in her mouth. Solemnly, she chews.

'Mary likes you.' She turns towards me and pins me with those beautiful, big blue eyes. 'She says: "sad now, happy soon".'

I gasp.

And as if on cue, the grandfather clock in the open hall strikes the half hour.

18

Friday dawns grey and sullen, and banks of dense cloud scud across a bruised sky. Although it's my day off, I hack Caspian while leading Indiana alongside. My right leg aches, a legacy of the car accident; I can always foretell a change in the weather. I'm more accurate than the Met Office! Both horses are fresh and react to the cool north wind, and I complete the ride around the country lanes, which usually takes a good hour, in forty minutes. I arrive back at the yard feeling invigorated and energised.

After making sure the horses and ponies have full hay nets and topping up their water buckets, I walk across the yard and open the door to my rooms. Situated at the rear of the house on the ground floor, away from the main living areas and next to Gyles's study, I have a cosy sitting room with a table and two chairs, a small sofa and television, and a large, simply furnished bedroom with a double bed, chest of drawers and a wardrobe. The compact shower room leads off from this. Although it's not what I'm used to, it caters for my needs.

I run a shower, but as I step in I back away smartly from the cold cascade.

'Damn!'

Even fiddling with the taps doesn't produce more than lukewarm, at best. The hot water at Foxcombe Manor peters out quickly, barely lasting more than the family's morning ablutions. I consider the clunking, groaning plumbing system; the Kinsmans must be a hardy lot to put up with it.

Gingerly splashing the cool water onto my body, I briskly wash my hair whilst contemplating how best to spend my day of leisure. Perhaps I'll explore more of the county, or venture into Bude and catch a film at the cinema. As I don't know anyone apart from the Kinsmans, it's something I could do on my own without feeling too much of a 'Billy No Mates'. But Ginny tells me Bude doesn't have a cinema and the nearest is a few miles away from the town. Once again, it highlights the differences between Sussex and Cornwall, and my current situation and the life I've become accustomed to.

'It's only about five miles further south at Treskinnick Cross,' she adds. 'There's plenty of parking and they show the latest big-screen releases.'

'It's a possibility, but first I'll see what else the town has to offer.'

Pulling open a kitchen drawer, Ginny rummages through its contents, her search resulting in a pen and notepad. 'I'll jot down a few places that may interest you.'

Several minutes later, armed with a list of attractions, I say goodbye and make my way out to the Peugeot parked in the open barn. As I cross the yard the heavens suddenly open, instantly turning the pale concrete dark grey. I break into a run and glance over at the gun dog enclosure. All four Labradors are sensibly sheltering inside their kennels. Checking that my waxed jacket is in the car, I turn on the engine and drive out of the open barn.

I've reached Poughill when I hear the text message arrive but, ignoring it, I carry on to Crooklets Beach. The car park is relatively empty, no doubt due to the weather having taken a turn for the worse and I park easily before making a dash for the beach café. Ordering a mug of coffee and a slice of cake, I sit at a window table overlooking the sea. All is grey... even the sand. A dozen surfers ride the rollers, oblivious to the weather. Suddenly I remember the message. Removing the mobile from my pocket, I check the screen.

David!

My heart leaps as my brain warns me to be prepared.

Come home, Sands. I miss you. xx

Home... Where is that exactly?
I text back.

Difficult without transport.

I gaze out of the window. At the far end of the beach, some distance from the others, a lone surfer manoeuvres his board broadside to a wave gaining height several yards out. I watch as he expertly judges the distance and turns at the last minute, powering hard before elegantly rising to his feet and riding the wave. Beauty in motion!

The phone beeps. Dragging my eyes away, I glance at the message.

Nothing we can't sort. Are you ready to return?

Am I? I've been away less than two weeks. Has anything changed in that time? I gaze out at the beach again. It's so different here and I haven't given Cornwall a chance. Surely it's too soon? I'm about to respond when another message comes through; one that makes me see red.

You've made your point!

Maybe it's the exclamation mark, but I have the impression David believes he's humouring a cheeky child... and one who doesn't *immediately* respond to his texts. At this time of day he will be between meetings, grabbing a few minutes to text his wayward girlfriend before entering the boardroom. An uncomfortable thought enters my head. Just how many girlfriends has he found time to text this morning?

'Argh!'

What am I to do? I miss him – my aching heart tells me so – but my head questions whether it's just the intimacy of being with someone. I can't deny it; it's tempting to return to all that's familiar. It would be easy to re-engage in the rules of a game I know only too well, but just how long will it be before that initial relief deserts me? And how quickly will that age-old frustration and lack of fulfilment take hold once again?

I text back.

Have you changed your attitude to our future?

I have to wait a further fifteen minutes before the next message arrives. I imagine David arguing a point with his team and laying out the strategy for a forthcoming marketing campaign, whilst also considering how best to answer me.

The weather has deteriorated and the beach is now empty of the early holidaymakers and dog walkers who were on the sands when I first pulled into the car park. It's only the diehard surfers who remain, chasing the next adrenalin rush. I watch the lone surfer, curiously mesmerised, and jump when the mobile alerts me to David's next message.

FFS. You sure know how to make a man run a mile! Stop messing and get back here where you belong. We will talk about it.

At least he's prepared to talk... and he is offering back my life.

I gaze at the ocean through the pouring rain. A seagull, buffeted by the wind, picks at an empty carton carelessly discarded at the base of a waste bin. I sigh. Why don't people take responsibility for the things that are important? Only slightly more effort by the perpetrator would have kept the area free of litter.

I think of David. I can't force him to start a family; he's

more than spelt that out to me. In any case, I'm not the sort of girl to deliberately trap a man. But he'll be forty in a few short years. How much longer is he happy to fool himself into believing he's a playboy? Either he's committed to me and willing to participate in all that that entails, or he isn't. He can't have it both ways.

As I stare out at the grey ocean, the rhythmic motion of the waves soothes my troubled thoughts and I hesitate before replying to his latest message. At the far end of the beach, the lone surfer emerges from the sea. Efficiently tucking his surfboard under one arm, he walks up the beach towards the beach café and I can't help but notice his graceful movements.

Not only beautiful in the water but also on land.

From across the sands, another surfer approaches and, oblivious to the rain, they chat as they walk together. Nearing the steps leading up to the café and car park, they briefly disappear from view, obscured by the rise of the land. A few seconds later they reappear and my eyes open wide as the surfer pulls his ponytail free, shaking his head to release long, sea-wet blonde hair. This is no man, but a woman possibly no older than me with a face of stunning perfection. Her athletic body moves with elegance and she carries the large surfboard with ease, as if she was born to it.

It's easy to see why I mistook her sex at a distance. The wetsuit hugs a boyish figure; small breasts, square shoulders and slim hips. As she makes her way to the car park she glances at the café and catches sight of me watching through the window. She smiles knowingly; as if aware I've been observing her in the surf. Awkwardly, I return her smile, but I'm peculiarly energised by the notion that here is a free spirit living life on her terms. No one tells her what to do.

And all at once I know what my response to David will be.

Sorry. Talking's not good enough.

19

The rain eases and I finish my coffee. Returning to the car, I set the windscreen wipers to intermittent. A movement in the side mirror catches my attention and I watch as the young woman and her surfing partner hoist their boards onto the roof of a VW camper van. They chat easily. Everything about this couple speaks of the freedom of the road, and it's so shockingly different to how I feel that I can't drag my eyes away. Altering the angle of the rear-view mirror, I gaze at my image. My eyes are still as startling blue as ever but they're dead; no sparkle. Where has the young girl gone who, despite her grey upbringing, was filled with hopes and dreams? I know she's in there somewhere. But as I stare at my reflection she remains hidden.

Repositioning the mirror again, I continue to watch the surfing couple. The stunning blonde, laughing at something her partner has said, punches him playfully on the arm before unzipping her wetsuit. Seemingly oblivious to other people taking refuge in their cars, she peels out of her neoprene suit to reveal a skimpy blue and white bikini. With a body like hers – attractively toned and sporting a flattering, already deep tan – why shouldn't she be brimming with confidence? The young man grabs a towel from the campervan and lobs it in her direction. Catching it easily, she bends over and vigorously dries her long blonde hair.

I know I shouldn't be watching – it's verging on voyeurism – but I can't help it. I'm mesmerised! Here is a snapshot of a happy, carefree life...

Straightening up, the surfer girl throws the towel inside the van as her companion pulls her into an easy kiss. Everything about this couple is so natural, and I can't help but be envious. Opening the driver's door, the man climbs in as the stunning surfer girl slides the side door closed and starts to walk around the van. Before disappearing out of view, she glances back at my car. Oh God... she knows I've been watching! Embarrassment engulfs me, but she simply raises her hand and smiles before disappearing from sight..

After the campervan has driven out of the car park, I sit motionless for a further ten minutes collecting my swirling thoughts. How awkward was that! What must she think of me? I cringe with shame. But, despite my discomfort, this naturally stunning woman and her partner have gifted me something of huge importance. They have shown me a way of being that resonates deeply with my troubled soul.

Now that the rain has abated, people leave their vehicles and venture down onto the sand once again. Should I do likewise? It's mid-afternoon and if I walk on the beach for an hour or so, I'll be back at Foxcombe early evening. But as I open the car door I hesitate. Do I want to be confined to my rooms after that? After all, my intention had been to explore the area. Closing the door, I turn on the ignition.

Although Bude is a small seaside resort, to my delight I discover it not only has a lively mix of independent retailers as well as high-street chains, but also an eclectic mix of art galleries, craft shops and numerous places to eat. It's an obviously popular town with a surfing culture that attracts the young, and I find it hard to comprehend why it doesn't have a cinema. The streets are full of people, no doubt drawn to the attractions of a town that offers an alternative day to one spent on the beach during inclement weather. I visit a couple of gift shops and a stationery store, where I buy a large wall chart and blocks of different coloured Post-it notes. I'm determined to introduce *that* rota. Then I find a café in the main street where I toy with a glass of apple juice for as long as I can get away with it.

The evening stretches before me. What shall I do? Maybe it's having witnessed a snapshot of the surfing couple's easy, carefree life that makes me feel so acutely alone. I'm used to my own company – *aloneness* is my default setting – but, somehow, this feels different. My earlier euphoria has turned to anxiety and I feel horribly unsettled.

There's only one other remaining customer in the café and he's settling up at the till. The assistant glances over in my direction and I can tell she's keen to finish her shift and close up. Perhaps there are events in the town this evening. If not, I can always find that cinema – at least it will kill time. I finish my drink and, getting up from the chair, walk to the counter.

'Was everything OK?' the assistant asks.

'Yes thanks.' Opening my purse I take out a fiver and hand it to her. 'Do you know if anything's happening in the town tonight?'

'Like…?' She rings up my bill.

'Live music, an art exhibition or something.'

She hands over my change. 'Probably. The Tourist Office

at the bottom of the hill will have a list of events, or a bit further on is The Wharf. There might be something going on there.'

I thank her and return to the table to retrieve my jacket from the back of the chair. Picking up the bag of stationery, I walk to the door, and as soon as I step out onto the street the door is locked behind me.

The wind has changed direction and the air has lost its earlier chill. I stroll down the street to the Tourist Office. The sign on the door says 'Closed', but I can see a woman inside who ignores my attempts at attracting her attention. The Wharf it is, then. Crossing the street, I enter a pedestrianised area with a canal alongside, where a number of rowing boats and pedalos are quietly moored. On the opposite side of the waterway is a whitewashed pub adorned with vibrantly coloured hanging baskets and window boxes, and from its roadside garden, a group of revellers laugh loudly. The neighbouring property, a majestic hotel, stands proudly at the head of a row of pastel-coloured houses all fronting the canal.

I walk past a popular bistro, judging by the number of people inside, and come to a selection of wooden-fronted workshops. One is a woodcrafter, offering high quality joinery products; another sells handmade fleeces; and the third is a gallery displaying artwork and jewellery. All are closed, or closing, so I continue on the pedestrianised walkway towards the sea. At the far end is a set of lock gates, alongside which a barge is moored, cleverly converted into a restaurant. A string of lights spanning its full length are suddenly switched on. It looks fun but I'm reluctant to sit on my own in a confined space, unable to dodge the inquisitive stares of other diners. What should I do? I could go to the pub. In a bar full of people it wouldn't be so obvious I'm on my own.

Slowly I retrace my steps, stopping to watch half a dozen ducks squabbling over something in the water. A cyclist powers by with a dog running level at his front wheel, and a couple of women walkers pass the time of day. As I approach the end of the pedestrianised area I notice a sandwich board outside the bistro. Large black lettering informs the casual passer-by that a book signing is taking place tonight from 6pm. I glance at my watch – it's almost that now. The building is full of people animatedly chatting with drinks in their hands. I surmise the author, whoever it is, must be very popular.

I continue walking, but as I reach the street I'm still undecided what to do with my evening. I turn back. A poster on the other side of the A-board is strangely familiar and I take a couple of steps towards it. I've seen it before! An arresting image of a tunnel of trees with, at its far end, appearing through swirling mist, a man standing with legs apart and arms folded.

Cornwall's Old Ways
Talk & Book Signing
with
Hunter Harcourt

'No way!' I stare in disbelief as a shiver teases its way up my spine.

It's the very image that had prompted me to buy *The Lady* magazine, which ultimately led to the discovery of

Ginny's advert. Little does the author know but it's because of him that I'm here in Cornwall.

'You're just in time,' says a man with a broad Cornish accent.

I look up. 'Oh, I wasn't…'

A shout from across the water, followed by raucous laughter, makes me glance in the direction of the pub. Perhaps a book signing is the more sensible thing to do. It's easier to be invisible in the midst of an engaged audience.

'Well, there again…' I smile at the man as he holds open the door.

'Still a few seats left. We'll be starting in five minutes. Help yourself to a glass of wine.'

20

With so many people inside the bistro, it's very warm. I remove my jacket and, as instructed by the man at the door, sign my name in the attendees' book, noting my address as Foxcombe Manor.

The restaurant's tables have been pushed to the back of the room and replaced by two wide columns of seats set out in neat rows in front of a large screen. Facing the audience is a single chair and halfway down the centre aisle, a small table supports a projector. As I help myself to a glass of white wine, I look around. The place is full to overflowing. There's a vacant chair in the front row but, deciding I don't want to be that visible, I make my way to the only other seat available. The rows of chairs are positioned closely together, I suppose to allow for maximum attendance, and as I make my way to the centre of the far column I have to apologise several times when people are forced to move their legs or stand up. As I settle in my seat, conversations around me take shape and I become aware of a mix of strong local accents and cultivated voices. The author obviously appeals to a wide range of people.

Suddenly the general buzz of conversation falls away as a middle-aged woman, dressed in a smart dogtooth skirt, twinset and pearls, steps out in front of the audience.

'What a marvellous turnout. Welcome, all.' She smiles expansively. 'We are so blessed to have the best-selling international author, Hunter Harcourt, with us tonight. Now, I know you're all keen to hear what he has to say, but before we meet him I have some necessary housekeeping rules to impart. In the unlikely occurrence of a fire, please make your way out through the entrance doors onto The Wharf.' Like an air hostess, she points to the door at the far end.

Next to me, an elderly man tuts loudly and mumbles under his breath. 'Where else would we exit?'

'Once there, please don't wander off,' continues the smartly dressed woman. 'I shall have to check you all against the signing-in book to make sure everyone is accounted for.'

She pauses for breath and takes a long look around the room. 'Now, Hunter says he is very happy to answer any questions, but please save them until the end. After all, we don't want to spoil what I know will be a fascinating presentation.' She gives a big, toothy smile. 'Following the talk, Hunter will stay for a while and sign copies of his books, which are available to purchase at the back.' She waves towards the rear of the bistro.

'Get on with it, woman,' mutters my vocal neighbour.

'Wine, soft drinks and nibbles are also available throughout the evening. So, without further ado, it is with the greatest of pleasure that I hand you over to the hugely popular nature writer, Hunter Harcourt.'

Honestly! You'd think she was announcing a senior member of the royal family.

The audience claps as the woman beams at a man making his way down the outer aisle towards her. I suppress a smile as she backs away and gives a little curtsey. She's obviously Hunter Harcourt's number-one fan! But, as the author turns towards us I gasp and receive a curious look from the man to my right.

Dressed in a pair of tan-coloured corduroy trousers, an olive green moleskin shirt and sporting black-framed glasses that afford him an air of intellectual authority, the person standing centre stage is none other than the man on the beach; the very one whose Great Dane made Dylan bolt and caused Caspian to dump me in the process. Heat rushes to my face.

'Good evening and thank you all for coming tonight.' His voice is soft and educated. 'I realise it's not exactly a heatwave out there…' laughter reverberates around the room '…but, nevertheless, Cornwall is blessed with many attractions and I'm touched that you should choose to make time for my slideshow.'

He nods to someone at the rear of the room and suddenly the lights go out. Picking up a remote control, he points at the projector and clicks. Immediately, a striking photo fills the screen – an archway of trees, diminishing in a tight tunnel of close-knit trunks and branches with, at its far end, a small circle of light.

'*Cornwall's Old Ways* – the title of my latest book – doesn't simply refer to hidden tunnels, secret passages, smugglers' tracks, coffin paths, and the like. I've also researched the older, ancient ways of people of yesteryear who inhabited this county and, sometimes, this has encompassed not just the living.'

As with the article in *The Lady* his words hold weight, and a strange thing happens. My heightened emotions drain away as my brain kicks in. Eagerly, I await the next piece of knowledge this man is prepared to gift his audience.

'During my lifetime, I have trodden hundreds of miles of sunken paths and routes that many centuries of wear have played a part in harrowing deep into the land. What is most apparent is that whilst walking these tracks, or old ways, there is always the suggestion of the past inhabiting the present; as if time has folded back in on itself.'

I sit up straight; hungry for more.

'In Dorset, for instance, these deep and shady lanes and tracks can be almost twenty feet beneath the level of the surrounding fields, worn down by the fretting of water and packhorses of a hundred generations.'

He clicks again and an image of rolling downland appears on the screen, a low tunnel of branches, little more than a hedge, the only feature visible in the open fields.

'This photo perfectly illustrates that. The tunnel top you see here is, in fact, the uppermost branches of a sunken path some fifteen feet deep.'

It's fascinating. I love the countryside, but I have never heard it explained in such a captivating way.

'In regions of the archipelago where the stone is soft,' Hunter continues, 'there are many old paths and tracks to be found in the landscape. In fact, some are more ravines than roads. As with the wear on the stone sill of a doorstep, dipped by the passage of many feet, they are the result of repeated human actions and relate to old ways that still connect place to place, and person to person. They are landmarks that speak of habit.'

My focus turns from the screen to the man. At ease in front of all these people and comfortable in his own skin, he appears to know exactly who he is. And for the second time that day I'm aware of being shown other lives.

'In Cornwall, where granite is predominant, the tracks tend to ride the hard surface of the land, a clear example being the many smugglers' tracks found around the coastline. But in the shadier and leafier parts of the county there are many old lanes that began as ways to markets, the sea, or sites of pilgrimage. Some were boundary markers and their routes are noted in Anglo-Saxon charters. Many consider old ways as places where it's possible to slip from this world to where ghosts softly gather.'

He pauses to assess the audience's grasp on this revelation before continuing. 'Old paths are linear only in a simple sense; they also have branches and tributaries. Within these rifts time might exist only on the surface and, whilst walking such paths, you may disturb strange pasts.'

''Tis true,' says the man next to me. 'You don't believe it do you, maid?'

I turn to him with a brief smile. 'I do, as it happens.'

I didn't grow up in the shadow of the South Downs and Chanctonbury Ring without being imbued with the strange stories surrounding the area.

'In fact,' continues the author, 'only the other day I was walking my dog in the woods that surround my house when something spooked him. We have traversed the tracks in that particular area many times, but on this day he refused to venture further along the path. He stood his ground and stared at something beyond me with his fur bristling and his eyes full of fear.'

I listen intently. Is he referring to the day the Great Dane bounded out of the woodland into the field?

'I called to him but he refused to come. I walked back to him and then continued along the path and called again, but he refused to move. Somewhat cautiously, I carried on alone and then stopped. Again, I enticed him to join me, but he circled away and took another path through the woods. Now he refuses to take that particular track.'

The fascinating evening flies by. All too soon the lights are switched on and the audience is invited to ask questions. Several people query specific old ways in the locality and Hunter Harcourt carefully considers each question before answering in a well-rounded and educated manner.

A woman sitting near the front raises her hand. 'Thank you, Hunter, for sharing your wonderful photographs and for such a fascinating talk. I wonder what your take is on Cornwall's haunted houses.'

'Ah… Cornwall's haunted houses. Always a popular subject.' He smiles graciously at her. 'Well, no ancient manor house is complete without at least one resident ghost. We'd be foolish to think otherwise.'

Several heads nod.

'In fact, I was recently invited to a property not a million miles from here to investigate a newly discovered pathway, which proved to be an old smugglers' tunnel. The manor is probably known to many of you – the oldest, continually inhabited, ancestral family home in England with origins in Saxon times. It was held by the wife of Edward the Confessor before passing to the Count of Mortain. The current house dates from the late medieval period and is based around a hall, which was then added to in Tudor times. It's thought to be the first house in Britain with a purpose-built bedroom. The manor has a long and, sometimes, turbulent history and the family that moved there in the twelfth century retained ownership for over five hundred years, until the Crown took the property during the Jacobite Rebellion.'

'Penfound Manor,' mutters the man next to me.

'The ghost is said to be that of the daughter of a prominent Royalist, Arthur Penfound, who owned the house during the English Civil War. Kate Penfound was in love with John Trebarfoot, whose family was staunch Parliamentarian. Knowing their families would never agree to a match, the young couple planned to elope. Legend has it that on the twenty-sixth of April, Kate climbed from her bedroom window to the courtyard below to meet John, but her father caught them. The ensuing argument quickly turned into a swordfight, in which John was killed and Kate injured by her own father when she stepped in to stop the two men fighting, later dying from her wounds. Her father, too, died. Since this time, strange happenings have been reported. Kate has been seen in her bedroom and on the main staircase, and on the anniversary of their deaths a replay of the duel has been witnessed in the courtyard.'

A low murmur echoes around the room.

At the far end of the front row, the woman who introduced the author rises to her feet. 'Are there any other questions?' Her gaze sweeps over the audience. 'No? Well, if not, perhaps we could all form an orderly queue at the back for Hunter to sign copies of his wonderful books.'

Before I realise what I'm doing I find myself standing, and as the author's eyes focus on me I'm struck mute.

Whatever has possessed me?

'Do you have a question?' asks the woman.

I feel faint at my brazenness and my cheeks burn under his gaze. 'Err, yes...'

'Well ask away then.' The woman sounds impatient.

I notice a small smile lift the corners of Hunter Harcourt's mouth. Obviously, I amuse him.

'Go on, maid,' encourages the elderly man sitting next to me. 'Ask your question.'

'That's a very sad story.' My voice comes out in a squeak.

'Speak up! We can't hear you,' says the woman.

I clear my throat. 'That's a very sad story,' I say, speaking more loudly this time.

'Indeed,' Hunter Harcourt responds.

I take a deep breath. 'I wondered if you knew of any goings-on at Foxcombe Manor?'

He doesn't answer immediately and I scrutinise his face. It's unfathomable.

'Where's that?' asks a man in a plummy voice on the far side of the room.

'In the parish of Morwenstow. That manor, too, is of Saxon origin and I believe there have been a few sightings.'

Although Hunter Harcourt answers the question, his intelligent gaze never leaves my face and I have the distinct impression he's gauging me. His previous answers were so full and complete that I'm surprised by his reticence to offer any further information. Suddenly I feel awkward and obvious.

I'm about to sit down when my mouth takes over. 'Just how many ghosts are there?'

Again, I'm aware of his assessment. 'I believe there are three, possibly four.'

A gasp comes from the audience but he swiftly closes the session. 'Ladies and gentlemen, we've covered a lot tonight and I don't know about you, but I'm parched! Allow me to grab a glass of something and then I'll happily chat with you and sign books.'

Clicking the remote, he switches off the projector and makes his way to the rear of the room.

Uncertainly, I sit down. Why didn't he elaborate? What is there to hide? Ginny hasn't given me much. In fact, I've learnt more from the children.

As the rows of seats empty and people flock to the tables piled high with Hunter Harcourt's publications, I glance at my watch. The evening has flown by and I'm relieved to find it isn't too pathetically early to return to Foxcombe. Picking up my jacket and the bag of stationery, I follow the throng of people to the rear of the bistro and decide to treat myself to one of the author's books. His talk tonight has made me feel less empty. It will be good to have his written words to dip into.

As Hunter Harcourt chats to people and signs copies of his various books, I observe him. It's obvious he spends a great deal of time outdoors; his tanned skin and dark blond hair laced with sun-kissed streaks testament to the fact. The black-framed glasses suit his pleasant open face, suggesting educated authority. Randomly, I wonder what he's done with the Great Dane tonight. Suddenly, I find myself face-to-face with the man and a brief, uncomfortable pause ensues before he smiles.

'So... you decided to give the *stupid oaf* another chance?'

Amusement flickers in his hazel eyes, and heat rises in my cheeks. I'm flattered he should recognise me – after all,

I was wearing a riding hat on our previous encounter – but I feel as awkward as hell.

'I'm sorry. I didn't mean it. I was concerned about Zac.'

Casting my eyes down in embarrassment, I notice his tanned hands – square, the veins standing proud, with practical fingers and beautifully shaped nails.

'Yes, but he appeared to be enjoying the speed at which he was travelling when I last saw him. I trust he is all right?'

Despite my nervousness, I laugh. 'Thankfully, he's fine. And you're right, he thought it was cool. Zac says Dylan has never gone that fast before.'

Hunter Harcourt gives a small laugh. 'So, you have an interest in Foxcombe Manor?'

'I do. I'm staying there.'

'I see.' He hesitates, his eyes searching my face 'And the reason for your question? Have you experienced anything unusual?'

I shake my head, and then recall the odd sensation of silk trailing across my body.

'Not really. I haven't witnessed any apparitions, but the children have.'

'Your children?'

'No. The Kinsmans.'

He smiles at me – even, white teeth and kind, sincere hazel eyes – and my stomach does something odd.

'It's often youngsters who pick up on these things. They are yet to be tainted by life.'

I glance at him curiously. I can't imagine Hunter Harcourt knowing anything about being *tainted by life*.

A long, awkward pause, and another amused look.

'Would you like one of my books?'

'Oh yes!' Suddenly I remember why I'm standing in front of him. 'A copy of *Cornwall's Old Ways* please.'

Sliding off a copy from the top of a rapidly diminishing pile, he picks up a pen and opens the front cover. 'Would you like it dedicated to anyone in particular?'

I shake my head.

He writes something on the title page and I glance around. Clusters of people are desperate to chat with him but he seems in no hurry to end our conversation.

'Are you staying at Foxcombe Manor for long?' he asks casually, as he closes the cover and hands the book to me.

'I'm not sure. It all depends.'

'Well, maybe we'll see each other again.' His eyes twinkle. 'And I promise in future my dog and I will do our utmost not to upset the horses.'

I laugh and turn away.

'And rest assured,' he adds hurriedly, 'Foxcombe's ghosts are benign.'

So he *does* know more! Immediately I turn back, but several people have surged forward and now demand his attention.

Walking out into the still night air, I pause outside the bistro and gaze across the canal. Floodlights now bathe the hotel's façade, and sounds of a fun evening drift over from the neighbouring pub. I look up at the ink-black sky, so unpolluted in this part of the country and awash with stars, and then I glance back inside the bistro. Hunter Harcourt, observing me through the window, grants a warm smile before turning to his next customer. Despite the cool night air, I break out into a hot flush. Curious to know what he's written in the book, I open the front cover.

*To the enigmatic young woman who doesn't mince
her words!
Until we meet again...
Hunter H.*

21

On Monday morning, having spent an hour training Biscuit and Dylan in the sand school, I enter the back porch and, using the cast-iron bootjack, ease off my boots. Both ponies responded well this morning and enjoyed being schooled in the arena at the same time. It blows me away how engaged horses become when worked *at liberty*, and these two rascals have proved no exception. Although this is a new concept for them, by the end of the session they were working in harmony.

As I open the back door I hear voices, and a cosy scene unfolds. Ginny and Gyles sit at the kitchen table drinking tea. Gyles greets me. There's only the slightest hint of a Cornish accent and I wonder if he's always owned this voice, or whether his private boarding school education erased this element.

'The kettle's just boiled,' Ginny says.

'Thanks.' Picking up a mug from the kitchen drainer, I cross to the Aga. 'The ponies were very well behaved this morning.'

'Yes, I saw you through the study window. You appeared to have them well under control, twirling around each other.' Gyles gives an amused smile.

'There were a few shenanigans at the start but they soon settled.' I spoon coffee into the mug. 'They enjoy working together.'

'I'm pleased you're giving them something to concentrate on other than how to get round their small owners.'

'It's always wise to keep ponies occupied.' Lifting the kettle off the hob, I pour on hot water.

'When you consider the other applicants who responded to your advert, Ginny, there's little wonder you picked Cassandra.'

Pulling out a chair, I glance inquisitively at my employers.

Ginny smiles at me. 'There was no contest.'

'Did many apply?'

'Luckily, I only had to interview half a dozen before we found you. There were a couple of girls straight out of school with no experience whatsoever.' Ginny takes a sip of tea. 'And a middle-aged couple with two dogs and a cat to accommodate. Can you imagine? Roly, Pumpkin and Marmaduke would never have allowed that! Then there was a male nurse who wanted to leave the NHS and start afresh. I wasn't so sure about having *another* man about the place. One's quite enough!' Ginny pulls a mock grimace.

I laugh.

'And don't forget the Scots woman who knew her way to a man's heart,' Gyles teases, patting his stomach.

I raise an eyebrow.

'Oh yes, the cordon bleu chef.'

'Now, that would have been interesting.' He winks at me.

'Too much of a good thing never did anyone any good,' Ginny says in a no-nonsense voice, and having dealt with her husband she looks me straight in the eye. 'As soon as *we* spoke, I knew there was no one else I wanted to interview. Apart from the variety of your skills being a good fit for our lifestyle, I instantly liked you.'

'Well, that's good to hear,' I mumble, suddenly shy.

Ginny places her mug on the table. 'Now, Cassie, are you free this Saturday evening?'

'Yes.'

What else would I be doing?

'Good. I hoped you'd be around. We've invited a few people over for supper.'

Ah, they want me to help out with their dinner party.

Ginny's advert in *The Lady* stated she wanted someone prepared to tackle anything life threw at them, and I've certainly had plenty of experience at playing hostess.

'Of course. How many are coming?'

'Six, so far. There may be another couple but they have yet to confirm.'

'You've met some of them,' says Gyles. 'Brian and Colin, and their better halves. My partner, Neil, who you haven't met, is also coming, along with his wife, Camilla. She brings on young eventers and I imagine the two of you will have a lot to talk about.'

I like Brian, Gyles's farm manager, and Colin, who helps around the farm. Both are down-to-earth local men.

'That sounds fun. What would you like me to do?'

Ginny's eyes grow round and Gyles laughs.

'Do? We don't want you to *do* anything,' Ginny exclaims. 'We're inviting you!'

They're inviting me… for my own company. Tears spring to my eyes as I gaze at the couple sitting on the opposite side of the table.

'You silly girl, we want you there as our guest.' She bequeaths a warm smile.

'It's nothing formal,' says Gyles. 'Just supper with a few friends.'

'Thank you.'

God, I hope I don't sound too pathetically grateful.

In the open hall, the grandfather clock strikes eleven.

'Well, as much as it's a pleasure spending time with you ladies, I can't sit around here all day. There are chores to attend to.' Gyles rises to his feet. 'Talking of which, Cassandra, at your interview you said you had experience of company accounts.'

I nod.

'I'd like you to help out with some accounting for me. You don't need to come into the Bude office. It can be done from here. I thought you could incorporate it with admin over two mornings a week, perhaps starting tomorrow after stable duties. How does that suit?'

I smile at Gyles. Even though he's my employer and pays my wage, he is still gracious enough to ask if it *suits* me. Ginny has found herself a good man.

'Of course. It will do me good to apply my accounting brain.'

He raises an eyebrow. 'Don't get too excited. It's only simple farm accounts and probably nothing as complicated as you're used to. Nevertheless, I hope you will find it challenging enough.'

'I'm sure it will suit me just fine.'

'Good, that's sorted then. I'll see you ladies later.'

As he walks from the room, I turn my attention to Ginny. 'Who are the other people you've invited?'

'Luke and Amanda Metcalfe. We've known them for years, although we know Luke better than his wife. They divide their time between here and London. Amanda has a high-flying career, which keeps her upcountry most of the time.'

So many different ways to live...

'Now,' Ginny says, suddenly business-like. 'This afternoon I'd like to tackle the children's playroom. There's far too much stuff in those cupboards and I want to take some to the charity shop. Let's have sandwiches and soup, say, twelve-thirty, and then we'll have a good few hours to get stuck in before collecting the children from school.'

As I leave Ginny in the kitchen and cross the open hall towards my rooms, I contemplate how odd it must be for the Kinsmans to have a stranger living in their home. However, both husband and wife seem genuinely concerned for my wellbeing. Again, unbidden tears spring to my eyes. How is it possible that they show such understanding and care towards someone they hardly know when David is unable to express the same concern?

Opening the door to my bedroom, I walk to the chest of drawers and pick up my mobile phone. No missed messages or calls. With a heavy sigh, I flop on the bed and log onto the internet. Against my better judgement, I type in 'David Ashcroft, Ashcroft Enterprises', and instantly the screen fills with images. I know I'm being a fool, but I can't help it. As I scroll through the pictures the knot in my stomach tightens. Here he is at an industry awards dinner, looking dashingly handsome and debonair, dressed in a sharp black suit. Holding on firmly to his arm is a pretty, buxom blonde. Reading the accompanying blurb, I learn that he has been awarded 'Innovator of the Year' at an industry bash at the Hilton, Marble Arch.

There are numerous images of the evening and I recognise quite a few of the other nominees, all experts in their own field. Many of David's employees are in attendance, amongst them his Head of Finance. At one time I'd worked closely with him when David had the idea I should help out in the accounts department. His Head of HR is also there to see David pick up his award, as are John and Veronica Price. Everyone looks suitably glamorous in the lavish surroundings, seated at round tables covered with white linen tablecloths, each set with fine porcelain crockery and crystal wine glasses.

Jealousy stabs deep. This is my old life. If I was still David's partner, I, too, would be at the celebration. I spot Denise looking worse for wear, draped around a young man, and I wonder if the photograph was taken at the end of the evening or if she'd made sure she drank as much as she could as early as possible. If she's been unsuccessful wheedling her way back into David's personal life, I know she'll make damn sure to take full advantage of his hospitality.

As I flick through the remaining photographs I grow sadder by the minute. David features in many, I suspect not only because he is 'man of the moment' but also the photographer recognises the camera loves his movie-star looks and effortlessly captures the charismatic persona shining through. I don't recognise the girl with David. She's pretty – not unlike Melanie – and he towers over her. Her strapless evening dress clings to a body of womanly curves and only just manages to contain her ample assets. It's obvious she thinks David is something special and I notice he takes full advantage of her adoration. His hands are everywhere! And then I notice her jewellery – a beautiful diamond necklace plunging teasingly into her fine cleavage with a matching pair of sparklers at her ears.

'Bastard!'

Is it possible to feel any more wretched? David presented me with the same diamond set only last Christmas. Cynically, I wonder if the jeweller had secured the sale by offering him a discount for bulk purchases.

Hearing a soft knock at the door, I glance at my watch. Where has the time gone?

'Cassie, are you there?'

'Just coming, Ginny.'

I switch off the mobile, place it on the bedside table and cross over to the mirror to remove any traces of tell-tale tears. Finally, I force a bright smile onto my face.

22

That night I dream David and I are together again. It's probably because of my foolish trawl through the internet, but it's *me* at the awards party sharing his success, adorned in diamonds and wearing the strapless evening dress. David is attentive and considerate, and I bask under the heat of his appreciative gaze as he includes me in all his networking moments. That, alone, should have warned me it was only a dream because, in reality, he would have abandoned me and left me to my own devices while he enjoyed being the centre of attention. Apart from the many venomous looks Denise shoots in my direction, everyone is friendly. I am welcomed.

It's odd how the rational mind cannot differentiate between what's real and what's mere smoking mirrors; the dream seems so real. Slowly emerging from that rose-tinted world, I open my eyes, aware of unfamiliar warmth surrounding my heart. The ache has gone, but swiftly my hand covers my chest as the fracture reopens. Perhaps, if I'm quick, I will return to the bliss of that dream. However, as hard as I try, sleep eludes me.

Eventually, I sit up and switch on the light. My watch tells me it's 3am. Sighing deeply, I pick up the copy of *Cornwall's*

Old Ways from the bedside table and start to read. Three hours later my alarm goes off and I drag myself out of bed, exhausted, but also comforted by Hunter Harcourt's words.

The day of the supper party arrives, and at 6pm Ginny announces we should all get changed. Gyles has assured me it's an informal gathering but I check with Ginny what she's wearing. I don't want to stick out like a sore thumb. As it turns out, it is fairly relaxed. However, not wanting to disgrace myself or cause my employers embarrassment, I select a simple, short black skirt over leggings with a matching T-shirt and a long, grey waterfall cardigan. Pulling on my ankle boots, I stand in front of the mirror and critically assess my appearance. Is the outfit too sombre? The only striking colour is my eyes. I've lost weight since first arriving at Foxcombe, no doubt due to the toll of having abandoned my life. However, my legs, although slimmer, are still shapely, and I hear David's voice pointing out they were one of many assets that had first attracted him. A deep, gnawing ache takes hold.

For God's sake, forget him!

Scooping a hair tie from the top of the chest of drawers, I pile my long, black locks into a high, messy ponytail and tease out a few lengths to frame my face. In defiance of David, I wear the diamond necklace and drop earrings – the same as those that now adorn the decorative, buxom blonde. Glancing at my reflection for one last time, I leave the sanctum of my rooms. As I cross the open hall I hear voices, and I enter the kitchen.

Gyles lets out a low wolf whistle. 'Ginny, would you take a look at what's just walked in.'

His wife turns from the kitchen sink. 'Oh you are beautiful!'

I colour in embarrassment.

'A fine filly indeed,' Gyles agrees.

'I like your necklace and earrings.' Rhea gets up from her seat at the table and rushes towards me.

I smile down at the girl.

And not to be outdone, Tegan pulls at my hand. 'I like them too!'

'Now, girls, don't maul Cassie. She's off duty tonight.' Ginny throws me a warm smile.

Shyly, I glance at Gyles. He's still staring.

'And, Gyles, you can remove that goofy look from your face,' she adds good-humouredly.

'Don't think I can. I've only ever seen Cassandra in riding clothes. My word, young lady, you certainly scrub up well.'

'Well, in that case, husband dear, make yourself useful.' Ginny gives me a wink. 'Pour Cassie a glass of wine.'

It's not long before the Kinsmans' guests arrive. Gyles's partner, Neil, and his wife are the first. As soon as introductions have been made and we all have drinks, Camilla takes me to one side.

'Gyles tells me you're a keen horsewoman.'

'Yes.'

'And what do you do? Show jumping, eventing, dressage?'

'A bit of dressage, but mainly natural horsemanship and classical training.' I have the distinct impression she requires more. 'I enjoy helping horses to change physically, mentally and emotionally over time.'

Camilla considers me for a long moment. 'I know you've probably got your hands full with this mad household but if you ever consider a change of scene and want to give me a hand bringing on the youngstock, I'd be more than happy to have a conversation with you.'

'Thank you. I'll bear that in mind.'

From the kitchen, Ginny and Zac enter the open hall with plates of nibbles.

'I'd make it worth your while,' Camilla adds in a whisper, before turning abruptly as Zac approaches. 'Hello, young Zac. Helping out tonight?'

'Yes,' he answers politely, holding out the plate.

'Good boy.' She selects a smoked salmon canapé.

'Thanks, Zac,' I say, helping myself to a goat's cheese and cranberry tartlet. 'When it all gets too much just let me know and I'll take over.'

'You're not allowed to. Mum and Dad said so.'

'Quite so, Zac.' Camilla winks at the boy.

A sudden loud rapping makes us all turn and, crossing the room, Gyles opens the front door to Brian and his wife.

'Welcome,' says Gyles. 'Come on in.'

'Colin's just pulled up,' Brian says, as he follows his wife into the house.

Gyles steps outside and raises his voice to give directions. 'That's fine, Colin, just park over by the wall.'

The next minute he re-enters the house, followed by Colin and his girlfriend; a fresh-faced redhead around my age. It's not long before the open hall resounds to the easy chatter of good friends who seem willing to embrace me, even though I'm the outsider. Colin's girlfriend,

Clare – as down-to-earth as her boyfriend and obviously well-liked – is a school teacher at the local primary school, which all the Kinsman children attend. I've been chatting to her for a while when Ginny catches my eye from the kitchen doorway and beckons me over.

'Luke assured me he and Amanda would be here by seven-thirty, but it's now seven-forty. Everything will be overcooked if we don't sit down soon.' Ginny chews her lip. 'I do hope Amanda isn't having one of her strops.'

I raise an eyebrow.

'What to do?' Ginny says under her breath.

'Why don't we all go through to the dining room? By the time we've settled they're bound to be here.'

'Good idea.' She squeezes my arm. 'Cassie, I don't know if I've ever told you this, but I don't know what I'd do without you.'

'A few times, Ginny!' I give her a smile. 'As I've said before, I'm here to help.'

'OK, then. Let's get everyone seated at the table.'

It takes a while to gain everyone's attention but eventually we move from the open hall into the formal dining room. As with the other rooms in the main house, this, too, is fully oak-panelled, but only used for Sunday lunches and entertaining, the Kinsmans preferring to eat at the large refectory table in the kitchen most of the time. In the centre of the beautiful mahogany table are a couple of silver candelabras with red tapered candles while, in addition, wall lights cast a warm welcoming glow around the room.

'Everyone, find your nameplates.' Striking a match, Gyles lights the candles. 'It's boy, girl, boy.'

We do as instructed. At the head of the table is a nameplate bearing Ginny's name. Zac and I have seats to her left, whilst Tegan and Rhea are allocated places on the other side of their mother, beside the two empty seats reserved for the missing guests. To my left sit Colin and Clare, then Neil and Camilla with Gyles at the far end. Seated on his other side are Brian's wife, June, and then her husband, then the vacant chairs opposite me.

Gyles circles the table, pouring wine. 'If Luke and Amanda are no-shows we can all spread out.'

As Ginny and her two oldest children bring in the starters, I rise to help.

'Sit, Cassie,' she commands.

Clare laughs and, leaning forward, speaks across her boyfriend to me. 'It doesn't do to go against Ginny's wishes.'

'Absolutely,' confirms Ginny.

'Ah, that sounds like our elusive guests.' Gyles places the bottle of wine on the table and heads towards the door.

'Cassie, have you met Luke and Amanda?' Clare helps herself to a roll from the basket on the table.

'No.'

She raises her eyebrows. 'Once met, never forgotten!'

I'm intrigued. Is she referring to them as a couple, or one or the other? But before I have a chance to question her further, Gyles reappears in the doorway closely followed by the late arrivals.

'I think you know everyone here, but for one. This is Cassandra. Luke and Amanda, our neighbours.'

My eyes open wide; his light up.

'Pleased to meet you.' Amanda crushes my fingers in a surprisingly firm handshake.

'Likewise,' I say, unable to take my gaze from the man. My brain refuses to compute: how can *he* be Luke?

'Me too, although Cassandra and I have met before.'

It's the way he says my name...

'Oh really?' Amanda glances sharply at her husband.

This exchange gains the attention of the other guests seated at the table.

'Twice, to be precise. Once, when Byron spooked the horses and Cassandra unfortunately ended up on the ground, and then again at the talk I gave in Bude.'

Faces turn towards me.

'You came off?' Ginny exclaims.

I nod shamefacedly.

'Luke! You have to take more care of Cassie. We can't lose her now, not when we've only just found her.'

I grow red under his gaze.

'Sit yourselves down.' Gyles pulls out a chair for Amanda.

'How was the talk?' asks June. 'I was hoping to make it but our spaniel showed signs of whelping that night so I had to stick around. She had six puppies, all healthy I'm pleased to say.'

Luke smiles at her. 'It went well, thanks, at least from my viewpoint. You will have to ask an attendee to find out what she thought.' His eyes are playful.

'It was very interesting,' I say. And I meant it. It helped combat the emptiness that evening... as have his written words since.

'Tuck in, everyone.' Ginny fastens a large napkin around Tegan's neck.

Up until that moment I was ravenous. Now, self-consciously, I doubt I'll manage a morsel.

Easy conversations roll around the table, but I'm so aware of the man sitting opposite me that I find it hard to concentrate.

'So, Cassandra.' His voice is soft… and there it is again, that stirring in my belly. 'How are you finding the book?'

How can I tell him it's my comforter for those occasions when I feel lost and bereft?

'Illuminating,' I manage to say, while attempting to swallow a mouthful of salmon.

He raises an eyebrow. 'Any particular part?'

I put my fork down. 'Although I grew up in the countryside, you present a very different angle. It's as if I'm experiencing it for the very first time.'

'Then I have achieved what I intended!' The smile reaches his warm, mischievous, hazel eyes. 'In what part of the country did you grow up?'

He helps himself to a bread roll. Again, I notice the strong, square hands with those capable fingers and beautifully shaped nails.

'Sussex. Not far from Chanctonbury Ring. Do you know it?'

'I do. It's a very interesting place, both from a geological viewpoint and a paranormal perspective.'

'Have you walked much of the South Downs?' Picking up my fork, I attempt another mouthful. I don't want Ginny to think I dislike her starter.

'Yes. On those occasions when I grow tired of London, its people and the concrete, I head south. It's the closest area that offers a suggestion of the openness of Cornwall.'

I know what he means. Raising my eyes, I meet his. Clear, intelligent and kind.

'Luke, honey.' Taking a sudden interest in her husband, Amanda turns away from the conversation at the far end of the table. 'You're not boring everyone with your woes about London living are you?'

Her jibe doesn't offend him and his voice remains easy. 'No, Mandy. Cassandra and I were discussing the South Downs.'

Her haughty gaze sweeps over me. I know that look. I've seen it in Denise's eyes a thousand times.

'Oh, and what's your association with them?' she asks archly.

'I was born there.'

'What? In a burrow?' Her laugh is loud and false.

'No, the local hospital,' I say, refusing to react.

Amanda pulls an unimpressed face. 'So what's brought you to Cornwall?'

Her tone is bored, suggesting she knows my answer will hardly be worthy of her attention, and suddenly I wish I was anywhere but here. I don't want to deal with her type again; I've had a bellyful over the past decade.

'My advert.' Cleverly involving her husband, Ginny comes to the rescue. 'I was beside myself wasn't I, Gyles, before Cassie responded?'

'She certainly was. We didn't know what to do.'

My lips twitch with the faintest of smiles.

'What do you do?' Amanda's cool gaze settles on me once more. 'Are you the children's nanny?'

'She's hardly *just* a nanny, Amanda!' Ginny reprimands. 'She's our "Superhuman".'

'Cassandra's whipping the admin and accounts into shape,' adds Gyles. 'She's even managed to persuade me to part with hard-earned cash and invest in an online accounting package!'

I catch Luke's assessing look.

'Cassie's great,' says Rhea.

'She's terrific with Dylan,' adds Zac.

'Cassie's my special friend,' announces Tegan, gazing at me with her beautiful, big blue eyes.

As I start welling up, I will myself not to lose it. Not in front of all these strangers.

23

'So, Mary speaks to you does she, Tiggy?' Clare gently probes.

The little girl looks across the table at her teacher and nods.

'Oh do tell. I do so love a ghost story.' Amanda's voice is insistent.

Ginny clears her throat. 'I'm not sure this is the right time to get into all that.'

'Whyever not?' Amanda exclaims. 'Everyone in the district knows Foxcombe's haunted, and it's not as if your children aren't aware of the spirits in their home.'

Ginny casts a nervous glance in my direction. 'I'm not sure Cassie wants to learn about them tonight.'

'What nonsense!' Amanda gives me a crafty look. 'I'm sure Cassandra can handle such things. Go on, Tiggy, when did Mary last speak to you?'

Tegan turns her unwavering gaze upon the woman further down the table. 'When Cassie fetched us from the playroom.'

Yet again, Amanda's cool gaze settles on me. 'Do you know anything about the ghosts of Foxcombe Manor?'

'Not a great deal. I understand Mary's a maid from the seventeenth century but I don't know much more than that.'

'Goodness, dear, you have a lot to discover!' She throws back her head and laughs.

I catch Ginny give Gyles a meaningful look.

He clears his throat. 'Anyone for more wine?'

As her husband tops up their guests' glasses, Ginny motions me to follow her from the room. Once in the safety of the kitchen, she dons a pair of oven gloves, opens the Aga door and removes a tray of beef Wellingtons; each a beautiful, golden brown.

'Oh good, caught them in time.'

'What would you like me to do?'

'Nothing, Cassie. I just wanted to give you a bit of a heads-up.' She grabs a large serving plate and slides the pastry parcels onto it. 'Amanda, as you've probably gathered, is rather full-on. It's her career that makes her that way. She's all-powerful in the workplace and doesn't know how to temper her character on social occasions.'

'Her husband seems so different to her.'

'He is. But what do they say about opposites attracting?'

I watch Ginny spoon mashed potato into a bowl.

'She won't let this ghost thing drop now, not until she's got what she wants, whatever that may be.' Ginny makes a tutting sound. 'She's like a terrier once she's got her teeth into something. But, if you hear anything tonight that unsettles you, you must promise to let me know and I will put right whatever nonsense she stirs up.' She looks at me beseechingly. 'Promise me, Cassie.'

'OK.' However, although I agree, I wonder what it is I'm about to discover.

'So it doesn't look suspicious, would you mind taking a couple of bowls of vegetables through to the dining room?'

'Sure.' I pick up the bowl of potato and another of steamed asparagus.

'And, Cassie…. I don't want to see you back in here tonight.'

I'm about to argue that point but she holds up her hand.

'I meant it when I said you were our guest and the evening is yours to enjoy. You do more than enough for us without having to play waitress to that egotistical woman.'

My eyes open wide. 'I thought she was your friend, Ginny.'

'She is, but she's incapable of knowing when to stop.'

I smile at my employer – *friend* to everyone.

As I re-enter the dining room, Amanda is still in interrogation mode. I place the bowls on the table, acutely aware of Luke's eyes watching my every move. Shyly, I glance at him. He smiles warmly.

'Do you want a top-up, Cassandra?' Gyles holds aloft a bottle of red.

'Yes please.'

'So where do you see her?' Amanda quizzes Tegan.

'In the playroom,' the little girl replies.

'Tiggy sees her mostly, although I've seen her too,' says Rhea, pausing on her way out of the room. 'Come on, Zac. Come and help.'

'I also used to see her, but not so much now.' Zac hops off his chair.

'So, it's the youngest that has the ability to tune in to this spectre.' Amanda looks thoughtful.

'Not necessarily,' Luke contradicts. 'It's often the

most pure in heart that are gifted a sight into the spirit world, which tends to be hidden from us more mundane mortals.' He smiles sweetly at Tegan sitting at the top end of the table, blissfully unaware of her part in this turn in conversation.

'What does she look like?' Amanda pushes the little girl for more information.

Tegan frowns, pursing her lips in concentration. 'Like Daisy.'

'Who's Daisy? Oh don't tell me there's another!' Amanda peels with laughter.

I mask a wince, my eyes narrowing.

'Mandy, tone it down,' says Luke.

His wife shoots him a look. 'Oh, Lukey babe, can't you handle me?' She pulls a mock sad face.

She's a nightmare! How can Luke stand it?

'Daisy is Tiggy's rag doll,' I say in a level voice.

Amanda ignores me. 'And what does Mary wear, Tiggly-too?'

The little girl giggles at the name. Then, solemnly she says, 'A black dress and a funny white hat, like the one Mummy wears in the bath.'

Amanda hoots with laughter. 'Oh that's just brilliant!' As tears threaten to run down her cheeks, she wipes them away. 'Does she speak to you a lot?'

Tegan shakes her head, making her blonde curls quake. 'Only since Cassie's come.'

My eyes open wide, and Luke glances at me.

'Well, that's interesting. I wonder why that is?' Amanda casts another frosty look across the table.

'OK, enough of this.' Ginny re-enters the room with the

plate of beef Wellingtons. Behind her, Zac and Rhea each carry a bowl of vegetables. 'Let's change the subject.'

Other conversations take over. Ginny's homemade Wellingtons are delicious and, thankfully, I regain my appetite, but throughout the meal I'm aware of the man sitting opposite, observing me. It isn't obvious to the others; it's just me who's acutely tuned in.

Looking up, I smile. 'So, what's with the name?'

His eyebrows rise in surprise. 'Hasn't Ginny enlightened you?'

'No.'

'It must have been a bit of a shock when I turned up.'

'You could say that!' I load my fork with asparagus.

'Hunter Harcourt is my pseudonym. My agent thought it had more of a literary ring than Luke Metcalfe.'

'It's a great pen name.' But he also suits his given name.

'It's a combination of my middle name and my mother's maiden name.'

Luke Hunter Metcalfe...

'Names are weird. Some people suit theirs, but others don't fit at all.'

'What's your full name?' he asks softly.

'Oh, I have a ridiculously grand name. Cassandra Tallulah Shaw.'

His left eyebrow arcs.

'See, I did warn you!'

'A name for the stage, if ever there was one.'

I laugh. 'There is an acting connotation, as it happens. My mother named me after Tallulah Bankhead. She wanted Tallulah as my first name but, thankfully, my father put his foot down.'

'So, are you known as Cassandra or Cassie?'

'Either, but for the past ten years I've answered to Sandra, Sandie or Sands.' Just the mention of those names dampens my spirits and lessens the evening.

'So you, too, are known by a different name,' Luke says thoughtfully. 'I was right.'

I shoot him an enquiring look.

'An enigmatic young woman…'

I blush and quickly glance at Amanda, but she's in the midst of a heated debate about farming methods with Brian and Colin and isn't keeping an eye on her husband.

'Are your parents in Sussex?' he asks.

'In a manner of speaking. They're no longer alive.'

'I'm so sorry.' He sounds genuinely mortified.

'It's OK, Hunter… *Luke*.' I laugh awkwardly. 'It happened some time ago.'

I can tell he wants to continue our conversation, but his attention is diverted by Camilla enquiring about his latest book.

Presently, the children leave the table and head upstairs. Tegan wants me to read her a story but Ginny says it's too late. I do, however, put the little girl to bed. As she lies down with Daisy in her arms, she gazes unwaveringly at me for a long moment and then suddenly pushes herself up into a sitting position.

'What is it, Tiggy?'

She looks beyond me to the door, focusing on something. I know there won't be anything there but, nevertheless, I turn. As I glance back at her she smiles, throws her arms around my neck and kisses me on the cheek. Then she settles down with her rag doll once again.

'Sleep well.' I tuck her in.

'Mary says happy soon,' she says in a sleepy voice. Putting her thumb in her mouth, she closes her eyes.

I gaze down at the pretty little girl with the golden curls. Does she understand what she says? As I walk from the room and pull the door to, I fancy I hear the whispered swish of a gown, as if someone has just passed by, swiftly followed by the sensation of silk trailing softly across my body.

'I hope so, Mary,' I whisper. 'I really hope so.'

24

When I return to the dining room it's empty, everyone having adjourned to the sitting room for coffee. I join them and sit in a comfortable armchair next to Brian. Amanda, unable to resist, has reintroduced the subject of the haunting of Foxcombe Manor and I listen attentively to the conversation. Without the children present, perhaps I will learn more.

'Oh, for goodness' sake,' Ginny says in exasperation.

'You must admit it's interesting,' counters Amanda. 'Anyway, the children are safely out of the way and your darling Cassandra is a big girl. I'm sure she can handle it.'

Who does she think she is, discussing me as if I'm not present?

'Come on, then, let's get it over and done with.' Ginny's sigh is resigned.

Eagerly, Amanda sits forward in her chair. 'So, exactly how many ghosts are here?' She glances around the room, as if taking it in for the first time.

'Three, we believe.' Gyles helps himself to a chocolate mint from a colourful ceramic dish on the coffee table. 'Possibly four.'

'And who might they be? Do they only appear on

high days and holidays, or on the anniversary of some tragic event, or do they randomly appear while you're all having breakfast around the kitchen table?' Amanda chortles.

I cringe. She certainly likes to have command of the room.

'It's not a laughing matter, Mandy,' warns Luke softly.

'Oh, I'm not laughing at the ghosts. I know only too well how serious a subject it is. I haven't lived with you all these years without having had that drummed into my head.'

'Would you like a chocolate?' Gyles offers the dish to her.

'Thank you, Gyles.' She reaches out and takes one. 'So, we've heard about Mary, the maid. Who else resides here?' She pops the sweet into her mouth.

'Isn't there an old lady?' June volunteers.

'Yes. We believe her to be Margaret Venning.' Gyles confirms. 'She married Oliver Venning of West Combe, at Moretonhampstead in 1558, but when her husband died twenty years later she returned to Foxcombe. Her final resting place is in the local church.'

'So, what's her party piece?' Amanda persists.

I stare at Luke's wife. Fired up, her face is full of excited expectation.

I'd hate to work for you, Amanda Metcalfe.

'We haven't witnessed her.' Gyles breaks into a grin. 'But, apparently, she's been seen sitting where you are now.'

'What, in this chair?' Amanda leaps to her feet.

Ginny laughs. 'Not that *exact* chair, Mandy. The furniture has been replaced since the sixteenth century! She sits in a chair by the fire, warming herself.'

As Amanda gazes wide-eyed around the room, it occurs to me that it's she who is unable to handle the stories.

Abruptly, she crosses to the other side of the room and sits down next to June on the couch.

'Oh, Amanda, honestly. You baby!' Camilla makes no effort to hide her amusement.

Luke has been silent since I entered the room, but now he speaks. 'Ghostly appearances aside, it would be interesting to find out why the marriage service took place at Moretonhampstead, on the far side of Dartmoor, and not here in Morwenstow. A commonly held belief is that people didn't travel far in the old days, but this is frequently overturned by stories such as this.'

'Yes, it's a conundrum,' agrees Gyles.

'That's the second spirit, so who's the third?' Amanda's voice is less confident now.

Gyles's face softens. 'That would be our very own Lady Chatterley, although none of us has been lucky enough to witness her. I'm surprised you don't know about her, Mandy. Story has it that in the late nineteenth century, Anna Kinsman, the very beautiful younger sister of my great-grandfather, was to be married to a suitable young man from Bideford. Preparations were well under way, but Anna was beset with doubts. She didn't want to marry her suitor because she was in love with Daniels, the estate's gamekeeper.'

'And I should know this, why?'

'Daniels lived at Keeper's Lodge.'

Amanda pulls a blank face.

'Better known as Foxcombe Cottage.'

'Did you know this?' Amanda demands of her husband.

Luke nods.

'Why didn't you tell me?' she demands.

'It never came up in conversation.'

With a frown she turns back to Gyles. 'So what happened to this Anna?'

'I'm afraid it's a tragic tale. By all accounts she was a spirited girl and she refused to go through with the wedding. Unknown to the rest of the family, she continued her clandestine love affair with Daniels but, tragically, only a few months later he was killed in a shooting incident, something concerning poachers. With her spirit broken, the lovely Anna refused any further suitors her parents presented her with, and she remained a spinster for the rest of her life. Apparently, she took to wandering the woods and down to the cliffs, calling out for her beloved. She died young, aged only thirty; some say of a broken heart.'

'Oh that's so sad,' I whisper.

'Indeed, it is,' Luke responds quietly.

Our eyes meet, and for a brief moment I hold his gaze.

Amanda's eyes narrow. 'Oh, this is just too ghastly. If only I'd known.' She gives her husband an accusing look.

Luke responds in a calm voice. 'And that's precisely why I didn't tell you. Anyway, Mandy, the story doesn't have any bearing on the property of today. The lodge has been extensively developed since then.'

'I didn't know you were such a sensitive soul, Amanda.' Faint sarcasm threads Camilla's words.

Amanda glares at the woman. Composing herself, she turns her attention back to Gyles. 'So, who's the fourth?'

'Ah, that would be our son's namesake.'

'You don't mean to tell me you've named your son after a ghost! This conversation can't turn any worse, surely?'

Gyles chuckles. 'We liked the name. And don't forget, it's a family name.'

'I suppose so.' Amanda looks doubtful. 'What's special about this Zac?'

Gyles grins. 'He's impish, is Master Zachary. When I was a lad I slept in what was his bedroom. He had a habit of making objects disappear.'

'Oh now come on! No spirit can make an object physically disappear.'

'You're right, Mandy. It was more a case of veiled vision. For instance, I'd put down my watch or a book, or some other object, and when I looked for it again I couldn't see it. But, a few minutes later, it would reappear. Also, Zachary had a habit of drawing back the curtains.'

Amanda opens her mouth to speak, but then closes it again.

'Not literally. I'd close the curtains at night but I'd often wake to find moonlight shining in through the windows. However, when I got out of bed to close the curtains I'd find them already drawn.'

'My goodness, he does sound a mischievous soul,' comments Camilla.

'Yes, but it all got a bit much. I must have been around ten at the time. One night I awoke to a shadowy image of a boy standing at the foot of my bed. That spooked me, I have to admit, and I pulled the covers up over my head. However, the next minute I had the strongest sensation of the covers being pulled down off my body.'

Amanda's hand flies to her throat.

'Of course the covers hadn't moved, but that's what it felt

like. I kept the light on for the rest of the night and never slept in the room again. It's now used as a store room.'

'Oh, this is all too much. If it's not my husband discussing the comings and goings of Parson Hawker, seen to this very day in Morwenstow Church, my dear friends, Ginny and Gyles, share their home with not just their children but four or, who knows, maybe more spirits!'

I must admit – although it went against the grain – I had to agree with her.

Amanda glances at her watch. 'I think we ought to get going, Luke. It's fast approaching the bewitching hour and we don't want to get caught out by things that go bump in the night.' She rises to her feet. 'Thank you, Ginny and Gyles, for a thoroughly enjoyable evening, although I may never sleep soundly again.'

I watch as she makes her goodbyes. Professional to a fault, it's obvious she's used to dealing with people. When she finally makes her way round to me, she grasps my hands and looks searchingly into my eyes. Well used to Denise's attempts at subterfuge, I'm immediately on high alert.

'Cassandra, dear, I do hope these stories haven't upset you too much.' She lowers her voice. 'I know I wouldn't want to stay here overnight, but I can see you're made of much sterner stuff.'

I don't bother to respond.

As she steps away, Luke takes her place. Politely, he holds out his hand to me. It feels safe and warm, and he gives my fingers a gentle squeeze. Bashfully, I meet his gaze.

'Ignore my wife's histrionics. She finds it hard to resist a drama.' He smiles wryly. 'Don't forget what I said about the ghosts of Foxcombe Manor. They're a benign lot and pose no threat.' He squeezes my hand again and turns away.

Silently, I watch as he walks from the room.

25

After all the ghostly tales, I enjoy a surprisingly uninterrupted sleep for the first time in several weeks and awake to an unusual sensation: a lingering memory of a gentle touch. Turning over, I pick up my watch from the bedside cabinet and peer at its face. It's late, by my standards. Quickly, I wash and dress, and make my way to the kitchen to find Gyles and Ginny at the sink, washing up.

'You will leave some for me to do, won't you?'

Glancing over her shoulder, Ginny gives me a bright smile. 'Don't be daft! We don't expect our guests to clear up.'

'Ah, there's the girl I know.' Gyles runs his eyes over my everyday work clothes of jeans and shirt.

'Yes, Cinderella has returned,' I say with a sigh. 'She's never far away.'

'Where? I don't see her, do you, Gyles?' Ginny instantly says.

'Nope. Can't see her.'

They're being kind, and I give a small smile.

'What do you want for breakfast, Cassie?' Ginny asks.

'Just coffee. I'll make it.' I walk over to the Aga.

'Young lady, you must have something more than that,' Gyles admonishes. 'We can't have you fading away.'

'OK, I'll have a slice of toast to keep you happy.'

As I prepare my breakfast, Gyles and Ginny resume the washing-up. Their banter is light-hearted and cheerful, and when Ginny flicks Gyles with her tea towel at a cheeky comment he makes, I smile. It's heart-warming to see that after several years of marriage and three children this couple are still good friends. David and I don't enjoy such light-heartedness.

'It's a beautiful morning and I'd like the children to have a riding lesson later, Cassie. But what do you say to us going for a hack first? Gyles can keep an eye on the *little darlings*. It will blow away those cobwebs.'

Two hours later, having ridden around the village, Ginny and I navigate the perimeter of Foxcombe's large field that borders the woods. We walk the horses on a loose rein, allowing Caspian and Indiana to stretch their necks. Cotton wool clouds dot a cornflower blue sky and the long grass, swaying in the breeze, gleams under a strong sun. As I ride alongside Indiana, I draw the pure Cornish air deep into my lungs and gaze appreciatively at the beautiful countryside.

'Hopefully, the summer will continue in this vein,' I comment.

'So the weather forecasters have predicted. We get such extremes in this part of the country it would offer us farmers a welcome break. Last year's harvest was dismal, but if this weather continues we can start haymaking.'

I consider Ginny's words. Even though Gyles is a land

agent, these 'salt of the earth' people also depend on the success of their farming enterprise each year. It isn't like that for David. Although he owns thirty acres and keeps a flock of sheep, he's a hobby farmer. He doesn't depend on the farm for his livelihood; Ashcroft Enterprises provides that. Stone Farm is simply part of his extensive playground.

Reaching the bottom of the field bordering the woodland, we turn left and follow the treeline. Ahead of us, on the track, Amanda opens the five-bar gate at the top of the drive leading to Foxcombe Cottage. She looks incongruous in these natural surroundings, dressed in a smart, totally impractical, cream-coloured trouser suit and high-heeled shoes. Briefly, she disappears from view before reappearing at the wheel of a flashy, red Mercedes Sports.

'I never know how she manages to navigate the track in that sports car of hers,' Ginny says, giving her a wave.

Getting out of the Mercedes, Amanda closes the gate. 'Great day for a ride!'

'Certainly is,' responds Ginny.

'I'm going to London but I hope to be back for a few days next month. Can't miss out on Cornwall in the sun… It's such a rare phenomenon!'

'Have a safe journey. There's no stock in the field so you can leave the top gate open.'

Amanda gives Ginny the thumbs up and climbs into the car. As she drives along the track she glances back and directs an icy stare at me.

'Do Luke and Amanda own the thatched cottage in the woods?' I urge Caspian on to match Indiana's longer stride.

'Yes. Keeper's Lodge used to be part of the Foxcombe Estate. Gyles's great-grandfather substantially developed it in the thirties and changed its name because of the association with his sister's demise. We sold off the house several years ago to Luke before he was married.' Ginny glances at me. 'Mandy's work keeps her in London so they alternate between their townhouse in Chelsea and Foxcombe Cottage, although he's here more than she is.'

'She doesn't come across as a country lover.'

Ginny laughs. 'No. Mandy is more suited to the city.'

'She seems so different to Luke.'

'She is, but as I said last night, opposites attract. She has a wicked sense of humour and is good fun when not in micro-managing mode.'

'Does she micro-manage him?'

Ginny observes me. 'As you've probably noticed, Luke's quiet strength keeps Mandy's more exuberant character in check.'

As the horses step up onto the track and we head towards the barns, I consider what Ginny has said. She's right... it takes all sorts. Maybe I should simply accept my lot with David.

'Ride to the far end of the school and then come back at trot, weaving through the cones. Dylan first and then Biscuit. Make sure you give yourselves a good distance between each other.'

Tegan sits astride her beloved Inky. With her stirrups not even reaching the bottom of the saddle flaps, she looks the embodiment of a Thelwell illustration. As I lead the Shetland around the edge of the sand school, Tegan talks quietly to her pony.

I glance back at my young charge. 'You OK there, Tiggy?'
She nods.

'Inky's listening very closely to you today.'
She beams.

I look across the arena again. 'Right, Zac, off you go. Try
and keep your weave tightly into the cones.'

In the early afternoon sunshine, Zac and Rhea spend
the next thirty minutes engaged in gymkhana games
with their ponies. Tegan, Inky and I enter into the spirit
of the occasion. Jogging up the long side of the arena, I
coax the Shetland into a trot and teach the little girl to rise
in rhythm to her pony's action... more or less.

'Look, Byron wants to join in,' Rhea shouts.

Slowing Inky to a walk, I turn towards the top end of the
sand school. The Great Dane stands motionless inside
the post and rail fence, watching. He doesn't approach.

'Byron! Byron!' Tegan squeals, dropping the reins and
holding out her arms.

The dog – as large as her Shetland pony – cocks his head,
but doesn't move.

'Does he come into the sand school often?'

'Not on his own,' Zac replies. 'Luke must be close by.'

I lead Inky up to the fence and glance down towards the
woodland. Jogging up the track towards the sand school
and covering the ground at a steady pace is Luke. And there
it is again... that sudden thrill. I can't help but make the
comparison; unlike his wife, he looks as if he belongs in
these surroundings. He catches sight of me and waves. I
wave back.

'You must be fit to take that incline at a jog,' I comment,
as he approaches.

He laughs. 'It's my daily workout.'

Slipping under the bottom rail, the Great Dane walks to his master's side.

'I hope Byron didn't scare the horses again.'

'No. He stood still and just watched.'

'Good boy.' Luke strokes the dog's head.

'I saw Amanda earlier.'

'Yes. She has meetings tomorrow and had to get away early.'

'What does she do?'

'She's a hedge fund manager in the city.'

No wonder she handles us all as she does, but it doesn't explain why she's so icy towards me. I suppose I don't merit any effort, being merely the glorified nanny/groom.

'That's a full-on career. I bet she can't wait to get away from the stresses and strains of the job.'

'You'd think so, but Mandy thrives on the environment.'

'She must enjoy coming to Cornwall, though... to recharge her batteries.'

A small frown furrows his brow. 'She likes to recharge them in London. She doesn't come down very often.'

I'm *so* curious to find out how their marriage works, but that's way too personal.

'Come on, Tiggy. Time for Inky to go out in the paddock.'

Luke opens the gate. As I lead the pony out onto the track and turn towards the yard, he falls into step beside me. Byron trots at his heels.

'Rhea, Zac, another ten minutes and then come in,' I call across the school.

'OK,' Zac replies, trotting Dylan in a figure of eight around two cones.

As we cross the yard to the barn, I'm relieved to find that my awkwardness from the previous evening has gone and I feel comfortable with Luke. I help Tegan to dismount and, taking the reins over the Shetland's head, place them in her hands.

'Come on, Inky,' she says with great importance, as she leads her pony towards the barn.

Out of the corner of my eye I catch Luke's smile.

'I know... too cute for words.' I follow the little girl and her pony. 'Have you come to see Ginny and Gyles? I think they're both in the house.'

'No, I've come to see you.'

Without warning, my tummy flutters. 'Me?'

'Yes, you.' Kind, hazel eyes twinkle.

I frown.

'Don't look so anxious, Cassandra.' He chuckles. 'I'm not about to interrogate you.'

Entering the barn, I'm so thankful for its dim interior, which effectively masks my heightened colour.

'Yesterday evening you asked what I was doing the day you saw me on the foreshore. I thought maybe you'd like to come and find out for yourself on one of your days off. I assume the Kinsmans give you such days?'

'Yes.' I smile awkwardly. 'Fridays, but I can always change it, as long as there's nothing pressing with the children or animals.'

As I untack Tegan's pony, a range of confused emotions surge through me. I like Luke's intelligent company – perhaps a little *too* much – and his quiet strength lessens the gnawing void left by David's absence. But, what if I become dependent on him? Amanda's presence looms larger than life.

Luke stands at the open stable door waiting for my answer. I remove Inky's saddle and – stalling for time – ask him to place it on the pony's saddle rack on the far wall of the walkway.

'What about this Friday?' He turns back to me. 'The tides are right for a mid-morning exploration.'

I take a deep breath. 'I'd like that.'

He holds my gaze, and suddenly my awkwardness returns.

'Cassie, you'll never guess what,' cries Rhea, leading her pony into the barn. 'Biscuit's way faster than Dylan.'

'And how do you know that?'

Fleetingly, guilt sweeps her face. 'We raced each other from one end to the other.'

'It's true,' says Zac, appearing in the entrance with his pony. 'Biscuit was even faster than Dylan when Byron spooked him!'

I hate being a killjoy, but it has to be said. 'Look, kids, this is really important. I know it's great fun but you shouldn't race each other when I'm not there. Anything could happen.'

How would I explain that to their parents?

'We were only messing around,' Zac says in a flat voice.

'I understand, but it's when you're messing around accidents happen. Believe me, I know.' I frown. 'If something happened to any of you I'd never forgive myself. Also, I'd lose my job, and I really don't want to do that.'

If I lost this employment what the hell would I have left?

'We'll behave.' Zac says in a reluctant voice.

'Yeah, OK. We don't want you to go,' agrees Rhea.

'Good. Promise me we have an understanding.'

'Promise,' says Rhea.

'Yes,' mutters Zac.

'Don't go,' cries Tegan.

I smile down at the little girl and, lifting her up, I balance her on my hip. Playfully, she twists my long plait.

'I won't be going anywhere, Tiggy, as long as your brother and sister agree to play by the rules.'

'Play by the rules,' she tells her siblings, pulling a stern face.

'Now, come on, you lot. Untack your ponies and then we can go inside for a drink.'

As I place Tegan back on the ground, I catch Luke's eye and do a double take. He instantly averts his gaze, but it's too late... I've seen it.

A tender look that simply takes my breath away.

26

Friday dawns, and a clear sky promises a good day ahead. As I walk along the track leading to Luke's cottage, I can't ignore the jittery nerves besieging me and I draw in great lungfuls of clean, salty air to try and gain some clarity. Fumbling with the catch on the gate, I follow the drive as it twists through the trees, past a small orchard dripping with fruit, and on towards Foxcombe Cottage. As I turn the final bend, I see him waiting at the open door with an empty wicker basket at his feet. He smiles and I wave. Thankfully, I needn't have felt anxious because it takes only a few moments to relax, once in his company. Whatever this relationship is I welcome it. Luke wastes no time and we set out through the woods and across the stream, following the valley towards the coastal path, with the Great Dane gambolling ahead, only occasionally turning back to check on our progress.

'Several varieties of heather grow in Cornwall.' Luke indicates the numerous heathers blooming amongst the undergrowth of the surrounding coastal heathland. 'The one with the most brightly coloured purple flowers is "bell heather" due to its bell-shaped flowers. It's usually interspersed with ling or common heather.' He points out an example. 'You can see it has much smaller, paler and pinker flowers. A third kind – cross-leafed heath – is less abundant. It has pale pink, bell-shaped flowers growing only near the tips of the stems.'

He shares his knowledge generously. When the path narrows to a single track, making it tricky to talk, I fall behind and follow the man and his dog in comfortable silence. We come to a wooden walkway over a small stream and stop to catch our breath before continuing on, until reaching a flight of steps and a waymarked kissing gate. On the path, several yards ahead, a couple of lizards are sunning themselves but at our approach they immediately shoot off into the undergrowth.

'Lizards are cold-blooded.' Luke holds open the gate for me. 'They need to bask in the sun to warm up to their operating temperature, around thirty degrees Celsius. They usually do this with an area of cover nearby. It's their escape route from predators. They're most likely encountered in sunny spots on footbridges and footpaths. However, once they're aware of you they make a hasty escape. As we've just witnessed, they can move quickly once warmed up.'

'Do they hibernate in winter?'

'Yes. In cold temperatures they're too slow to catch any food – insects, spiders and the like. Nature is clued up, these being less numerous over the winter.'

I notice a number of robin-sized birds with black heads and orange breasts flitting along the cliff edge and ask what they are.

'Stonechats. They're common along the Cornish coast all year round. Did you know their name comes from the sound of their call?'

I shake my head.

'It's reminiscent of two pebbles knocked together.'

As with his writing, Luke's knowledge makes me hungry for more. It's odd, though. It's as if I already know these things, but, somehow, I've lost the understanding and need to be reminded.

Luke glances at his watch. 'We're making good progress. The tide will be on its way out.'

He turns away and carries on up the path. Ten minutes later, we stand on a wooden footbridge that spans another stream, gazing down upon a wild and remote sandy beach. At the far end of the bridge, Byron sits and watches the waves.

Luke rests one hand on the wooden guard rail. 'This cove has a rough and exhilarating character, shaped over the years by the tempestuous Atlantic sea.'

He speaks with reverence, and I drink in his words.

'We will probably have it to ourselves.' He glances at me and smiles. 'Not many people venture here; it's unsafe to swim and there are no lifeguards on duty. Occasionally, the more intrepid and dedicated surfers find their way here at low tide, when the sand is exposed, but due to its isolated location the beach is more often visited by seals. You never know, we may be lucky today and see some.'

I look down at the dark scars of jagged rock seaming across the sand towards the water, waiting to catch any foolhardy or unaware vessel that ventures in too close to the shore. 'Those fingers of rock are very dramatic.'

Luke nods. 'Each narrow ridge is an individual rock layer tilted on end by subterranean upheavals. The inexorable power of the sea has ground them level with the beach.'

I gaze up at the surrounding clifftops. Several sections have cracked and fallen away, and a number of sheep peacefully graze on closely cropped grassy bowers that hang in mid-air, seemingly unconcerned by what's not beneath them.

'Just up there...' Luke nods over my head '...is the somewhat eerie GCHQ "listening station".'

'Must be difficult to have secrets living here,' I say drily.

'Impossible!' He laughs softly, which does strange things to my insides. 'Although the station's activities remain classified, it's believed to specialise in the interception and decryption of domestic and foreign electronic communications.' He shifts the shoulder strap of his small rucksack. 'Let's make our way down to the beach.'

As soon as his master moves, Byron forges ahead. The narrow path clings to the cliff on its descent to the beach and, mindfully, I follow. One careless footstep could easily set me tumbling over the edge.

Luke steps onto the sand. Turning, he offers me his hand.

'Thank you.'

Grasping his steadying fingers, I meet his gaze... and my heart stalls.

Soft, warm eyes linger on my face. As if scorched, I drop his hand and concentrate on the surroundings.

It's a beautiful cove – natural and wild – and the gorse and heather in full bloom add swathes of yellow and purple to the grey backdrop of slate cliffs enclosing the beach. Luke is right. There is no one around. Byron gallops across the sand, his long legs effortlessly eating up the ground.

As I fall into step beside Luke, I comment on the blue shimmer at the shoreline.

'By-the-wind sailors,' he says, as we approach. 'They're often found stranded along this stretch of coast.'

I gaze down at the beached sea creatures, their central, clear plastic-like sails standing proud, as if waiting for the next gust of wind to relaunch them onto the ocean.

Bending down, Luke picks one up and carefully places it in the palm of his hand.

'Like jellyfish, they catch their prey using stinging cells not perceptible by humans, although some people can get a rash. The direction of the sail along the float determines which way they travel. Those with a sail running top-left to bottom-right drift to the left of the prevailing wind direction, whereas those with top-right to bottom-left drift to the right.'

I reach out and gently touch the blue creature. It feels cool; its body the consistency of solidly set jelly.

'Here's the science.' Luke grins. 'They're not a single organism, but a whole colony of coral-like polyps interconnected with a canal system that distributes food caught in the tentacles. Each colony is of a single gender. And if that isn't complicated enough, alternate generations are singular planktonic jellyfish-like creatures that don't form a by-the-wind sailor, but their offspring do!'

He laughs softly at the look on my face and replaces the creature with care on the sand.

The heat of the sun tempered by a gentle breeze close to the ocean's edge warms my soul. A dozen seagulls circle above the turquoise sea, and as I turn to join Luke I spot a pair of sparrowhawks hovering on the thermals, eyeing the cliffs below.

We approach a large pool. Mussels and limpets cover the

rocks and a pink alga grows in the more submerged areas. Setting the wicker basket down, Luke removes the rucksack from his back and places it on the sand. Then, untying the laces of his tan-coloured walking boots, he takes them off and removes his socks, stuffing them into one boot. I can't help but notice his neat feet. They're not at all like David's size elevens, with their long, crooked toes; his movie-star looks don't extend that far. And I try not to stare as Luke rolls up his jeans to reveal well-defined, tanned calf muscles.

He removes a penknife from the rucksack and slips it into his back pocket. 'And now we forage for lunch.'

Trying not to disturb the water, he steps into the pool and cautiously lifts a rock. Immediately, there's movement.

'Look, Cass, do you see?'

I smile – not just at the continuing education, but because he's referred to me by an abbreviated version of my name, as if he's known me for years. No one has ever called me *Cass*. I like it.

'What is it?' I peer into the pool.

'A common prawn. Look, there's another.'

I watch as the creatures dart through the water, their semi-translucent bodies covered in spots and lines making them appear ghostlike in the shallow pool.

'Wonderful,' I whisper.

Taking care not to trample anything underfoot, Luke takes a step and moves another rock. Suddenly the pool is teeming with marine life.

'How lucky are you? That's a Montagu's blenny.' He points to a small, olive-brown fish with bluish-grey spots and darker vertical bands on its flanks. 'It's easy to identify. This species has a uniquely shaped crest with a row of small tentacles between its crest and dorsal fin.' He looks up with excited eyes. 'It's only found in the South West.'

I'm being fast-tracked to a degree in marine biology and I can't ever recall feeling so *alive*. As the day continues, the hollow emptiness that has plagued me for so long lessens its hold.

We harvest seaweed – the reason Luke has brought me to this wild cove – and I absorb every scrap of information he cares to share. I'm in awe of his understanding of the natural environment and, as the minutes pass, it becomes abundantly clear why I'm so often frustrated with my lot. Through circumstance and totally unaware, I've only ever operated in first gear... and with the brake on!

Shielding my eyes from the glare of the sun, I gaze along the beach to the far end where Byron sniffs amongst an outcrop of rocks. A few yards away from him, half a dozen small birds run across the sand, busily turning over stones and seaweed.

'What are those birds doing?'

Luke passes a handful of seaweed to me and turns in the direction of my gaze.

'Searching for food. They're touchstones, one of our most familiar waders. They often frequent rocky beaches and harbours.'

'They're charming!' I lay the seaweed in the wicker basket.

'Depending on their age and time of year, their plumage can be a bit of a mishmash of brown, white and ginger tones, but they always show a dark bib. When they're in flight there are also flashes of white in the wings.'

As long-held angst starts to lift from my soul, I take a deep, healing breath and glance at Luke.

He smiles and holds out the penknife. 'Your turn, Cass.'

Cass...

'Always cut seaweed, never tear,' he instructs. 'The root-like structure that holds it to a surface is called the holdfast. Make sure you keep it intact. If seaweed fronds are pulled off, it breaks the holdfast and kills it.'

I remove my boots and socks, roll up my trousers and then step into the pool. Trapped in its temporary prison, the water is luxuriously warm. Following Luke's directions to the letter, I firmly grip the marine plant with one hand and make a clean cut with the knife held in the other.

'You're a natural,' Luke compliments.

I well with pride as he bestows me an easy smile.

'Never turn your back on the tide,' he continues. 'Weather conditions can change quickly and an onshore wind can bring it in unexpectedly fast.'

'Can anyone forage for seaweed?'

'No. In the UK, there's no law granting the right to pick for personal use. It's always necessary to obtain permission from the relevant landowner before removing growing or loose seaweeds.'

'So who owns this beach?' I gaze around at the ruggedly beautiful, unspoilt cove.

'As you probably know, the UK coastline below low water mark is owned by the Crown; the Queen. Above that mark, this cove is owned by your employers.'

'Gyles and Ginny?'

He laughs. 'Yes.'

'I knew their acreage was extensive, but I didn't realise it included a beach.'

'Several of their fields run down to coves, which they own. I'm very fortunate they granted me the right to forage. They know I can be trusted to harvest only for my own use and no more. Also, I keep records. That way, we can keep an eye on varying species on different sites. You see, seaweeds play an important role in our ecosystem. Not only do they provide habitat for a wide variety of species to forage in, feed off, spawn and nurse in, but also they offer refuge from predators for fish and invertebrates.'

He gives me a long, appraising look. 'They also assist coastal protection by dissipating wave energy, capturing sediments and nutrients, and providing a carbon sink. Care for these marine plants is essential for our wellbeing and that of our planet.'

Talk about an overload of information... but I welcome it. I feel like a student who, starved of education all her life, is suddenly offered a place at Oxford or Cambridge.

'I guess we should head back.' Luke bends down to pick up the basket, now filled with different-coloured seaweeds. 'Byron, come!'

The dog cocks an ear but continues to investigate the rocks. However, as we start to walk towards the steps leading up from the beach, the Great Dane suddenly looks up and gallops across the sand.

'Sometimes you can find fossils here,' Luke says, stopping to closely examine a cluster of dark grey pebbles.

Placing the basket on the sand, he picks one up and turns it over in his hand. Discarding it, he selects another. As I join in, I catch his sideways glance and secret smile. It feels so right. The two of us... out here in the wild.

'Here we go.' He holds out a small rock.

The pebble has been polished by the sea, and clearly visible on the surface is the fossil of an ammonite-like creature. Taking it from him, I caress its smoothness.

'How intricate.'

'Keep it... as a memory of this day.'

My mouth twitches into a smile but I can't meet his eyes, because I know I will keep the fossil forever. Not just as a memory of the day, but as a reminder of when Luke first opened my mind to the possibilities that could be present for the rest of my life.

27

'What can I do to help?'
The kitchen at Foxcombe Cottage is of traditional style, with a flagstone floor, bespoke solid wood cabinets, matching central island unit and a butler's sink. Through an open doorway, Byron laps water from a bowl in what looks like a utility room.

Luke places the laden wicker basket on the draining board. 'Not a thing. You are my lunch guest.' He glances up at a large clock on the wall. 'Or rather, high tea.'

'Please let me help.'

'Well if you insist, you can lay the table on the terrace. There's cutlery in the sideboard in the dining room. First door on the right.'

I turn away and walk down the hallway.

'You'll find wine glasses there too,' he calls out after me.

Foxcombe Cottage – I smile at the name – is a substantial, gentleman's residence with stone walls at least three feet thick. No doubt, they've weathered many a storm. The house exudes charm and a deeply calming atmosphere, hinting at the capacity to shoulder any drama. I suspect this has much to do with the character of its present owner.

I wonder what part makes up the original gamekeeper's lodge and make a mental note to ask.

The dining room is light and airy, decorated in varying shades of cream. A mahogany table with four chairs and two matching carvers sits centrally, and on the far wall a large tiled fireplace houses a wood-burning stove. Suspended on chains from the moulded picture rail around the room are a number of interesting paintings, and in a bay window with original, painted wooden shutters is an ornately carved, period sideboard.

Crossing over to it now, I glance out over terraced lawns, at once mesmerised by the unspoilt views down the valley to the cleft in the cliffs and the sea beyond. With no other human habitation in sight, it's as close to living amongst nature without actually being out in it. I smile to myself. It's fitting that someone like Luke should live here. Dragging my eyes away from the enticing vista, I open the top drawer of the sideboard and take out two sets of cutlery and a couple of napkins, and discover crystal wine glasses in the cupboard below.

Entering the hallway, I notice Byron standing in the kitchen doorway solemnly watching as I make my way through the house and peer into other rooms; each one traditional and comfortable. Then I come to Luke's study. The door is slightly ajar and, glancing towards the kitchen, I push it open. As with the dining room, this room is on the sea-facing side of the house and, positioned in front of the window, a leather-topped oak desk maximises on the magnificent view. What inspiration for a writer! Painted wooden shelves line the walls, filled with books, and on a mantelpiece over a beautifully tiled fireplace are several framed photographs. Checking along the hallway again to the kitchen, I glance down at Byron who has now joined me.

'Don't tell,' I whisper, as I slip into the room.

The photos are of Luke – or should I say, 'Hunter' – at various literary events in a selection of prestigious surroundings. He looks at ease. In the majority of the images he wears the black-framed glasses, which only accentuate his intelligence and authority. I approach the desk. A closed laptop sits alongside a number of notepads. Hesitantly, I lift the cover of one. His handwriting is neat, the characters carefully formed and, again, unwittingly, I make the comparison; David's handwriting is large and abandoned. In the margins are several rough but exquisitely drawn sketches of the subjects he references. I read a couple of pages, as absorbed in his words as if he was speaking directly to me. I hadn't realised the English language could be so fascinating. He would make an incredible teacher – of any subject – inspiring the most difficult of students. Closing the notebook, I gaze out of the window. What an idyllic life he has created.

Byron nudges my thigh with his nose.

'You're right. No more snooping.'

Quickly, I exit the room. Once I'm out in the bright afternoon sunlight, I turn back and gaze at the house. Nestled in a clearing with trees on three sides, it is sheltered from the worst of the weather; the moss-free thatch testament to the fact. On the stone terrace is a wrought-iron table and chairs and I set out the cutlery and wine glasses. Byron, having flopped down on the lawn, rests his nose on his paws and silently watches me as I fold napkins into triangles and insert them into the glasses.

A light breeze, interlaced with birdsong, teases through the tops of the trees and I welcome the breath of fresh air as I take in my surroundings. The natural environment encroaches upon the grounds of Foxcombe Cottage and the boundary is unclear. The garden appears to comprise two lawned terraces with a flight of granite steps connecting one to the other, and although there are several mature flowering shrubs, there are no fancy flowerbed borders.

A lock-up-and-leave home.

The thought makes me strangely anxious. Firmly crossing my arms, I walk to the far side of the lawn and peer into the shadowy woodland. Zac and I must have been lower in the valley the day we rode out and I spied the thatched roof through the trees, but it's odd that I didn't find the track when I walked to the cliffs on my day off. After all, there must only be a limited number of paths through the woods.

'Here we go.'

I turn at the sound of Luke's voice. He places a bowl of something green, decorated with a sprig of mint on the table, along with a plate of oatcakes.

'You haven't just baked those?' I say in amazement, as I join him.

He gives a lopsided grin, and I catch a glimpse of the boy he must once have been. 'As much as I'd like you to think highly of me, no I haven't. These are ones I prepared earlier.'

He'd like me to think highly of him...

'Herby oatcakes with gutweed.'

I pull an uncertain face and he laughs.

'I know. It doesn't sound very palatable, but postpone judgement until you've tried one.'

'And the green creation?'

'Broad bean and sea greens dip. Now, *that* I have just rustled up.' He stands and regards me for a moment. 'Go on; help yourself while I get the wine.'

Sitting at the table, I select an oatcake and scoop up a little of the dip. It's satisfyingly salty and makes my taste buds tingle.

'Happy with white?' From the front door, Luke raises the bottle in his hand.

'Perfect.'

I watch as he approaches. What a day! At last, a firmly bolted door has been well and truly forced open.

He pours the wine and holds up a glass. 'To you, Cassandra.'

'To lunch-come-high-tea.' We clink glasses.

'I hope you enjoyed our foraging excursion to the cove.'

'Very much.'

As he sits, he observes me thoughtfully. 'Have you studied natural history in any great depth?'

Inwardly, I cringe. This is when it all unravels. 'No. Is it that obvious?'

'Not at all. You have a refreshing hunger for knowledge, and your reactions and questions hint at a deep and wise understanding.'

I glance at him.

'I would even go so far as to say you are in possession of an ancient knowledge.'

My gaze turns to one of astonishment. I'd felt that too!

'I've always had an affinity with animals... from a very

early age. I'd spend hours in the garden observing the birds and other visiting wildlife, and as a toddler I was fascinated by insects, ladybirds and the like. Once, when I was called in for tea, apparently I placed an earthworm on the dining room table to show my mother.' I laugh diffidently. 'She was appalled and swiftly sent us both into the garden again.'

Luke grins. 'I should imagine that was a bit of a surprise.'

'For some reason I was never allowed pets of my own, but my parents didn't stop me from befriending and feeding the wild animals in the area. One year, I built a log pile hotel for small mammals and spent hours observing a family of resident mice, taming them with titbits. I'd core an apple and fill it with fruit – they particularly liked that – and I named them all and could tell them apart. Hedgehogs and foxes also loved our garden, and one season a vixen and her cubs learned to come to call for a tasty meal. I always made sure the bird feeders were full and a particularly brave robin would sometimes feed from my hand.'

I smile at the memory of the few happy highlights of my unusual childhood. This must seem so banal to him and, suddenly embarrassed, I stop talking. But Luke poses a question that makes me realise if only I'd thought of it – or someone had suggested its possibility – my life could so easily have taken a different course.

'Why didn't you pursue your interest in the natural world, Cass?'

I bite my lip nervously. I don't want to discuss my tedious life and run the risk of messing up our fledgling companionship.

'Oh, this and that. Life, I suppose.'

Feeling awkward, I glance at him, but his eyes are non-judgemental and his smile is kind.

'Yes, life... it has a habit of creeping up.'

We fall into conversations on safer ground, and Luke explains how the original Keeper's Lodge has been all but obliterated by the additions that have created the house of today.

'The gamekeeper's lodge was a fairly basic two up, two down, covering the area of the kitchen and utility and what is now a first-floor bedroom and bathroom. There's little of it in evidence, although some of the old beams are visible in the pantry and around the back door.'

It is bliss. The late afternoon sun is exquisitely warm, Byron snoozes happily on the lawn, the food is tremendous... and Luke's conversation fills me in a way I've not experienced before.

'Want to give me a hand with the next course?' He rises to his feet and picks up the empty bowl. 'I hope you like crab.'

'I do... to both!' Stacking the empty plates, I follow him inside.

He sets me the task of preparing a salad. As I chop avocadoes, spring onions, cherry tomatoes and some of the fresh velvet horn we harvested from the rock pools, I steal a glance across the central island at Luke, finely slicing ginger on a wooden chopping board.

'Crab and dabberlocks,' he explains with a smile. 'I've had to use dried seaweed as it's out of picking season, but it doesn't diminish the taste.' Sliding slivers of ginger into the bowl of crab, he adds coriander leaves and lemon juice before mixing the ingredients together.

It all feels so natural. David and I *never* prepare food together. We either eat out, or he expects a meal to be ready on his return from work.

The shrill ring of the phone is an assault to the senses and instantly shatters the relaxed atmosphere. When Luke doesn't immediately answer, I give him an enquiring look.

'I'll leave it,' he says, acknowledging my silent question.

As the answerphone kicks in, Amanda's strident voice fills the room.

'Luke, are you there?' Hesitating briefly, she sighs heavily. 'Walking the cliffs, no doubt. When you get back, phone me. I'm in *all* evening!' She says it as if it's a fate worse than death. 'Peter and Charmaine have invited us to their anniversary celebration, Sunday week. I've accepted.' She pauses again. 'Are you there?'

I continue to chop the salad, even though it's already prepared.

'I should get that.' Luke places the fork on the marble worktop and quickly crosses the room. 'Hi, Mandy. Just got in.'

I can't hear her side of the conversation, but his immediately reduces to monosyllables. The *open* man I've spent the day with has vanished and suddenly I'm conscious of being in her territory, enjoying a cosy meal with *her* husband. Awkwardness descends. Deciding I should give the couple some privacy I make to leave, but Luke turns and, smiling, motions me to stay. After a few minutes more he says goodbye to his wife and replaces the phone in its cradle on the wall.

'Sorry about that. Mandy and her organisational abilities can often leave one breathless.'

He picks up seamlessly from where he'd left off, but as the late afternoon stretches into early evening there's a presence between us that I cannot ignore. Despite being over two hundred miles away, Amanda's force of character has caused a division.

The evening sky offers up a fiery display. I watch, mesmerised, as the setting sun positions itself centrally above the cleft in the cliffs, bathing the surrounding countryside in a beautiful golden glow as it prepares to dip its toe in the ocean before gracefully sliding over the horizon.

'What an incredible sky.'

'Those builders of yesteryear certainly knew a thing or two. This house is perfectly positioned for sunsets and sunrises.'

'Clever builders.'

'Indeed.' Luke smiles. 'Do you know why the sky turns red?'

I shake my head.

'The setting sun sends its light through a high concentration of dust particles, which usually indicates high pressure and stable air coming in from the west. Basically, good weather will follow.'

'Well, it's been good weather up to now, but I wouldn't say no to more.' I glance at my watch. 'I should get back.'

Is that disappointment registering in those sincere, hazel eyes?

I pick up the empty glasses.

'Leave that, Cass. I'll do it later.' He gets to his feet. 'I'll walk with you up the track.'

'You don't have to do that.'

'No, but I'd like to.' We set off across the lawn.

'Byron, come.'

The dog rises to its feet and accompanies us along the tarmacadam drive snaking through the trees and, soon, we reach the five-bar gate at the bottom of the farm track. Luke lifts the catch.

'You really don't have to accompany me, Luke.'

He hesitates.

'Thank you for a fascinating day and a wonderful meal.'

'My pleasure, Cass.'

Smiling briefly, I set off up the track towards Foxcombe Manor. Fifty yards on I reach the second gate and as I open it, I glance back. Luke is still watching and I try to ignore the reaction deep in my belly. I raise a hand but he doesn't reciprocate and I carry on up the track, admonishing myself for feeling upset. When I reach the sand school I turn again, but this time there is no sign of man or dog. Taking a long, calming breath, I gaze up at the increasingly colourful sky.

'Red sky at night, shepherds' delight,' I whisper into the late evening air.

28

The next morning I rise early. Fortunately, I don't have to do a changeover as the guests in the Porter's Lodge have booked a ten-day stay and won't be leaving until Tuesday. Instead, I work Caspian in the sand school before the heat of the day kicks in.

My handsome buckskin boy looks up as I open the paddock gate and walk towards him. I haven't slept well. Images of Luke in a wild cove had morphed into images of David assuring me there was no one else in his life, and I'd awoken feeling out of sorts. But as soon as I feel Caspian's warm breath on my skin, my equilibrium is reinstated.

'OK, young man,' I say softly, 'time to find out if we remember any of Justin's training.'

As I lead him from the paddock, Indiana raises her head but quickly settles to grazing again. In the stables, I give Caspian a cursory flick-over with a brush before tacking him up and heading for the sand school.

There isn't a cloud in the sky and in the distance the sea shimmers enticingly. Even though it's barely past eight, the day promises to be as hot as the previous one, and several of the black and white farm cats stretch out amongst the long grass in the shadow of the barns. For the next ten minutes, I concentrate on working Caspian into a soft outline and it doesn't take long for him to yield to my aids. Time whizzes by and I forget my surroundings; I am simply lost in the moment with my horse. As I approach the bottom of the arena, I ask for collected canter and then haunches-in on a circle. Although several weeks have passed since we last performed this exercise Caspian remembers our training, and as he happily engages I feel his exuberant spirit grow. Stroking his dun-coloured neck, I reward him by increasing the size of the circle.

'OK, Caspian.' His ear flicks back, locking on to the sound of my voice. 'Let's see if we can do this.'

Once again, I ask for collected canter and, immediately, he offers haunches-in on a circle. I can't stop the wide smile. This horse is *so* intelligent. Our concentration is total as we work through the elements of the exercise. The world outside our sphere does not exist. Eventually I ask for pirouette and Caspian is light and responsive. With his body equally bent from head to tail in the direction of the movement and his hind legs remaining in the centre of the circle, his shoulders move in a larger ring around his hindquarters. I am euphoric. This is not an easy exercise, but my wonderful, loyal horse has performed this difficult manoeuvre as if it were a mere trifle.

Gentle clapping brings me back to the 'here and now', and I glance over at the gate. Luke stands with Byron at his side and my heart skips a beat.

'Beautiful. Just beautiful...' He holds my gaze for a long moment. 'The harmony between horse and rider.'

Foolish girl, to think he meant otherwise.

'Yes, I'm really pleased.' I allow the reins to slide through my fingers as Caspian stretches his neck. 'But that's enough for today.' I dismount lightly.

'What is that movement you just did?' Luke asks, as he opens the gate.

I glance at him, pleased by his interest. 'Pirouette. It was originally used in times of man-to-man combat to make the horse turn on the spot. That way, the rider could stay face-to-face with his opponent and prevent being attacked from behind.

'So, mastering the pirouette was important to survive in battle.'

'Yes.'

As I stroke Byron's head, Caspian lowers his nose to the dog.

'In the baroque period,' I continue, 'riding became an art. The skills of horse and rider were demonstrated in the pirouette, which can be ridden in walk, trot, canter and piaffe.'

'A very accomplished horsewoman,' Luke remarks, nodding as if to confirm the fact.

My soul expands. No one – apart from my horse trainer – has ever acknowledged the skills I've gained over the years.

'There's always more to learn, but horses are my passion.' I smile shyly, feeling as if I've just shared a secret.

Hazel eyes appraise me.

Suddenly Byron growls and Caspian throws up his head in alarm and spins round. As one, Luke and I turn towards the commotion and see Ginny rushing around the corner of the barns. She stops dead.

'Oh, there you are.' Her forehead creases into a frown. 'I thought you were returning to London, Luke.'

'Next Saturday,' he answers easily. 'Everything all right, Ginny?'

'Yes. No. I mean...' Flustered, she takes a deep breath. 'I've got to take Gyles to the consultant in Exeter. He has an appointment arranged for the end of the month but a cancellation has come up and they say they can see him today. I'm sorry this is such short notice, Cassie, but can you take care of the children? It's important Gyles doesn't miss this.' She chews her lower lip.

'Of course.'

'We can take them to the beach,' offers Luke.

I glance at him in surprise.

'Thank you,' Ginny says distractedly. 'I'm not sure what time we'll be back.'

'Don't worry. I'll give the children supper and put them to bed if you're not back in time. You concentrate on Gyles and don't worry about the family.'

'We are so blessed to have you.' She gives me a taut smile before turning away.

But before Ginny disappears around the side of the barn she glances back, and I see her troubled expression as she glances from me to Luke.

As I lead Caspian across the yard towards the barn, Luke and Byron fall into step beside us. It's as if we always walk together and, inwardly, I smile.

'Do you know what's wrong with Gyles?' I ask.

I haven't noticed anything amiss with my employer, and neither have I been aware of any hushed conversations between husband and wife.

'No. My friendship with Gyles and Ginny doesn't extend to discussing their personal ailments.' Luke's voice holds a serious edge.

I slide back the bolt to Caspian's stable door and let him enter.

'Which beach shall we go to?' Luke asks.

'I've only visited Crooklets.'

'Summerleaze is good for children. The water's safer there and, of course, there's the sea pool.'

I remove Caspian's saddle. 'It's very generous of you to offer to take us to the beach, Luke, but please don't feel obliged.'

He laughs. 'I don't feel obliged, Cass. We can take my Land Rover.' He checks his watch. 'I'll pick you up in, say, an hour?'

'That's great. I'll rustle up a picnic.'

He smiles warmly. 'Come on, Byron. We have things to do.'

As Luke and the Great Dane exit the barn, I consider the man. He is so different to any I have previously encountered.

The beach is a living, breathing entity, filled with the sound of happy families enjoying a carefree, hot summer's day on the sands. Luke carries the bag of towels and his red cool box while I follow with a picnic basket in one hand and Tegan holding on to the other. Zac and Rhea walk ahead, battling their bodyboards.

'Where shall we set up camp?' Zac asks, turning back to us.

'Over there.' Luke nods towards a low rise of dunes dotted with several clumps of culm grass.

Shifting his bodyboard into a more manageable position, Zac heads towards the area.

Tegan looks up at me with excited eyes. 'Are we going in the sea?'

'Yes, and we can go in the pool as well, if you like.'

She nods enthusiastically.

Luke sets down the cool box and the bag of towels. As he takes the picnic basket from me, involuntarily our hands touch and a surge of electricity makes us both blink. Immediately I'm flustered, but Luke simply smiles in that lovely, unaffected, generous way of his.

'Race you to the sea, Rhea.' Zac peels out of his clothes down to his swimming trunks.

As brother and sister dash off across the sands with their bodyboards, I drop to my knees and unzip Tegan's trousers.

She places her hands on my shoulders to steady herself. 'I like doing things with you, Cassie.'

'I like doing things with you too, Tiggy.' I slide the trousers over her slim hips.

Luke is busy sorting out towels, but I notice a smile playing on his lips. Having helped the little girl into her swimsuit, I leave her sitting on the sand with a bucket and spade.

Before leaving Foxcombe Manor, I'd put on a swimsuit under my clothes. Now, I remove my T-shirt and jeans and self-consciously glance over at Luke. There's no point in trying to hide the ugly and obvious scar on my right leg, but I'm relieved he doesn't comment on it. However, as I catch his eye, my insides begin to slide. If I didn't know better I'd say that was desire written on his face.

Whoa! This is way too much…

He turns away and concentrates on unbuttoning his shirt.

'Come on, Tiggy. Let's go to the sea.' I hold out my hand to the little girl.

We are several yards from the dunes when a voice rings out. 'Hello. I thought it was you.'

I shield my eyes from the sun. It's the stunning surfer girl.

'I saw you at Crooklets.' She holds her large surfboard with ease. 'I'm Robyn.'

'Hi, I'm Cassie.'

She nods at someone behind me and I turn to see Luke walking towards us wearing swimming trunks, his tanned body attractively muscled. I avert my gaze, but not before I've had visions of running my fingers through his chest hairs.

'This is Luke,' I say.

'Hi. It's a great day for the beach.'

'Indeed it is,' he responds.

Planting her surfboard in the sand, Robyn shakes his hand. 'I haven't seen you two here before. Are you on holiday?'

'No. We come from further up the coast.'

A thrill rips through my body. *We…*

'I only arrived a few weeks ago,' I explain.

'I want to go in the sea.' Tegan tugs at my hand.

'Can you see Zac and Rhea?' I glance towards the ocean.

'Yes!' she squeals excitedly.

Robyn observes us with interest. Something about her makes me feel as if I know her; but I don't.

'Well, I'll let you guys get on with your day.' She lifts her surfboard out of the sand.

'Good to meet you.' I smile.

'Likewise.'

Returning my smile, she nods to Luke. As she heads towards the sea, I watch her athletic, boy-like figure as it weaves through the families on the beach.

'Come on, Tiggy, let's join your brother and sister. Do you want to swing?'

The little girl nods and, turning to Luke, holds out her hand to him. As we follow in Robyn's footsteps, we swing the little girl with the big blue eyes and the corkscrew blonde hair through the air... and it's the most natural thing in the world.

After an hour of bodyboarding and jumping the waves, we picnic amongst the sand dunes. A welcome breeze cools the heat of the blazing sun as it beats down upon our bodies. Incredibly, I don't give David a moment's thought all day and for the first time in as long as I can remember, I feel free. Glancing towards the glittering ocean, I watch Robyn surf the waves. She's easy to spot, her elegance and grace setting her apart from the other surfers.

'Would you like a lager, Cass?'

'Please.'

Delving into the cool box, Luke passes over a can. Once again, our fingers involuntarily touch, and there it is again... that electrical charge. Looking into his eyes I see unperturbed acknowledgement.

'Gosh, it's hot!' I roll the cool aluminium can across my forehead.

He laughs and I smile uncertainly.

'Does anyone want more juice?' I ask, talking quickly to mask my jumbled emotions.

As the children hold out their plastic cups, Luke obligingly fills them. Steadying my nerves, I glance back at the ocean. Robyn is no longer in the sea but walking towards our area of dunes with her surfboard tucked under one arm. Although she's stunning, she isn't classically beautiful, more handsome; her naturalness perfect in this setting. I watch as a man approaches her and instantly recognise him as her companion from the day at Crooklets. She speaks to him, points in our direction and hands over her board before continuing on towards us. She notices me watching and smiles.

'You've found yourselves a great spot,' she says, taking in the children and acknowledging them.

'Would you like to join us for a drink?' Luke asks.

'That's very kind of you but, unfortunately, I have work to do before the day is out.'

My face twitches in surprise. I can't imagine her bound to something as mundane as work. She was born to *surf!*

'Did you kids enjoy bodysurfing?'

'Yeah, it was cool,' says Zac.

Rhea enthusiastically agrees.

'I noticed you two in the sea,' Robyn continues. 'You both have great confidence. You could stand on a board, if you wanted to.'

Zac's eyes light up. 'Seriously?'

She nods. 'Yes. If you want lessons I'd be happy to teach you.'

'Wow!'

She laughs at his enthusiasm.

'Just let me know.' She turns her attention to Luke and me. 'If you guys are free next Saturday I'd like to invite you to a barbeque.'

Chaos consumes me. Luke won't be here then. He'll be in London... with Amanda.

'That's great,' says Luke. 'Where and at what time?'

My eyes open wide in surprise.

'Here, in the dunes... from eight 'til late. Just follow the music.'

'Should we bring anything?'

'The food's sorted. Maybe some beers, but mainly yourselves.' She looks directly at me. 'Though it kills me to leave the beach on this fabulous day, sadly the office calls.'

Surfer girl... confined to an office! What does she do?

Her eyes sweep over the children again. 'You have a great family.'

'Oh, they're not ours,' I say in a rush. 'I mean, we're not together.'

'No?' Momentarily, her eyebrows knit together. 'Oh well, whatever. See you Saturday. Don't forget... just follow the music!'

29

I don't see Luke for the rest of the week, but I do spot him in the distance walking towards the cliff path with Byron. I know he's delaying his return to London because of the beach party, but foolishly I daydream that it may also have something to do with me.

Ginny and Gyles returned in high spirits from the appointment with the specialist and when I enquired how it had gone, Ginny simply answered, *'It was a false alarm, but you can never be too careful about these things.'* She offered no further information, and it wasn't my place to enquire further.

Fortunately, I'm kept busy as school has broken up for the summer and the children ride their ponies daily. However, the days still drag and I try to ignore the misplaced excitement building in the pit of my stomach. The weather continues to be good. Ginny suggests we all spend a day at the beach and she introduces me to Sandymouth, a spectacular stretch of sand spanning two miles and set against a dramatic backdrop of sheer cliffs. It even has its own waterfall tumbling onto the beach. As with other coves along this wild and dangerous stretch of coast, it, too, has fingers of jagged rock reaching menacingly towards the sea, and Zac enthusiastically informs me that at low tide he's seen a shipwreck buried in the sand. As we swim in the safe zone between the red and yellow flags, I observe the many families and surfers, and it's hard to believe Ginny when she tells me that Sandymouth is much quieter than Bude's other main beaches.

Finally, Saturday morning arrives. Having cleaned the Porter's Lodge earlier in the week, I ride early with Zac and Rhea to avoid the heat and insects prevalent later in the day. It's cool in the barn, as we clean the tack, accompanied only by the sound of Caspian, Dylan and Biscuit contentedly munching hay nets. Suddenly, my mobile rings.

It's David.

'Tell me when you're coming home, Sandie.'

My heart races traitorously as my stomach ties itself into a sickening knot.

I put down my sponge and motion to the children that I'm going outside to take the call. Walking to the mounting block, I sit on the cool granite and gaze out of the yard towards the paddocks. In the shade of a tree, Indiana and Inky stand listlessly together with only an occasional swish of a tail – I must bring them in after the call – while half a dozen chickens peck and scratch at the dry ground around their hooves.

'Sands, are you still there?'

'Yes.'

'I miss you.'

I *so* want to believe him. My gaze slides over the landscape to the ocean. It's another beautiful day – we've been so lucky this week – and the sea is aquamarine.

'Stone Farm is empty without you.' He waits for my response but I remain silent. Sighing expansively, he changes tack. 'Tell me about your days. What do you do?'

'They're full, David,' I say in a matter-of-fact voice.

'That tells me a lot! How do you fill them?'

'I look after and exercise five horses and ponies. I help out with the school runs and ferry the children to their various clubs and appointments. I also help Ginny run the holiday let and with general housekeeping; Foxcombe is a sixteenth-century manor house and it requires quite a bit of upkeep. I also provide admin assistance for Gyles and I've just started doing the farm accounts.'

David is quiet for a moment. 'Sounds like they're keeping you busy. Hope you get time to think about me.'

If only he knew. He fills my waking and, more often than not, sleeping hours. But I'm not about to admit that.

'From time to time.'

He doesn't say anything and my gaze settles on the gun dogs, all sensibly lying in the shade in their outside enclosure.

'I see you've been out on the town.'

'So, you *have* been checking up on me!' His voice is triumphant.

'No. But when you're splashed all over the internet it's hard not to notice.'

'That was a great night.'

'I'm so pleased.' My voice is deadpan as I push away the vision of the pretty, buxom blonde adorned in *my* diamonds.

'Oh, come on, Sands. There's no need to be petulant.'

'Petulant!' I gasp. 'What makes you think I'm being that?'

'Your tone.' He laughs.

And there it is again. He's reduced me to being a naughty child.

'I'm not being petulant,' I protest, shocked at how sulky I sound. 'It *did* look as if you were having a great night, judging by the accessory hanging off your arm.'

He laughs again. 'No need to be jealous either, Sands.'

'I'm not jealous.'

Why can't I say anything without David putting a spin on it?

'Jen's a sweet girl.'

'Oh spare me, please.'

'You don't expect me to be a monk while you're away playing at "happy families" do you?'

Why does he always gain the upper hand? Grappling with my emotions, I'm unable to speak.

'She may be a bit dense but she's a good prop for these occasions.'

Suddenly I'm angry... for her. 'I bet she'd be thrilled to hear you referring to her as that.'

'Sands, if you're not around to accompany me and share in my successes...' He lets the sentence hang, waiting for my response, but I refuse to rise to it. 'I'm not going to be without a partner. A man has needs, you know.'

Squeezing my eyes tight shut, I will his remarks not to affect me. But the fissure in my heart widens a little further.

'As has a woman,' I say in a small voice.

'Just so, but until you come back I will continue to fill that void. Jen hasn't replaced you, Sandie, she just satisfies my sexual needs. Nothing more.'

I can't believe he said it! How does he think that makes me feel? In my mind's eye, I see the adoring blonde's ample assets spilling out of her skimpy, strapless evening dress with David's hands all over her body. At once, the red mist descends.

'OK, I get it. She satisfies your needs. But why did you have to buy her the diamond necklace and earrings?'

'Sandie, Sandie, Sandie.' His tone is patronising, as if pacifying a moody child. 'Don't get your knickers in a twist. It's just jewellery. The girl deserves something.'

'But why that particular set? I thought you'd bought it especially for me.'

'I did buy it especially for you. It looks great on you! As you know, I like the designer's style and if you're not around and I think it would look good on someone else, well, what's to stop me from gifting it to them? There's no exclusivity, Sands. Come on!'

How dare he be so flippant with my feelings? I want to scream and shout, but I know that's the reaction he's trying to force from me.

'Goodbye, David.'

Ending the call, I switch off the phone and stare wildly around. He's right. What the hell am I doing in the middle of nowhere without a home or family of my own, filling my days helping Ginny and Gyles with theirs? My life is such a mess. A sudden, crippling stomach cramp sends me doubling over and taking fast, shallow breaths, I beg it to stop. After a while, I tentatively straighten up. What was all that about? I can't afford to lose my health in addition to everything else in my life. Hearing David's voice and the callous nature of his phone call has upset me beyond measure. Isn't time supposed to be the great healer?

I glance at my watch and groan. The beach party is only a few short hours away. It's the last thing I feel like doing now, but I can't bail out. Luke has postponed his trip to London because of it.

30

A warm breeze blows in from the sea and although it's almost eight in the evening, the beach is alive with people determined to make the most of the last of the sunshine. I watch as a boy runs along the sand, encouraging a bright yellow kite into the air. Suddenly, from out of nowhere, two dogs appear and chase the kite's tail before tearing off on some other mission.

Opening the rear door to the Land Rover, Luke extracts a picnic blanket and a pack of beers.

'Any idea where they're likely to be?' I ask.

'Robyn said to follow the music.'

I wait as he locks the door and tucks the key into the back pocket of his jeans. Then, together, we walk onto the beach through a gap in the dunes.

It's easy to locate Robyn's party. Away to the left, a group of people have gathered. The beat of the music is loud and insistent and tantalising barbeque smells waft on the evening air. All at once, the sombre mood brought on by David's earlier phone call begins to lift.

I glance across at Luke and smile. 'Thanks for doing this for me.'

'What's that?'

'Postponing your trip to London, so I can have a social life.'

He gives me a curious look. 'That's not the reason I postponed my trip. I wanted to go to a beach party.'

'Cassie, Luke!' Extracting herself from a huddle of people, Robyn rushes towards us. She looks fantastic, her athletic body shown off to perfection in a bikini with a sarong wrapped around her lower half. 'I'm so pleased you made it.'

Immediately she links arms with me and I'm suddenly reminded of my childhood friend, Shannon; thick as thieves and partners in crime. She introduces us to her friends who are an eclectic and interesting mix, ranging from children to doting grandparents.

'Find a spot and grab some food.' She indicates a couple of barbeques on the beach.

Standing behind one, holding a long-pronged fork, is her partner.

Robyn shakes her head when Luke offers her the pack of beers. 'Keep them. We've plenty here.'

'Where shall we park ourselves?' Luke asks, turning to me.

'Let's try up there.' I point to a nearby dune.

He sets off, climbing with ease. I follow as best as I can, but the fine, loose sand combined with my sandals makes the going difficult.

From the summit, Luke looks down and grins. 'Having a bit of trouble there, Cass?'

'You could say that!'

He stretches out a hand and, gratefully, I accept.

The view from the top is expansive. To our right is the

natural sea pool, a popular bistro, judging by the number of people sitting outside, and a number of cheery, brightly coloured beach huts. In the opposite direction, on the cliffs to the south, is an octagonal stone tower.

'What's that building over there?'

Luke looks up from spreading out the picnic blanket. 'The Pepper Pot. It was built as a refuge for coastguards. Its designer is said to have fashioned it after the Temple of the Winds at Athens. The points of the compass are carved in a frieze below its moulded cornice.'

'How old is it?'

'I believe it was built around 1835 for Sir Thomas Dyke Acland who owned Ebbingford Manor, in Bude. He played a large part in the town's nineteenth-century development. The canal was partly built on Acland land.'

I nod, pleased that he so willingly shares his knowledge with me. Closing my eyes, I breathe in the senses and sounds of the beach and store them to memory: laughter and shouts; breaking waves; the warmth of the sun; a gentle breeze; aromas from the barbeque; and the music. When I open my eyes, Luke is watching me.

A warm smile graces his face. 'Come on, let's join the party.'

As soon as we descend the dune, Robyn grabs my hand and introduces us to her partner.

'Jamie, this is Cassie and her friend, Luke.'

'Good to meet you. Robyn said she'd invited you.' He speaks with a gentle, West Country lilt. 'Grab a plate and let me know what you want.'

Up close, he is pretty, verging on effeminate, but his looks perfectly complement Robyn's stronger, more handsome countenance.

Taking two plates from a stack perched on a picnic table, Luke hands one to me. As we decide what food to have, Robyn sorts out our drinks. I am mesmerised by her. She is so naturally confident and at ease with people.

She is how I want to be; as I used to be with Shannon.

But, somehow, over the years I'd messed up.

'Here you go.' Robyn hands me a glass of wine and passes a cold beer to Luke.

'Cheers.' He takes a long draught.

'So, what do you guys do?'

I cringe. This is where I always came unstuck. 'Luke's a writer,' I say quickly.

'That sounds interesting.' She looks at him inquiringly. 'Anything I might know?'

'Possibly, if you're into nature and landscape writing,' Luke answers modestly.

'He writes under the pseudonym Hunter Harcourt,' I add.

Life moves in mysterious ways. It's hard to believe I'm standing on a Cornish beach with the man whose image first caught my attention in a Sussex service station only a matter of weeks ago. That day seems so distant...

'Didn't you give a talk the other day in town? I think I saw it advertised in the local paper.'

Luke nods. 'I did.'

'How did it go?'

'It went very well. I met Cass there.'

Robyn smiles.

'Although we'd met before.' His eyes twinkle mischievously. 'Only on that occasion I incurred her fury.'

She shoots me a quizzical look.

I turn crimson at the memory. 'It was a misunderstanding, Luke. You know I was concerned for Zac's safety.'

'Love is never straightforward,' Robyn states.

'Oh, we're not...' But I don't finish the sentence.

'That's true,' Luke agrees, with an easy smile.

I frown. I'm lost in this conversation. It's as if they know something I don't.

'Take Jamie and me, for instance,' Robyn continues. 'I came to Cornwall for a career move and left my husband in Nottingham to organise the sale of our house. He was to join me once he'd accomplished that, only I met Jamie in the local sandwich bar before he managed to secure a buyer. Here we are, two years on, and husband's nowhere to be seen.'

I stare wide-eyed. It doesn't compute. She is the girl born to surf without a care in the world, not one to be fettered with such mundane, messy problems as having a husband *and* a lover.

Robyn catches hold of my arm. 'It's true, Cassie. Cornwall attracts many a soul with baggage, but it welcomes us all and makes no judgement on the flotsam and jetsam that end up on its shores.'

'I assumed you were born here!'

She laughs. 'Noooo. Cheshire's my home county. I was brought up in Warrington and went to university in Manchester. It was my husband who introduced me to Cornwall and, well, once discovered, never forgotten. But enough of me! Tell me, Cassie, what's your line of work?'

I squirm. This is the question that confirms I'm a complete waste of space. What have I done with my life? Where others are driven to reach lofty goals, I drift along without any firm destination in mind.

'Cass is an accomplished horsewoman. She helps the Kinsmans organise their young family and assists with the guardianship of Foxcombe Manor.'

I could weep with gratitude. Luke has saved me from myself.

'I know Gyles Kinsman and he doesn't suffer fools,' Robyn says. 'He must think very highly of you to trust you with his children. And as for horses... I love them, but I'm afraid we don't gel. I much prefer surfboards.'

I laugh. 'When you ride the waves it's as if you don't have one beneath you.'

'Thank you, Cassie. That's what all surfers strive for; to be at one with the ocean.'

'Hey, Robyn!' calls out a tall blond man fast approaching with a dark-haired girl.

'Carl, Samantha. Good to see you.' She turns back to us. 'Excuse me while I play hostess. Enjoy the food, and I expect to see you dancing later.' She walks towards the newcomers.

As the sun descends towards the horizon, streaking the sky red, orange and purple, laced with pink, we relax into party mood. It's an intoxicating mix: sand between my toes – now that I've abandoned the sandals – good music, plenty of food and drink, Robyn's honesty and Luke's closeness. Without warning, contentment creeps up and takes me by surprise.

It's not long before the sun slips over the edge of the

world, and the ever darkening night sky is pinpricked with stars. Someone lights a fire and I watch as Robyn dances uninhibitedly with a group of people. Her sarong is no longer tied around her waist but now secured at her neck, cleverly reinvented into a floaty dress that shows off her attractively square shoulders. When God created Robyn he'd bestowed upon her many attributes.

Suddenly she looks across at me, calling out over the sound of the music. 'Come and dance, Cassie.'

I shake my head. She pulls a disappointed face.

'Go on,' Luke encourages gently.

I turn. His eyes are soft and tender.

'Why not?'

'I'm not a good dancer.'

'I don't believe that. The harmony you have with your horse shows a sensitive and caring nature. I bet you have great rhythm.'

I bet you have too…

I glance back at Robyn. She's still watching.

Oh what the hell! I get to my feet.

Silently she claps.

At first I'm stiff and self-conscious, but before long I dance with a freedom and passion I didn't know I possessed. As Robyn and I respond to the pulse of the music, we sway and circle each other. It's good being in the company of someone who feels like a kindred spirit.

'See, it wasn't so bad.'

'Out of practice.'

'Don't fight it, Cassie. Let Cornwall help find your equilibrium.'

I look at her askance. Is it *that* obvious I'm broken and

hollow inside? But before I have a chance to slink off and retreat into my shell, she grabs hold of my hands.

'I recognise a soul sister when I see one. In fact, I recognised it that day at Crooklets when I saw you watching me from the beach café. It doesn't matter what's gone before. Let the past be the past and look to the future.' She smiles. 'And what I see of your future looks kinda good to me.' She tosses her head in Luke's direction.

I glance over towards the dunes. He's watching us.

'He's not my future, Robyn.'

'No?'

I shake my head. 'He's married.'

Her laugh is deep and sexy. 'And so am I... just not to Jamie!'

'Do you think you ever will be?'

'Maybe. Who knows? It's not important. What *is* important is being true to yourself and not living life on someone else's terms. We're stronger than we know. Hell, just getting here takes strength! Be the wild spirit you've always wanted to be.'

I smile uncertainly. Is it really that easy? And how does she know me so well? Perhaps she truly *is* my soul sister. After all, I did feel a connection with her the first moment I spotted her surfing way out at sea.

'I'm going to get your man. He looks lonely all on his own.'

She skips over to Luke and speaks to him. With a nod, he gets to his feet. At first, Robyn joins us in the dance but then she discreetly withdraws. As Luke and I move closer together, the other partygoers become vague shapes on the periphery of vision. He smiles down at me and the beat of the music works its magic. He doesn't speak – it's unnecessary – and, as I guessed, he has great rhythm.

When the song comes to an end and is immediately replaced with a slower tune, Luke reaches out and gently, almost reverently, draws me to him. Slowly, exquisitely, we move together, and as the full length of his body presses lightly against mine, once again I succumb to a delicious sliding sensation deep within. I thought I'd feel awkward, but there's nothing remotely uncomfortable about our closeness. It's as if I've known the strength of his arms and the feel of him all my life. Still we don't speak, and as I lay my head against his shoulder I close my eyes, blissfully aware of his every stroke of my hair. For once in my life, I am in the right place at the right time. Perhaps Robyn has a point. Maybe I shouldn't fight it but, instead, allow Cornwall to reshape me into what my soul yearns for. Wild spirit… what would David think of *that*? My lips twitch in amusement.

All too soon the melody finishes and Luke extracts himself from our embrace. Immediately, I feel the cool of the night air.

'Let's go for a stroll, Cass.' His voice is hardly recognisable.

As we walk away from the barbeque, the noise of the party diminishes. There are several people on the sand; couples walking hand in hand, while others embrace beneath the starlit sky. Once again, my *aloneness* threatens to strangle me. Who the hell am I trying to kid? Wild spirit! I'm just a sad soul without direction, sharing time with a married man who I've simply borrowed for the evening.

We walk on in silence. The only sound is the waves gently lapping the shoreline as the waxing moon, almost full, shines its silvery light across the water. Under different circumstances it would be seriously romantic. Passing the seawater swimming pool, we carry on towards Crooklets Beach and I consider my life with David. However unfulfilled, it is a comfortable one and there are no concerns about money. But – and I still don't understand how I've allowed it to happen – David has shaped me into what he considers a fitting partner, so why, then, did he need to have an affair... or affairs? The thought makes me shiver. Was I really so blind as to not see the signs? And why did I grant him the power to take away my strength over the years?

I join Luke at the edge of the ocean and gaze towards the horizon, as the inky water laps at our feet. In this wilder, more remote stretch of beach there isn't a soul about. Some way out, silhouetted against the moon, the dark shape of a guillemot sweeps low over the sea. Suddenly, I sense Luke's gaze upon me.

'I'd do anything not to go to London tomorrow. The city has lost its appeal. I have several meetings but I'll return as soon as I can.'

I don't know what to say.

'Do you know why, Cass?'

'No.'

It will have something to do with the wildness of Cornwall, its flora and fauna.

He takes my hands in his. 'Ever since I was on the receiving end of a particular person's wrath she's been on my mind.'

My eyes open wide and I swallow the gasp rising in my throat.

'I had no idea who you were, but as you were with Zac

and riding on Kinsman land I presumed you knew the family. I hoped I'd glimpse you again, or see you at one of their gatherings. I couldn't believe it when you attended my talk in Bude.'

My heart hammers inside my chest but I manage to find my voice, albeit only a whisper. 'I couldn't believe Hunter Harcourt was you.'

He squeezes my hands. 'Cass, please believe me when I say I have your back. You are not some enigma, as I wrote in that foolish dedication. You possess a warrior's soul, which was plain to see that day Byron spooked your horse.' He laughs apologetically. 'And tonight, when you danced with Robyn, I saw your wild gypsy spirit shine through.'

I am astounded; he describes me in a similar way to Robyn. It isn't someone I recognise, but how can they both be wrong? Why can't I see her?

'Say something, Cass.'

'I – I don't know what to say.'

He hugs me gently.

'I don't know what's going on in your life, but I suspect at some point you've been denied the opportunity to be you.'

I squeeze my eyes shut in a futile attempt to hold back the tears. In a film, this would be when the hero kisses the girl. But this is no film. This is my sad, sorry life.

He holds me away from him and I open my eyes.

'You know, Cass, you will make a wonderful mother when the time is right.'

This time I can't hold back the gasp. This is too much! He's hit the nail on the head.

'Just watching you with the Kinsman children, it's obvious.'

Quickly I turn away and wipe my face as the tears fall.

'Hey, don't cry.' He turns me towards him. 'It's true. Just let life happen, Cass. Don't force it. But while you're doing that please don't forget I'm here for you as a friend... always.'

I nod. Even though my body refuses to see him as a friend, responding in a way that it shouldn't, I can live with that offering. After all, what *is* our relationship? He belongs to someone else.

'Come on, we should get back to the party,' he says softly.

As I fall into step beside him, Luke casually drapes his arm around my shoulders... just a couple of pals returning from a stroll on the beach.

31

The night sky is full of stars as we drive back from the barbeque. Luke points out the various constellations, adding a not inconsiderable smattering of valuable education as he describes their different characteristics. As always, I find it fascinating. Not for the first time, I marvel at how one man can absorb so much knowledge.

It's just after 3am when we reach the manor house. So as not to wake the sleeping household, Luke stops the car on the farm track at the entrance to the quadrangle of barns.

I turn in my seat. 'Try to get some sleep before your journey later.'

'I hope to, but it hardly seems worth it. I'll be leaving in less than five hours.'

'Well, drive safely... with the window open, if need be.'

He laughs softly. 'Good advice.'

'Thank you for this evening, Luke.'

'My pleasure, Cass.'

Opening the car door, I climb out and switch on the flash light on my mobile phone.

'I'll wait to make sure you arrive safely at your door.'

I'm about to protest, but then decide not to. It won't make any difference.

'Thanks.' I give him a smile. 'Have a good week in London. I hope all your meetings are successful.'

'I hope so too. That way, I won't have to go up again for a while.' He pulls a resigned face.

I chuckle. 'Bye, Luke.'

'Goodnight, Cass.'

As I walk across the yard towards the dark bulk of the manor house, two of the gun dogs emerge from their kennel and stand at the wire fence, watching my progress. I talk to them soothingly as I pass by and hope they won't start to bark. The last thing I want is for Gyles and Ginny to think there's an intruder attempting to steal their prize gun dogs. Goodness knows what they'd do. Probably appear with guns at the ready!

As I reach the door to my rooms, I turn and wave. Luke still watches, the moonlight catching the contours of his open face. He looks so wholesome and right. Quickly, I remind myself... *friends*.

He returns my wave, and as the car moves off I unlock the door and enter the house.

That night I enjoy a dreamless sleep and wake feeling calm and at peace with the world. Glancing at my watch, I realise that Luke will have been on the road for at least an hour. Sundays are more relaxed for me in the Kinsman household, as Ginny sees to the children and gives them their breakfast, and it only leaves me to deal with the horses. It's not confirmed, but I suspect it's because she's aware of how full-on the work is and it gives me the chance to draw breath and prepare for whatever the forthcoming week may bring.

Today, Zac, Rhea and I ride around the village and across fields being cut for hay. Weekends are just another working day in the farming calendar, and we wave to Colin in the cab of his tractor. The family tradition of Sunday lunch in the formal dining room at 1pm sharp is something Gyles likes to uphold, and it's already approaching noon by the time we return to the barn. Hurriedly, we stuff hay nets and refill water buckets before leaving the horses and ponies contentedly munching in their stables.

After a quick freshen up and a change of clothes, I close the bedroom door and make my way along the corridor. As I enter the open hall, I hear a curious noise and stop to listen. As usual, the manor's timeless serenity drapes thickly in the air. But, no… there it is again. What *is* that noise? It sounds like someone's crying. Whoever can it be? Heartfelt, strangled sobs float down from the minstrels' gallery, but as I cross the hall the noise diminishes. I can't imagine any of the children crying in that fashion, but if one of them is hurt I need to find out.

I start to climb the stairs and feel a flutter of unease. As I make my way across the galleried landing and enter the passageway leading to the playroom, the sobbing starts up again. It sounds odd, as if coming from a very great distance and muffled by cotton wool. I open the door to the playroom. It's empty. I move to the next closed door and tap softly.

'Rhea, is everything OK?'

No reply. I open the door and peer in. Again, the room is empty. I turn away, puzzled. Am I imagining things? But I can still hear crying. It's such a pitiful sound and my heart aches. I cross the hallway to Zac's door and knock. There's no response and I enter. He's not there. However, with some satisfaction, I notice he's taken note of my request to keep his room tidy and not as it was when I'd first arrived at Foxcombe.

Backing out of the room, I gaze along the passageway at the other closed doors. It doesn't sound like Tegan crying; it's an older voice. But I need to be sure. I walk to her bedroom, knock and enter, but the room is empty. Where *are* the children? Perhaps it's later than I think and they're already in the dining room. I glance down at my watch. Damn! The battery must have stopped. It displays just before twelve-thirty, but I know that's not so. It was that time when I changed into a fresh pair of jeans.

And then I hear a heart-wrenching sound from further along the passageway. Surely, it's not Ginny? I can't imagine her crying over anything. Approaching the door to her personal reading/hobbies' room, I stop and listen. The muffled wailing emanates from within. It's a desolate, harrowing sound, as if she's in agony. Why is she so distressed? Softly, I knock on the door.

'Ginny, may I come in?'

The heart-rending sobs continue, so I repeat the request a little louder. Still no response. I turn the handle but as soon as the door opens the crying stops, and I stand, paralysed, staring into the empty room. There's a distinct chill in the air and a sliver of fear coils its way up from my stomach.

I will not freak out. I won't!

'Cass, lunch is ready.' Zac's voice filters up from downstairs.

'Coming,' I call out in a shaky voice.

Forcing myself to move, I close the door again and make

my way back along the passageway, half-expecting the disconsolate weeping to resume. Fortunately, it doesn't. However, as I cross the galleried landing and approach the top of the stairs, I have the strongest feeling I'm not alone and the hairs on the back of my neck bristle. I turn. There's no one there, but I recall Gyles's words that first day I undertook office work when he'd noticed me standing behind him in the doorway. '*I thought I sensed a presence.*' Does he still *feel* the spirits that wander the corridors of Foxcombe Manor?

I start to descend the stairs but get no further than three treads before I hear the faintest, whispered swish of a gown, as if someone has just passed by, followed by the sensation of silk trailing softly across my body.

'There you are,' says Zac from the dining room doorway. 'What were you doing upstairs?'

'I thought I heard one of you crying, but it must have been the wind.'

'Wasn't any of us. We're all in here waiting for you,' he says in a matter-of-fact voice before scuttling back inside the room.

My heart dances a rapid beat. Stoically, I tell myself that if Zac can take this in his stride then so can I. However, when I glance down at my watch I'm not so sure. Bizarrely, both the hour and minute hands are whizzing manically around the clock face, coming to rest at five minutes past one.

As I step down onto the next tread, from out of the corner of my eye I see a movement up on the minstrels' gallery. With my nerves already at breaking point, my head whips round sharply and I'm blinded by shafts of sunlight streaming in through the tall, upper-storey stone-mullioned windows. White, cream and grey; like a heavy veil. But as I focus on the hazy aura, other colours emerge – strands of teal, peacock blue and gold. No, not gold... chestnut. And I swear there's a shape suspended in the mote-filled rays, as if caught in a fold of time. For the briefest of moments, I fancy I see a young woman peering over the gallery's balustrading, her lustrous chestnut hair falling in gentle curls around a face of exquisite, yet haunting beauty.

Below, Ginny emerges from the kitchen with a bowl of roast potatoes in her hands. She glances up at me standing motionless on the stairs.

'Come on, Cassie. You'd better get stuck in before my hungry mob scrape the bowls clean.'

32

Escaping the hustle and bustle of the busy street, Luke and Amanda step into the glass lift and ascend twenty floors to a place of sanctuary. Delicate lavender and olive trees elegantly line an extensive roof garden, immediately transporting diners to the South of France. Only the romantic, picturesque view across London's jaw-dropping skyline gives away the restaurant's true location. Strategically placed leafy trellises create private seating areas, furnished with velvet upholstered couches and chaises longues with complementary plump cushions, flickering candles and cosy rugs. Centre stage, a vine-covered pergola groans under the weight of a plethora of ripening black grapes. Arched antique mirrors and an eclectic mix of antique pots and planters add to the ambience, creating a relaxing, luscious entertaining space a million miles away from the city streets below.

From the far side of the terrace, an elegant brunette waves at the couple as they step out of the lift. Excusing herself from her group of friends, she sets off towards the new arrivals.

'Charmaine's looking well,' remarks Luke, as their hostess approaches.

'She has the knack,' Amanda says out of the side of her mouth, her beaming smile not slipping an inch. 'Even when she's just stepped out of the sauna and her make-up's sliding off her face.'

It's a balmy evening and Luke takes a long, steadying breath. As he draws air deep into his lungs, the stress of having had only a few hours' sleep before driving up from Cornwall reduces. Earlier in the week, when he'd advised his wife of his change of plans to travel up today instead of Saturday, she'd been less than impressed.

'Hello, darlings.' Holding her glass at arm's length, Charmaine kisses Luke and Amanda on the cheek whilst summoning a nearby waiter holding aloft a tray of glittering flutes filled with champagne. 'So pleased you made it, Luke. How's the book coming along?'

'I've completed the first draft.' Taking two glasses from the tray, Luke hands one to his wife. 'That's why I'm in London. I've meetings with my agent and publicist this coming week.'

'And then you'll disappear back to the depths of the countryside once more?' Charmaine takes a sip of champagne, observing him thoughtfully.

'At the first opportunity,' Amanda says pointedly.

Charmaine laughs. 'But don't you find it frustratingly dull, darling? Oh, don't bother to answer that. I already know your reply.'

'Different strokes for different folks.' Luke gives their elegant hostess an unruffled smile.

'I make sure he attends plenty of cultural events while he's in the city so he doesn't stagnate,' Amanda announces loudly, ensuring her words are heard by Peter, Charmaine's fast-approaching husband, and the small blonde woman with him.

'If there's anything that captures my interest.' Luke nods a welcome to the newcomers.

Amanda pulls an exasperated face. 'You know, I'm lucky he's here at all!'

'Why so?' asks Charmaine.

'A rare and exotic species has recently arrived on the Cornish scene. It's rather grabbed his attention.'

The small blonde woman joins in the conversation. 'Oh, what species is that?'

'I believe it's called a "hireling".' Amanda snorts disdainfully.

'A what?'

'See, I told you it was rare!' Amanda laughs, her eyes glittering dangerously as she takes a long swallow of champagne.

Luke frowns. There's a time and place for Amanda's shenanigans, and *now* is neither. He throws his wife a warning look.

'There are many interesting and different species that capture my attention, none more so than any other.'

Rattled, Amanda retaliates, 'I suppose you have to give it your undivided attention whilst it's under your radar. After all, you never know how long it will stick around.'

Linking arms with the small blonde woman, she turns and marches away.

Luke watches his wife and her friend make their way across the roof terrace towards a number of tables laden with food.

'What was all that about?' Peter asks.

'Just Amanda being facetious.' Luke tips back his glass and swallows a large mouthful of champagne.

'Not to worry,' soothes Charmaine, putting her arm through Luke's and patting his hand. 'We all know what she can be like. Amanda wouldn't be our *dear Amanda* if she wasn't. Let's help ourselves to the buffet while there's still some available.'

Much later, Luke follows his wife along the hall of their Chelsea townhouse towards the lounge, depositing his keys on a side table as he passes by. The sound of nails tapping on wooden flooring heralds the arrival of the Great Dane in the doorway.

'Good boy, Byron.' Luke strokes the dog's head. 'Keeping an eye on things in our absence?'

The dog gazes up with big, soulful eyes.

'Well, that was a good evening,' Amanda says, flopping heavily onto the sofa and kicking off her shoes. She picks up a large, oversized cushion and hugs it to her chest. 'Isn't it marvellous how a few glasses of bubbly loosens tongues?' She gives a sharp, flinty laugh. 'I had no idea Rupert and Diana were in the throes of a passionate affair! They've done well keeping that to themselves.'

Luke sits down next to her. Reaching for the remote control lying on a glass-topped coffee table, he switches on the television. Byron settles at his feet.

'Did you have any inkling?'

'Hmm...?'

Amanda glances at her husband's profile and sighs. 'Rupert and Diana! Did you know about their affair?'

'No, but then that's hardly surprising. I haven't been around much.' Flicking through the channels, he settles for an old movie.

Amanda purses her lips tightly. She doesn't want to watch TV. She wants to discuss this latest bit of juicy gossip, but her husband obviously isn't in the mood.

'How long do you expect to be in London, Luke?'

'Not sure. It depends how negotiations go this week.'

'I've been thinking.'

'That sounds ominous.'

Putting the cushion to one side, she sidles up to him. 'I'd hoped to come down to Cornwall next month, but I doubt I'll get away much at all over the next few months. I've got a huge amount of work on, what with the new account, and it's imperative I'm here to oversee it. But I can't bear the thought of us being apart for that length of time. Do you *have* to go back? Can't you do your rewrites and edits here in London?' She flutters her eyelashes.

Inwardly, Luke sighs. How many times have they argued this point? 'I could, but as you well know it's better for me to be *in situ.*'

'But it's so boring when you're not around.'

Luke snorts. 'I don't think so! *The* socialising queen, bored?'

'A girl has to entertain herself while her man's away,' she says, defensively.

'It all depends on the outcome of this week's meetings,' Luke says, squeezing his wife's knee, 'but I promise I'll come up to town as often as I can.'

She frowns.

'Don't worry, Mandy. I'll do my utmost to save you from dying of boredom.' Suddenly, his hand stills. 'After all, we know where that's led in the past.'

Amanda looks at him sharply. 'You're not still stressing about *that*, are you? Move on, Luke. Life's too short. It happened, but it's behind us now.'

'I have moved on, Mandy.' Swallowing his irritation, Luke removes his hand. 'But once infidelity enters a marriage and one's beliefs have been put to the test, it's not always easy to regain trust in the other.'

'Oh for goodness' sake!' Amanda moves to the end of the sofa. 'You always take things *so* seriously, Luke. How many times do I have to tell you? Simon was just a fling. A mere distraction from the boringly, mundane business of life here without you. Anyway, we've been through all this in counselling. I promise to behave myself, however many men flatter and ply me with gifts, but you can't blame them for trying when you insist on being an aloof and distant husband.'

'Them?'

For a fleeting moment Amanda's face registers guilt. 'Yes, *them*. In case you hadn't noticed, the financial industry is full of young men striving for lofty goals. Ambition is a turn-on, Luke, I can't deny it…'

'Do our marriage vows stand for nothing, Amanda?'

'Oh, of course they stand for something. I'm just saying that when men wine and dine me and they don't see a husband around, it's easy for them to forget there is one.'

'And how easy is it for you to conveniently forget him?'

She lets out an exasperated sigh. 'You know entertaining is a way of life for me, Luke. It's important I make connections for work. Networking is everything, and it's ongoing. I can't just stop. I'd be no good at my job!'

Luke stares blankly at the television screen. As someone who values fidelity above all else, he was shaken to the core when he'd uncovered his wife's affair... but they'd come back from the brink. At least, he had. Amanda didn't think she'd committed any great crime and, judging from her attitude tonight, still doesn't. The differences between them ensures their marriage stays sharp, giving it an edge, but the far-reaching ripples of the affair – even though it was several years ago – still bite deep.

'Where does that leave us regarding starting a family?' Luke turns to his wife. 'You always said we'd have one by the time we reached forty. That's only two years away.'

Amanda's expression freezes and she quickly turns away. 'Oh, I'm far too busy to think about that now,' she says dismissively.

'But if we don't think about it *now* the opportunity will pass us by.'

'Women have babies well into their forties these days.'

'That's true, Amanda, but it's safer to have your first before then.'

'I can't be dealing with this now, Luke. Work is full-on and I don't intend swapping that for changing dirty nappies and being trapped here, losing my mind.'

'You have a very negative view of what being a parent means. In any case, after a while you could return to work. We would organise day care.'

'And would you visit occasionally to see your child?' Amanda turns to face her husband.

'I'd be hands on, of course.'

'How... from Cornwall?'

Luke sighs. 'Things would have to change.'

'Yes. You would have to move back to London. I tell you now, Luke, it would be bad enough confined to these four walls, so I certainly wouldn't entertain being buried in the depths of Cornwall with a baby.'

Luke stares at his wife. 'I think we may have hit an impasse.'

Amanda smiles uncertainly. Softening her voice, she purrs, 'Only for the time being, Lukey.'

She turns to the screen, but it's no use; she doesn't want to watch TV. And she doesn't want to continue this conversation either. It's far too heavy and certainly doesn't fit in with her current plans, although she knows at some point she will have to give Luke the family he wants. She can't put it off forever. Glancing sideways at her husband, she sees he is once more, seemingly, absorbed by the movie.

Yawning loudly, Amanda rises from the sofa. 'Well, it's been a long week and I'm off to bed.' She drops a kiss on her husband's mouth. 'Don't be late, Lukey. We've got a lot of catching up to do in that department.'

'I won't be long.'

'Better not,' she answers brightly before exiting the room.

Half-heartedly, Luke watches the film. It was good catching up with Peter, Charmaine and the others – his and Amanda's circle of London friends are diverting and entertaining company – but now, his thoughts drift to the beach party. Was it really only yesterday evening? It seems an age ago. A vision of Cass and Robyn dancing on the sand comes to him. Two goddesses; one exotically dark and the other naturally fair. Unable to take his eyes off the women, he'd watched as Cass lost her inhibitions and an increasingly vibrant, wild and untamed side come to the fore. He'd always suspected it lurked just beneath the surface.

On the first day he'd met her – when she called him a 'stupid oaf' – she'd displayed her warrior spirit by leaping onto her horse and speeding off in hot pursuit of Zac and his pony. He smiles at the memory. But now a wild gypsy soul is becoming evident. He finds her fascinating; she with the long, sleek black hair and astonishing sapphire-blue eyes. Why *is* she so unaware of the effect she has on those around her? Who, or what, has happened in her life to make her so adrift from her true self?

Astounded at the level of anger consuming him, Luke raises a self-deprecating eyebrow. He knows his wife was only being wittily clever earlier that evening, but her observations were characteristically accurate. Cassandra Tallulah Shaw is, indeed, a rare and exotic creature, and one who deserves to reach her fullest potential.

'Lukey, babe, come to bed.' Amanda's seductive tones float down the stairs.

'Coming.' Luke presses a button on the remote and the television plunges into darkness.

The Great Dane watches as his master rises from the sofa and walks towards the door.

'Byron, bed.'

Obediently, the dog gets to its feet and heads towards the kitchen.

Luke takes one last look around the room before switching off the light and climbing the stairs.

33

The sound of a car engine makes me glance up from clearing weeds in the sand school, and as the Land Rover's nose slides into view a fluttering sensation takes hold in my belly. The beach barbeque, no more than eleven days before, seems a lifetime ago, but I've been unable to forget the warmth and companionship Luke extended to me during our evening together.

Friends... I remind myself.

Bringing the car to a stop alongside the post and rail fence, Luke lowers the passenger window. 'Hello, Cass.'

'Hi. How did it go?'

'Good, thanks, although I'm relieved to be back. The city is swamped with people.'

I pull a sympathetic face and rest my chin on the rake's handle.

'It's your day off on Friday, isn't it?'

I nod. It's not really a question; he knows the Kinsmans give me Fridays off.

'Have you anything planned?'

'Nothing that can't be altered.'

His face lights up and my foolish heart beats that little bit faster.

'Come to the cottage for ten. I'd like to introduce you to Parson Hawker and the legacy he's left on this landscape.'

'Sounds interesting.' I straighten up. 'Ten it is.'

'Good.' He gives me a look that sets the butterflies in my tummy swirling into a maelstrom. Then, grinning, he points to the far side of the arena. 'Think you may have missed a bit.'

'Thank you, Mr Metcalfe, for pointing out the bleeding obvious,' I say in a mock-stern voice.

He laughs. 'See you Friday, Cass.'

I watch as the Land Rover carries on down the track towards Foxcombe Cottage. What am I to do? I can't allow myself to fall for him. That's a one-way ticket to nowhere.

'He's just being nice,' I growl. 'Get over it, Cassandra.'

Attacking the weeds with the rake once again, I resume my chores with formidable, renewed energy.

Luke navigates the track, keeping one eye on the rear view mirror and Cassandra standing at the sand school fence. As he gets out of the Land Rover and opens the bottom gate he glances back, but she's no longer there. Proceeding along the winding tarmac drive through the trees, he parks in the stone-chipped circle at the side of the house, switches off the engine and stares through the windscreen, deep in thought.

It's only when Byron starts to whine that he rouses himself and lets the dog out of the car to relieve itself on the lawn. Luke stands with feet apart, stretching his arms high above his head and interlocking his fingers as he gazes down the valley to the cliffs and the sea beyond. Navy blue today.

On Friday morning, Luke and I walk through the woods and over the fields to the church of St Morwenna and St John the Baptist. I've not visited the place of worship before.

'This is pale and haunting,' I say, standing in front of a white figurehead in the churchyard.

'It's a replica of the figurehead from a brig wrecked on Sharpnose Point in 1842. The original figurehead is inside the church. The *Caledonia* went down with captain and all crew, but for one. They're buried here in a mass grave.'

I gaze at the memorial in silence. Sporting a tam-o'-shanter and sporran, the woman holds a cutlass in her right hand; in her left is a round shield bearing a carved flowering thistle. Although she wears a bracelet, fancy socks and a kilt falling in soft folds, all marking her femininity, her upper body is clad in chainmail of mermaid-like scales. A sash drapes across her left shoulder to the opposite hip.

'The Reverend Robert Stephen Hawker,' Luke says, 'or Parson Hawker, as he's affectionately known, served as vicar to the smugglers, wreckers and dissenters of the area from 1834 to 1875. He was an eccentric and compassionate man who, I believe, was born out of time. He's famous for burying many drowned sailors washed up at the bottom of Vicarage Cliff at his own expense. He also wrote poetry, including the Cornish National anthem, Trelawny, which is based on his poem, *Song of the Western Men*.'

'Who, or what, is Trelawny?'

'Bishop Trelawny was one of seven bishops imprisoned by James II after Monmouth's failed rebellion. Parson

Hawker also brought the medieval custom of the Harvest Festival back into the church.'

'What a benevolent man.'

'Indeed. He was unstinting in his efforts to ensure drowned sailors received a Christian burial. Story has it that he would scramble down the cliffs when there was a shipwreck and carry back the bodies for a church grave. Until Hawker, those poor souls were often buried on the beach where they were found without Christian rites, the belief being it wasn't possible to tell if they were Christian or not.'

I shake my head. How awful to be buried on some random beach you just happened to wash up on.

'When Hawker arrived at Morwenstow there hadn't been a vicar here for over a hundred years,' Luke continues. 'Smugglers and wreckers were numerous in the area. Apparently, Morwenstow wreckers *allowed a fainting brother to perish in the sea without extending a hand of safety".'* This place of worship was known as the smugglers' church.'

I raise my eyebrows.

'There are many fine memorials here.' Luke glances around the churchyard. 'Some are adorned with what is probably Hawker verse.'

In contemplative mood, we walk amongst the gravestones and come upon a Celtic cross.

'This, too, is in memory of shipwrecked sailors buried here.'

'It's not unlike the one in the garden at the manor. Ginny told me Gyles's great-grandfather discovered a Celtic stone cross buried upside down in a field beside the church path.

Apparently, before it was moved to the garden, livestock used it as a rubbing post!'

Luke nods. 'I've seen it. It's believed to have been constructed in the time of the Third Crusade, around 1190. It's also one of only four crosses in Cornwall made of grey elvan, the hard metamorphic rock that forms many clifftop rock outcrops. Have you noticed its unusual carved design?'

'No.'

'Take a good look. Although based on the fairly common pattern of a cross on a wheel head, each limb of the carved cross is itself crossed with a transverse bar close to the tip.'

'I'll have to be more observant,' I say with a rueful smile. He laughs.

As Luke enters the church porch beneath a lovely Norman arch, I gaze out at the Atlantic and wonder about all those drowned sailors now laid to rest in the cemetery. Over the centuries this remote church must have witnessed many tempestuous storms, but today the atmosphere is tranquil. This churchyard is an ancient place and, silently, I pray that those lost souls have finally found peace.

As we enter, I take a cursory look around. It's cool inside and we are the only people present. The church is a conventional shape with nave, two aisles and a fine, open wagon roof. There's a single chancel with tall wooden sedilia, the rood screen making it dark and secluded, and three lovely arches decorated with bird-beaked faces in surprisingly good condition. The pew ends are interesting, carved with original fifteenth-century Gothic tracery featuring the usual symbols and grotesques, but also sea monsters.

As we walk around the interior, Luke shares his

knowledge and, once again, I feel my soul expand as he makes his intelligent observations.

'The font is believed to be of Norman origin. It's unusual in the way it slants towards you, as if inviting you in.'

'I like its ropework decoration.'

'The pulpit incorporates blind tracery woodwork, and look at the wall plates, Cass. What do you see?'

I gaze up. 'Oh, that's wonderful.'

At the base of the roof, a carved vine winds its way around the church with figures of angels spaced at intervals.

'The angels are carved directly out of the oak; not pegged on.'

Listening attentively, I learn that the chancel screen incorporates sixteenth- and seventeenth-century carvings, and that the remnants of a mural painting of St Morwenna on the north wall dates to the late fifteenth and sixteenth centuries. I find it remarkable this was painted at around the same time as Foxcombe Manor was built. We study the original life-size figurehead of the *Caledonia* and a memorial window depicting Reverend Hawker and his dog.

Presently, making my way up the north aisle, I come to a slab in the floor and stop to read the inscription carved in the slate.

'The resting place of Charlotte Hawker,' Luke says, joining me. 'She was the reverend's first wife for over forty years.'

'That's going some!'

'Indeed. He was born in 1803, the son of a poor Cornish curate. So, to pay for his own Oxford education, at nineteen, he married a woman aged forty-one with a private income.'

'Not for love then...'

'It must have been, eventually. Anyway, people marry for all sorts of reasons.'

Something in his tone rocks the comfortable companionship we share.

'The year after his wife's death, Parson Hawker, then aged sixty-one, married a nineteen-year-old Polish girl who was a governess to children of a neighbouring reverend.'

'Goodness, I bet that set a few tongues wagging.'

Luke raises an eyebrow. 'I expect so. But the marriage must have suited them both as it produced three daughters.'

'So many different ways to live...' I say to myself; at least, I thought I had.

'Very true, Cass.'

He holds my gaze. Quickly, I look away.

'Come on,' he says, curtailing the unsettling undercurrents threatening to consume us. 'I want to show you Hawker's Hut.'

34

As we leave the sanctuary of the church, I glance back at its solid tower.

'Why are there no bell openings on this side?'

'There's no point. Only the sheep will hear!'

I nod at the logic in this and fall into step beside him. Making our way through the churchyard, we climb over a stile at the far end into a field.

'There's the vicarage Hawker designed and had built.' Luke says, pointing to the right.

Across the field is the handsome Victorian house with the unusual chimneys. Its ornate, diamond-paned windows glint in the late morning sun that suddenly peeps out from behind a bank of cumulus cloud.

'The chimneys are modelled on church towers where he served as vicar,' explains Luke. 'Tamerton, where he was a curate; his other living at Welcombe; Magdalen College, Oxford; and the tower here at Morwenstow. Apparently, the old kitchen chimney is a replica of his mother's tomb.'

'He obviously had a great sense of connectivity and appreciated the beauty of art.'

'I think you're right. Everything he undertook indicates

that Parson Hawker had an understanding of the bigger picture. He also liked isolation and seclusion, as you will see from the next building he built.'

Thankfully it's not too hot, making for good walking conditions, and we carry on down to join the coastal path. The views are superb and we navigate the narrow pathway along the cliff edge in single file until reaching a slate plaque announcing, 'Hawkers Hut'. Taking a lower track, within a matter of yards we arrive at a wooden door set into the cliff face.

'The National Trust's smallest building,' announces Luke with a grin. 'Hawker constructed it out of driftwood salvaged from wrecked ships. He's said to have spent many hours here contemplating, writing poetry and smoking his opium pipe.'

'Zac told me it was where the reverend *did drugs*!'

Luke laughs. 'In a manner of speaking. Look, Lundy's clear today. I'll take you there one day.'

I glance out to sea. On the horizon the island beckons enticingly.

'I'd like that.' With a twinge of conscience, I wonder what Amanda would say.

'This way you can see along the coast to Cambeak, Tintagel and Pentire in the distance.'

I turn and gaze at the magnificently rugged vista spread out before us.

We are alone on the cliff. Luke opens the door to the hut and I enter. The interior is tiny; the wooden walls and bench seats covered in carved initials. It's peaceful and still inside but outside all is energy, and we sit and watch the swell of the Atlantic through the open doorway. White horses crest the waves surging towards the shore, and a number of gulls keep an eye on the ocean beneath them as they soar through the air.

'Have you sat here on stormy days? It must be a spectacular sight.'

'I have,' Luke replies. 'I leave Byron at home on those days. He's sensible on the cliffs, but if anything happened it would be tricky to rectify with a dog of his size.'

'It's easy to imagine Reverend Hawker sitting here in quiet contemplation, putting the world to rights.'

'Yes, but he didn't only visit for the sake of isolation. He also entertained guests here, the likes of Alfred Tennyson and Charles Kingsley.'

'Goodness! I'm in the presence of greatness.'

'Well, thank you, Miss Shaw,' Luke says with a grin.

'Oh, I didn't mean…' I stop before digging a deeper hole. Luke chuckles.

I glance at him in embarrassment, my cheeks flaming, and then I burst out laughing. 'You know what I mean.'

'I do.' He smiles warmly.

'Tell me more about the reverend. He sounds a fascinating man.'

'Well, let me see.' Two small lines of concentration form between Luke's eyebrows. 'He was ordained a priest in 1831 and was offered the rectorship of Morwenstow Church in 1834 by the Bishop of Exeter. Apparently, he was more than happy to accept because he'd visited as a child and loved the remoteness of the place with the sea crashing on the rocks below the church.'

'Sitting here in his hut, you can tell he loved nature.'

'There's a lot to commend.'

I gaze across at Luke. I can't imagine him being comfortable in London.

'Hawker was a legendary eccentric. He dressed up as a mermaid and excommunicated his cat for mousing on Sundays.'

'No way!'

'Apparently so.' Luke grins. 'His fashion sense was daring for the time; a claret-coloured coat, blue fisherman's jersey, long sea-boots, a pink brimless hat and a poncho made from a yellow horse blanket. He claimed it was the ancient habit of St Padarn. He also talked to birds, invited his nine cats into church and kept a huge pig as a pet.'

'So did George Clooney... keep a pig, I mean. But, I'm sure Reverend Hawker's parishioners weren't too happy about having cats in the church.'

'They were all country folk, so I expect they accepted it as yet another one of his eccentricities.'

'What a character.'

Looking across the small divide, I meet Luke's gaze. So much passes between us in that moment and he smiles. I love the way his eyes crinkle at the corners when he does. Without warning, my heart beats a little faster.

Friends, Cassandra...

'Has Amanda visited the Hut?'

At once, Luke's demeanour changes. 'Under protest.'

'But why? It's such a wonderful experience.'

'For some. Amanda feels safer in a city environment. She prefers pavements beneath her feet.'

The Metcalfes seem poles apart; chalk and cheese. Once again I wonder what makes their marriage work.

'How did you two meet?'

He hesitates before answering. 'University. She was studying Finance and Economics, while I was there for a Geography and Environmental Science degree.'

It all sounds so self-assured and purposeful, forging through life without any doubts. I want to shrivel up, crawl away and hide in the darkest corner.

However, digging deep, I carry on. 'Ginny said you divide your time between the cottage and a London home.'

'Yes. Amanda used to be in Cornwall a lot more, but as she's progressed up the career ladder she spends most of her time in London. It's me who tends to make the journey these days.'

'Don't you get lonely here?'

'Lonely?' Luke seems genuinely surprised by my question. 'No, never lonely. There's always something of interest going on, and while I'm at the cottage I can write without interruption.'

I wonder if I possess the strength of character to be truly on my own. During my unusual childhood my parents were always in the background, and my role in the Kinsman household makes me feel involved. But, as David has accused, am I simply gate-crashing their family life?

Luke's gaze never wavers from my face. 'What have I said to make you so thoughtful, Cass?'

'I was just thinking of my own situation.'

'And what situation is that?' he asks gently.

I straighten up. So far during our acquaintance I've divulged very little of my life. I'm too embarrassed by my uneventful and meaningless existence compared to the one this clever, grounded man leads.

'You don't want to know about me. It's way too boring.'

'On the contrary, Cass, I do want to know about you.' His voice is soft.

Shyly, I meet his gaze. There's sincerity and strength in those hazel eyes.

'Only if you want to reveal anything,' he adds, with a kind smile. 'I'm not prying.'

And so, taking a deep breath, I recount my life: the unusual childhood, only saved by my friendship with Shannon and our shared obsession with ponies; the car accident that changed everything; meeting David and his wooing of me while I was in hospital for those three long months; moving in with him once I was discharged; and a cursory summary of our life together.

Luke listens without interruption and makes no judgement. I'm so thankful for that. As my sorry story unfolds, his support and warmth wraps around me like a comfort blanket in the small space that we share.

'And then, one day on the Downs, I witnessed something that made me doubt David's loyalty.' I bite my lip, as I recall his clandestine behaviour with Melanie. 'It made a mockery of my life with him, and as I discovered more, it dawned on me that I was living a lie.'

'So that's how you ended up here,' Luke says quietly.

'Yes. It's odd how that happened. He sent me to refuel his car and while I was waiting to pay I saw a copy of *The Lady* in the magazine rack. It was the edition with you on the front.'

He raises an eyebrow.

'That image of you standing at the end of the tunnel of trees resonated with me for some reason and, on a whim, I bought a copy. David was late home that evening, so while

I waited for him I read your article.' I flush at the memory the huge impression his words had made... and still do. Quickly, I hurry on. 'It was then that I came across Ginny's advert. Anyway, that night David and I argued badly and he moved into the guest bedroom, where he remained until I left Stone Farm. I didn't have many options but I knew I had to make a decision, so I contacted Ginny. The rest, as they say, is history.'

Although a lump has lodged in my throat, talking about this has eased some of the heartache.

Luke gazes at me with understanding and compassion. Leaning forward, he takes my hands in his.

'Has David contacted you since you've been in Cornwall?'

I nod. 'He says I should grow up and stop playing at "happy families" with someone else's children and return to where I belong.'

Is it my imagination or does he tighten his hold?

'And will you?'

I shake my head sadly. 'I've told him the only way I'll consider returning is if he faces up to his responsibilities and we start a family. We've been together ten years and I don't see a future together unless there are children in it.'

'And what has he said to that?' His voice is barely more than a whisper.

I give a small, derisive snort. 'It's not so much what he's said as what he's done. He's found a new girlfriend – at least I think that's what she is. *She* hasn't made those demands on him... yet.'

Luke looks down at my hands. Gently turning them over, he examines my palms. When he looks up again, the strength of emotion on his face makes the breath hitch in my throat.

'Men can be such idiots.'

I think that's all he's going to say, but then he speaks again.

'I know it's really hard, Cass, but you have taken the first steps towards taking control of your own life. When you had nowhere to turn, nothing short of magic would have rescued you from what you saw as your broken life, and that's what materialised. Things don't happen by accident. The day David sent you on that errand to refuel his car he placed you directly in the path of that particular copy of *The Lady* and Ginny's advert.' Luke smiles. 'You should thank him for that.'

I pull an unconvinced face.

'You know, each of us owns a specific type of magic. As soon as we align with the natural rhythm of the universe we begin to heal and an intrinsic beauty shines through. We grow into who we are meant to be. By recognising our own nature as being part of the natural world we become entwined within creation in a way that brings belonging, comfort, wisdom, peace and strength. Don't fear what lies within, because as we reclaim our inherent nature we feel safe in ways we've never experienced before. It's a homecoming.'

Tenderly, he strokes my hand. 'You may not believe it now, Cassandra Tallulah Shaw, but you will become whole.'

Tears prick my eyes. No one has *ever* talked to me in this way.

'People are usually unaware of the chains of cause and effect created by their actions,' Luke continues, 'but life is a blending of choices that opens doors to new experiences. Essentially, we are constantly reshaping our futures.' He gives my hands a gentle squeeze before letting go.

Swiftly, I brush away the tears about to spill.

'Just remember, Cass. You may not be able to control the wind but you can control your sails.'

35

'So what do you think?' I peer over Inky's half stable door.

'It's only six weeks since we removed her shoes but I'm pleased how she's responding,' replies Darren, the barefoot trimmer. 'The soles are hardening and there's a good amount of growth to the hoof wall.'

Holding onto the Shetland pony's head collar, Rhea beams.

'It's good Inky's transitioned without any problems, as have the others,' I comment. 'Unlike Indiana. Her feet are very poor by comparison. I suppose it's because she's a thoroughbred.'

Releasing the Shetland's foot, Darren straightens up and stretches his back. 'Just keep an eye on her. Mrs Kinsman hasn't had her that long. I believe she got her from upcountry and the mare's most likely still acclimatising to the different soil and grasses.' He starts to gather his equipment. 'With a little care and application she has every chance of success.'

As I open the stable door for Darren, a shadow falls across the entrance to the barn.

'Ah, there you are.' Gyles walks towards us with a piece of paper in his hand.

'Mr Kinsman.' Darren nods deferentially.

'Hello, Darren. And how are these expensive toys?'

I hear Rhea whisper to Inky, 'Don't listen to my dad. He doesn't mean it.'

'The ponies are doing very well. Of course, the buckskin gelding's used to going barefoot. It's just the thoroughbred we have to watch.'

'As you know, I have a more traditional approach to horse care. My hunters were always shod but I'm slightly outnumbered these days.' Gyles winks at me. 'If it's not one thing to expect an old stick in the mud like me to accept horses going barefoot, it's another thing entirely getting my head around riding without a bit!'

I smile sheepishly. Since I've been with the Kinsmans I've introduced the children to riding with halters. Even Ginny prefers Fairweather Indiana in a bitless bridle these days.

'Shall I tack up Dylan?' asks Zac, peering over his pony's stable door.

'Yes. I'll settle up with Darren and then we can start your lesson.'

As the trimmer carries the tools of his trade to his van, Gyles and I follow. A set of worry beads hang from the rear-view mirror and on the front passenger seat, curled up asleep, is his faithful, elderly mongrel, now grey around the gills. He told me he'd rescued it as a puppy from a beach in southern Spain. For someone in the equestrian industry, Darren is a one-off.

'Robyn called by the office earlier today.' Gyles holds out the paper to me. 'She asked me to pass this to you.'

'Thanks.' Taking it from him, I unfold it. Written in flowery, rounded handwriting is her name and a telephone number. 'How do you know Robyn?'

'Everyone in Bude knows her.' He chuckles. 'She's a handsome woman and tends to stand out in a crowd.'

A look passes between Gyles and Darren.

'But I know Robyn on a professional basis,' continues Gyles. 'She's a fine solicitor and I've had cause to use her firm several times in the past.'

My eyes widen. Of all the professions I'd considered, solicitor had not crossed my mind. But it makes perfect sense. Her confidence and assuredness speak of someone who knows her rights.

'I'll leave you to settle up, Cassie,' says Gyles. 'Do you have enough money?'

'Yes thanks. Ginny gave me her share this morning.'

Nodding to the trimmer, Gyles strides off across the yard towards the outdoor kennels. All morning, the gun dogs have watched the comings and goings with interest. Now, as their master opens the door to their enclosure, the Labradors rush out, circling madly with tails wagging. As Gyles and the dogs set off towards the fields a couple of chickens wander into the yard and, taking the opportunity of empty kennels, they check out the dogs' food bowls.

Darren removes his beanie and shakes the dreadlocks free. Reaching into the van, he extracts a well-used diary from one of the wooden compartments built around the sides, in which he stores his trimming equipment.

He thumbs through the pages. 'Six weeks brings us to the nineteenth of September. Same time suit you?'

'Yes, I'll be here.'

He jots down the appointment. Around his wrists are a number of beaded bracelets and plaited surfer bands, while his open-necked shirt reveals several chains and a Celtic cross. A free-spirited hippy at heart – one more akin to living unencumbered by such things as mortgages and a nine to five. However, I know Darren has responsibilities of the more mortal kind and he lives in a cottage in the village with his partner and young family. Once again, I'm reminded of the many different ways to live.

Sliding the van door shut, Darren climbs into the driver's seat and fires up the engine. The sleepy dog looks up and gazes at me through milky eyes.

'If you have any problems with Indiana just give me a ring.'

'I will. See you in September.'

As he drives out of the yard, Darren waves.

I glance down at the note in my hand. I'll phone Robyn this evening. Apart from Luke, she's my first true friend in Cornwall.

Two evenings later, I sit in the kitchen with Ginny, Gyles and Rhea while waiting for Luke to pick me up. When I'd followed up on Robyn's note, she invited us to join her and Jamie for 'music night' at a local pub. I wasn't sure if Luke would want to do this, but, as with the beach barbeque, he'd surprised me and immediately accepted the invitation.

'You're getting out and about quite a bit these days,' Gyles says, conversationally.

'Cinderella is finding her feet,' I say, as I weave Rhea's thick hair into a long plait.

Ginny makes no comment.

I'm keenly aware that this *night out* could be mistakenly viewed by others as a 'date', and associated guilt settles uncomfortably around my shoulders.

'Where are you off to tonight?' Gyles asks.

'Stratton. The Tree Inn.'

'Ah, a pub close to my heart! Ginny and I met there many moons ago.' He smiles fondly at his wife.

I glance at them in surprise. 'I assumed you'd known each other since childhood.'

'No, we didn't meet until we were well into our twenties. Surprising really, seeing as we're both from the area. But, being a few years apart, our paths never crossed.'

'No harm in keeping a man waiting,' Ginny says drily.

'There you go, Rhea.' I secure the soft hair tie in place. 'It suits you having your hair off that pretty face.'

'Thanks, Cassie.' She turns and beams at me.

I watch as she runs from the room and stands in front of the hall mirror, gazing at her reflection.

'Well, as much as I'd like to, I can't sit around here with you two ladies. This man has things to do.' As Gyles gets to his feet, the legs of his chair scrape jarringly across the slate flagstones. 'Enjoy your evening, Cassie.' Flashing me a smile, he walks to the door.

I glance across at Ginny. She's unusually quiet.

'Everything OK?'

Her lips twitch into a half smile, but there's a troubled look in her eyes.

'I'm worried about you.' She frowns. 'You and Luke, actually.'

'Don't be. He's a friend.'

'That's good. Only…' She pauses.

'Only what, Ginny?'

She sighs deeply before continuing. 'I don't want you getting hurt.'

I'm touched by her concern. 'I won't. Luke's just showing me the area and including me in things. That's all.'

'That's very generous of him.' Her tone is surprisingly sarcastic and I watch as she purses her lips together.

'It is.'

'Don't fall for him, Cassie. Never forget he's married. Although Amanda may not be in Cornwall often, they have a life together. Their living arrangements are not conventional but they work for them.'

My heartbeat increases as my cheeks turn red.

'I won't forget,' I say quietly.

How can I? Amanda's dominant character has a way of making itself felt, even when she's hundreds of miles away.

We sit in silence for a few minutes, avoiding eye contact, and it's only when Zac pokes his head around the door announcing Luke's Land Rover has pulled up in the drive that I spring into action.

I look across the table at Ginny and smile. 'Thank you for worrying about me, but please don't. I know where I fit into the scheme of things.'

Did I?

Rising from the table, I walk towards the door nervously biting my lip.

36

'They're good, aren't they?' Robyn says as she sways to the music.

'They're great!' I agree.

'Especially the lead singer.'

I study the man centre stage, surrounded by his bandmates. Thick, floppy sun-kissed hair accentuates a rugged, tanned face, and the tight shirt and snug-fitting jeans suggest a muscular body lurking beneath. Overall, he wouldn't look out of place on a surfboard. No wonder he's on Robyn's radar!

'Yes, *especially* the lead singer.'

She gives a throaty laugh. 'You've noticed too!'

'Kind of hard not to.'

'Kind of hard not to what?' asks Jamie, as he and Luke return from the bar carrying drinks.

'Kind of hard not to love living in Cornwall,' Robyn says without missing a beat. She gives me a wink.

'Here you go, Cass.' Luke hands a glass of white wine to me.

'Thanks.' I take a sip. 'Do you know this band?'

He turns his attention to the four men singing and playing their hearts out at the far end of the courtyard. 'Don't think

I do. They're good.' Raising the pint glass to his mouth, he takes a long draught.

'What are you drinking?'

'Splendid Tackle,' he says with a smirk.

Teasingly, I pull a shocked face. 'There's no clean answer to that!'

'According to Skinner's Brewery, *"A golden ale, zesty and bold"*. They're not far wrong.'

'Have you been here before?'

'A few times. The Galleon restaurant's good. Its beamed ceiling is salvaged timber from ships wrecked on this coast. I'll treat you to dinner here one evening, to give you a break from seaweed concoctions.'

I laugh. 'I don't need a break. Your concoctions are culinary delights.'

But a meal out with Luke, just the two of us. Like a date. Ginny's warning rings in my ears.

As the song comes to an end, the lead singer works the audience. I'm surprised he has such a strong West Country accent. It's not obvious in his singing voice.

'So, not before time, here we are back at The Tree... despite having to endure many miles to get here in our trusty vehicle.' He turns to the lead guitarist. 'How far have we come tonight, Tom?'

Holding his chin, Tom looks up to the sky with exaggerated consideration. 'Oh, must be six miles, give or take.'

A ripple of laughter reverberates around the appreciative crowd.

'You haven't seen our van!' The singer grimaces. 'Believe me, some miles in *that* bone rattler.'

As the crowd responds again, Robyn turns to me with one eyebrow raised in amusement.

The lead singer confers with the rest of the band before turning back to the crowd. 'This next song is from our second album, due out next month. Because we enjoy playing The Tree and you always make us feel so welcome, don't go telling anyone but you are the first audience to hear it *live*.'

'I bet he's said that at every gig this month,' whispers Luke in my ear.

He's so close; I can feel the heat from his body.

'He's a great front man.'

Luke nods. 'Got the looks too.'

'Oh, I hadn't noticed,' I say with a mischievous grin.

He laughs and takes another swig of ale.

Everything with Luke is so easy. If I ever dare say anything like that to David he subtly punishes me for the remainder of the evening, and sometimes into the following day. The thought of David wipes the grin from my face.

Why did he have affairs? What is so wrong with me?

Meeting Luke's eyes, I force a smile back onto my face. There's no point being melancholy and I won't let my estranged partner spoil an evening out with friends. But I can't help but wonder what it is about both David and Amanda that makes their characters so keenly felt at such a distance.

'Penny for them.'

I shake my head. 'Not worth even a penny.'

'In that case, let's dance.'

'What?'

'You started something at the beach party. I've discovered

a passion for dancing...' he holds my gaze '...with a certain young lady in possession of a warrior spirit and a gypsy soul!'

His eyes twinkle with mischief and my forced smile becomes genuine.

Placing our glasses on a side table, we walk to the area in front of the band where two girls are already dancing. Without interrupting his singing, the lead singer acknowledges us with a nod and waves for more people to join in. Instantly, Robyn and Jamie are at our side.

'Anything to get closer to that hunky singer,' she whispers out of the side of her mouth.

I respond with a wicked grin. I can't remember ever feeling this carefree. It's as if I'm in exactly the place I'm meant to be. I look at Luke dancing only a couple of feet from me, and his fluid movements make my body react in a way that it shouldn't. I give in.

Sorry, Ginny, I can't fight it. What will be, will be...

Several songs later, we return to our drinks.

'This pub looks very old,' I say, gazing around at the courtyard's ancient walls.

'It's a former manor house with a colourful history. Parts of it date back to the thirteenth century.'

I expect Luke to expand on the subject, as is his usual custom, but he doesn't.

'Go on. Tell me more.'

Smiling, hazel eyes gaze into mine. 'Always so eager...'

Attempting to quash sudden embarrassment that threatens to turn into a blush, flippantly I say, 'Never satisfied until in receipt of the full facts.'

Luke moves closer to be heard above the sound of the

music and cups my elbow in his hand. Immediately, searing heat shoots up my arm and into my chest.

'Anthony Payne, the Cornish Giant, was born here. He's known by that name because he stood seven feet four and weighed thirty-eight stone. He lived much of his life in The Tree, when it was a manor house. He died at the grand old age of eighty-one in 1691 and his coffin was so enormous that part of the ceiling had to be dismantled to get it out. He's buried in Stratton church.'

As always, my mind unfurls to Luke; like a flower blooming beneath the life-giving warmth of the sun. As he imparts this information it's as if we are the only two people in the crowded courtyard. Even the loud music seems miles away.

'Payne was an English Civil War hero and manservant to the Royalist, Sir Bevil Grenville. Later, he was also manservant to Sir Bevil's son, Sir Richard, at the Plymouth garrison and it was there, in 1680, that Charles II commissioned Sir Godfrey Kneller to paint his portrait. During the English Civil War, the manor house was used as Sir Bevil's headquarters after the famous battle of Stamford Hill on 16th May 1643. Before the battle, Stratton was occupied by the "rebels" under the Earl of Stamford's command. But, that night, Sir Bevil and his troops rested in and around the town and were responsible for guarding the Parliamentarian prisoners.'

Releasing my elbow, he gives me a sheepish smile. 'Let me know if this is information overload.'

Information overload? I can never get too much.

I laugh. 'Here am I, out for casual drinks with friends and, instead, I'm receiving an impromptu history lesson!'

He grins. 'Well, continuing your potted *history lesson...* The Cornish giant was at Sir Bevil's side when he was killed at the Battle of Lansdown, near Bath. Immediately, Payne threw Grenville's sixteen-year-old son into his father's saddle and bellowed at the Cornish army: "A Grenville still leads you!" The boy led his father's men to a resounding victory over the Parliamentarians.'

'Thank you, Luke.'

'For what?'

'For bringing Cornwall to life for me.'

Emotion flickers in his eyes. 'You have no idea how welcome you are.'

I give a small, nervous laugh.

He runs a hand over his face, and when he looks at me again the emotion has cleared. 'Are you free on Friday, Cass?'

'I could be. Why?'

'I'd like to show you somewhere extremely special.'

'Sounds intriguing,' I say, playing it cool.

'It's a date then.'

Ginny won't be pleased.

From out of the crowd, Robyn approaches. 'It's the last chance for a dance. Come and join us.'

'Don't have to be asked twice,' says Luke, grabbing my hand and leading me through the crush of people towards the band.

37

The next few days drag unbearably. I attempt to follow Ginny's wise counsel, but intense feelings for Luke have me examining the minutest details of our evening with Robyn and Jamie. It takes superhuman effort to pack away the blindsiding emotions and firmly close the lid.

On Wednesday morning, during breakfast with Ginny and the children, I hear the sound of tyres crunching across gravel. Glancing out of the kitchen window, I watch the Royal Mail van draw nearer.

'Be a gem, Zac, and fetch the post,' says Ginny, studying the colourful chart pinned to the kitchen wall.

Obligingly, the boy hops off his chair and dashes from the room.

'Damn,' she mutters, removing a pink post-it note and turning to me. 'It's just as well you suggested setting up this timetable. The children's dental appointment clashes with Zac's judo display. I'll have to phone the dentist and change it.'

Her son returns a couple of minutes later clutching a fistful of envelopes. He scans through them, hands several to his mother and passes one to me.

David's handwriting instantly leaps out; his large, abandoned scrawl a spider's drunken trail. Why is he writing to me? What news does he have to disclose? In anticipation, my stomach contracts as my breathing shallows and my heart starts to pound. I glance around the table, half-expecting the Kinsmans to be watching with bated breath, but I am unobserved. Life continues in its usual fashion for the family. Is David writing to tell me he's put his relationship with Jen on a more permanent footing? If so, I'm not sure how I'll react and I don't want Ginny and the children to witness me falling apart.

'See you children at the stables in half an hour,' I say, as I push back the chair and rise to my feet.

'Can we jump today?' asks Zac, through a mouthful of thickly buttered toast.

'OK. I'll set up the barrels.'

'YAAAAASSSS!'

Ginny looks up from opening her post and I'm acutely aware of her eyes following me as I walk to the door. Since our *little chat*, I've caught her observing me on several occasions.

Once back in the safety of my rooms, I close the door and sit on the bed. For several minutes I stare at the envelope, fearing its content, and a deep frown contorts my features as numerous possibilities surge through my mind.

Sighing deeply, I tear open the envelope and remove an innocuous notelet. On its front is a photo of horses galloping through a field of poppies with a range of hills in the background, not unlike the South Downs. Cautiously, I open the card.

Sands,
Please come home.
I miss you! ☺
David xxx

Short and sweet... but I know what it has taken him to write it. David *never* lays his feelings bare. He believes it puts him at serious disadvantage.

As I stare at his words, countless emotions course through me. Am I trying to achieve an unrealistic pipe dream? David offers *real* life, but how can I abandon the Kinsmans now? And what about Luke? He's planned a trip for us.

Closing the notelet, I ease it back into its envelope and slip it into the top drawer of the bedside cabinet. There's no point beating myself up. I will simply concentrate on the day ahead.

At long last, Friday arrives. Luke picks me up from the sand school gate, as arranged. Riddled with guilt at wanting his friendship, yet knowing he's married, I didn't want him coming up to the manor house and alerting Ginny to our spending more time together. I know she's concerned for me, but her strong moral judgement isn't helping my own guilt trip. As it turns out, she sees us anyway. As the Land Rover drives past the manor towards the parish lane, she's busy harvesting vegetables in the kitchen garden. Shrinking down in the passenger seat, I watch in the side mirror as she straightens up and stares after the car. A gloved hand sweeps her hair out of her eyes, revealing a deeply etched frown on her face. My shame heightens – a naughty child caught in the act – and I glance uncertainly at Luke.

'It's all right, Cass, you can sit up now.' Luke's eyes twinkle with mirth. 'We've cleared the danger zone!'

I check the side mirror again before inching up the seat.

'So, are you ready to experience something rather special?'

'That would be nice,' I mumble, still grappling with my conscience.

'You won't be disappointed. It's Cornwall's best-kept secret and one of the truly remarkable, sacred places this county has to offer.' He concentrates on turning the corner. 'Not only is it a place of outstanding natural beauty but also a spiritual pilgrimage since the fifth century. There are many myths and legends surrounding it, from King Arthur and his knights to ghostly sightings.'

'Really?' As always, Luke has my attention.

'Yes, really!'

Hearing the amusement in his voice, a smile tugs at the corners of my mouth.

'Sometimes crystals, ribbons and other offerings are left in small shrines around the area, like a sort of clootie well.'

'A what?

'A clootie well. It's a Celtic tradition based in paganism that still thrives at sacred sites around Britain. At places of pilgrimage, near water sources, wells and springs, usually with a tree growing beside them, people leave strips of cloth or rags tied to branches as part of a healing ritual.'

We follow the coast road for a while before turning off. The day is fair and wispy clouds drift languidly across a pale blue sky. Ignoring the turning to Boscastle, we continue on towards Tintagel and presently come to a car park situated just off the road. Parking up, Luke switches off the engine and retrieves his backpack from the rear seat of the Land Rover. A mild breeze persists – perfect conditions for walking. There's very little traffic and we cross the road before heading up an unmade lane, past an inscribed Roman pillar that announces the property behind it is a former monastery.

As the lane reduces to a track, Luke says, 'Here we go… the start of a magical journey through a spiritual glen.'

Ancient, ivy-clad woodlands hug the banks of a meandering river, and a number of intriguing pathways lead enticingly through the valley, their slate beds worn into steps by generations of travellers. As with Foxcombe Manor, there's a sense of time suspended; time eternal. As we make our way along the path, neither of us speaks. That would, somehow, break the spell. A gentle wind ruffles the trees and in the distance I hear the sound of waterfalls. It's a world of deep tranquillity and as I listen to the birdsong and the music of the water, I forget my troubles.

'There's poetry in the air,' I murmur.

Intelligent eyes observe me. 'There is, Cass… and more besides. Fairies and piskies play here amid the animals and birds.'

Why doesn't it surprise me that this grounded, educated man can also accept the possibility of mystical beings? However, the ecologist is never far away.

'This area has been appointed a Site of Special Scientific Interest due to the rare specimens of plants growing here.'

I smile to myself, as warmth hugs my heart.

On a particularly slippery stretch of path, Luke holds out

his hand to me. His grip is firm and safe, and as I meet his gaze I hear a whisper. What is it? An older understanding? I know Luke hears it too because he smiles in mutual acknowledgement. But as soon as the connection is made, he squeezes my fingers and lets them go before continuing along the path ahead.

'We're not far from the waterfalls,' he calls, over his shoulder.

And sure enough, a few minutes later, we arrive at the first. I stand in awe at the natural beauty of the place; it's as if nature embraces us.

'It's hard not to be moved by the atmosphere,' Luke says.

Slowly, I nod. Before us, a spectacular sixty-foot waterfall cascades through a hole in the rocks into a beautiful lower valley.

'The river has carved its way through Late Devonian slate and eroded a hole through the original basin.'

'The water is so clear.'

'It's reputed to have healing properties, watched over by the spirits of past guardians of the glen.'

Carefully, we continue down the slippery path to the foot of the waterfall where mosses, ferns and grasses drape the rock face.

'It's so wild and unspoilt,' I whisper, spellbound.

Ribbons, crystals, photographs, inscriptions, prayers and devotions adorn the foliage and walls, and in the river are several carefully placed stone pillars.

'What are those?'

'Faery stacks. Some are in memory of loved ones who have passed; others are for wishes. Since ancient times, offerings such as these have been part of the heritage of sacred wells. Its continuing practice will always link us to that past.'

'This is one of the most beautiful places I have ever visited.' I turn to Luke with shining eyes. 'Thank you for sharing it with me.'

He smiles. 'I thought you'd like it.'

Has he brought Amanda here? Somehow, I doubt it.

'Let's explore the lower waterfalls,' he suggests. 'That way we can build up an appetite for the cream tea I'm going to treat you to in the café. Then we can visit the gallery.'

38

The next day, it takes a good three hours to clean the Porter's Lodge in preparation for the incoming PGs expected that afternoon. Satisfied that it's up to Ginny's standards and the guests will have nothing to complain about, I store away the hoover and cleaning materials. Making sure there are the complimentary half-dozen eggs in the bowl and butter, milk and bread in the fridge, I give the holiday let one last critical scan before pulling the door to. As I cross the driveway and enter the manor house, Ginny appears in the kitchen doorway across the open hall.

'Everything OK in the lodge?'

'Yes. That last couple left it in quite a state, but it looks immaculate now.'

'Good. Nothing broken?'

I shake my head.

'Cassie, I've made new curtains for Rhea's bedroom. The current ones are ancient! I'd like you to give me a hand hanging them. It won't take long.'

'Sure.'

I start following her upstairs, but suddenly she stops in front of a large oil painting set in an ornately carved, gilt frame.

'This is the painting of Anna... our Lady Chatterley.'

Although I've noticed the portrait before I never paid it much attention, but now, having heard the tragic tale, I study the image with interest. The young woman sits for the artist in the formal drawing room; the wood panelling and mullion window recognisable behind her. Her skin has the appearance of porcelain and at her neck is a delicate string of pearls. Long, lustrous chestnut hair falls gracefully in loose curls around a pale face of exquisite delicacy and beauty. However, it's the grey, haunted eyes observing me that make me gasp. Their unhappiness mirrors my own.

'What is it?' Ginny asks.

'Nothing. It's just...'

What is it 'just'?

'Her eyes are so sad and she looks so delicate. It's hard to believe she endured such tragedy.'

Ginny gives a small smile. 'She didn't though, did she? I firmly believe she died of a broken heart.'

'Have you seen photos of the gamekeeper?'

'Yes, there are a few in one of Gyles's old family albums, taken on an official shoot. Unfortunately they're rather grainy, but he looks as if he carried himself well. Their love affair was a scandal the family played down, especially during the early part of the twentieth century.' Ginny steps up onto the next tread. 'This is her father, Gyles's great-great-grandfather.'

I study the neighbouring portrait. An aristocratic, middle-aged gentleman sporting a fine moustache stares back at me through stern eyes; his strength of character evident to all. Anna never stood a chance. I glance back at the young woman's striking image. She wears a teal-coloured dress with a peacock blue shawl draped loosely around her shoulders; perfect shades for her colouring. But it's the way the artist has painted the material that catches my attention, the soft sheen giving the impression both garments are made of silk. Goose bumps prick my arms and I shiver.

Is it you who brushes past me?

'Are you OK, Cassie? You've turned rather pale.'

I rub my skin. 'I'm fine. It's just…'

There I go again. What is it *just*?

Standing on the stairs beneath Anna's portrait, I find myself explaining a little of what has brought me to Cornwall. I don't give much away, but I do offer some detail of my estranged relationship with David.

Ginny listens sympathetically. 'Have you heard from him since he claimed your vehicles?'

'Yes. He tells me I should get back to where I belong.'

She inhales sharply and cautiously says, 'Well, you must do what is best for you.'

'I've told him I won't.' I smile sadly. 'Even though I couldn't believe my luck when he chose me.'

'Why would you think that, Cassie?' She frowns. 'You can have anyone you want.'

'No, that's not true.'

She shakes her head in bewilderment. 'If truth be known, I expect it was he who couldn't believe his luck.'

She's being kind.

'I don't think so. You see, when I met David I didn't have much life experience and he was my first boyfriend. We've been together ten years and I always assumed we'd start a family one day, but he doesn't want to. It seems he's only interested in keeping me in a gilded cage, at his beck and call.'

'Men! Who do they think they are?' Reaching out, Ginny gives my arm a comforting squeeze. 'Let's get on with sorting out those curtains.'

She turns away and continues up the stairs.

'You know, Cassie,' she says over her shoulder, 'true love never did run smooth. The trick is in believing all will be sorted in time.'

39

From across the street, Robyn waves to catch our attention. Glancing both ways, Luke and I cross the road and make our way through the crowd towards her.

'Hi, Robyn.' I give her a friendly hug. 'Love the hat!'

On her head is a bright and cheerful, multi-coloured boater.

'It gets an airing each jazz festival!' She smiles broadly. Turning to Luke, she gives him a kiss on the cheek. 'Jamie's working in the sandwich bar today – takings are too good to miss – but I said we'd meet at the bandstand at five if we haven't hooked up before.'

The town bustles with people of all ages. Most have entered into the spirit and dressed for the occasion, and bobbing above the heads of the crowd is a sea of vibrantly coloured, heavily decorated sun parasols. Musical acts appear everywhere and discordant sounds tumble out of shop doorways, unlikely-looking buildings, pubs and hotels. The atmosphere is electric. It's easy to understand why the jazz festival has become so popular over the years. When Robyn suggested Luke and I join her for the event, she'd informed us this was the festival's thirty-second year and that it now offered four days of music from forty bands playing at over sixty gigs.

'I'm passionate about my adopted town and I work hard to support Bude and its inhabitants,' she'd explained. 'When I first joined the firm two years ago I suggested we support the event. I intend to continue our sponsorship.'

I glance sideways at Robyn now as we make our way through the crowd – my confident, outward-looking friend, who so effortlessly embraces the bigger picture. Many people stop to chat with her, and those who recognise Luke engage him in conversation too. Seamlessly, he slips into 'Hunter Harcourt' persona. There's no doubt I'm in the presence of local celebrities but, unlike when I accompany David to events, I'm not pushed to the periphery. Both Luke and Robyn include me, and not once am I made to feel inferior. Inwardly, I hug myself as ingrained defences, which always come to the fore at social gatherings, swiftly evaporate into thin air.

A while later, as we walk along the high street towards the canal, Luke stops at one of the many pop-up stalls that have temporarily appeared in and around the town.

'I think we need to engage more with the programme, Cass.' He grins. Picking up a straw boater with a pretty red and white ribbon around its rim, he passes it to me before selecting one for himself.

Someone has suspended a mirror on a chain from one of the stall's corner posts and I walk towards it, setting the boater at a jaunty angle on my head.

As I gaze at my reflection, over the noise of the crowd I hear Robyn comment, 'She's lovely isn't she, Luke?'

My heart pounds loudly. Keeping my gaze firmly on the mirror, I strain to hear his reply, but it's snatched away to merge with the general noise circulating the stall.

Luke refuses to let me pay for the boater.

'It's a gift, Cass,' he says, with a gracious smile. 'Now we can truly integrate!'

We immerse ourselves in the numerous musical acts, and as the shadows of the afternoon lengthen, we stop and listen to a band of seven men – the youngest surely in his early sixties. Their particular blend of saxophone, trumpet, trombone, piano, bass, drums and guitar is intoxicating and it soon has us tapping along to the catchy numbers. I glance at Luke and Robyn standing amongst the onlookers and try to recall a time when the simple pleasure of an occasion made me feel so relaxed and full of *joie de vivre*. With sudden, shocking clarity I realise that the sensation flooding my body and seeking out all its secret hiding places is *happiness*. Tentatively, I dare consider that maybe… just maybe… life is finally beginning to fall into place.

Luke stares at the ceiling, unseeing. The room is in darkness and he turns his head to check the clock on the bedside table. Late, or early, depending on your point of view. Sleep is far away. Reaching for the lamp, he switches it on before swinging his legs out of bed and walking across the room. He grabs the dressing gown hanging on the back of the door and slips it on as he heads towards the stairs.

Byron is asleep in his bed in the utility room, but at the sound of footsteps on the stairs he stirs and looks up expectantly. As Luke makes his way along the hallway, the Great Dane rises to its feet.

'Sorry, boy, for waking you,' Luke says, flicking a switch and flooding the kitchen with light. 'I know, it's unfair the two of us having a disturbed night.'

Affectionately, he strokes the dog's velvety ears.

Crossing over to the sink, he turns on the cold tap, allowing it to run for a while before holding a glass under the stream of water. He walks to the study, leaving the door open to allow light from the hallway to spread into the room, and in semi-darkness, crosses over to the bay window. As Luke stares out at the view, he raises the glass to his lips and savours the refreshingly pure water that comes from the cottage's private borehole.

The moon rides high in the sky, lightly swathing the surrounding woodland and valley in spun silver gossamer. In the distance is the serene, dark, weighty presence of the ocean. An undisturbed, tranquil scene... and yet Luke's expression is troubled as he casts his mind back over his life. It's one that has always had purpose. Even as a lad he knew what he wanted, and he'd planned and charted his way to this day. 'Focused' is how his parents describe their second son, when asked. He'd applied himself to study, excelled in his chosen subjects and, ultimately, gained a First Class Honours degree.

He'd met Amanda at university – he hadn't plotted *that* into the equation. Both driven and intelligent, her sharpness made life interesting and they were a good fit. But as Luke considers his wife now, a frown tugs at his brow. Armed with their respective degrees, they'd ventured forth into the wider world and he'd quickly found fame as an author. Amanda, too, had developed at the same pace, snapped up by the first financial firm to interview her. They were a successful couple and if their life was a little unconventional, it was a good one. Or so he'd thought... until Amanda's bombshell of an affair with Simon Hughes.

Pushing this thought aside, he takes another sip of water and reflects on the afternoon's visit to the jazz festival with Cass, Robyn and Jamie. They are so unlike his and Amanda's friends, and he wonders if he's a different person when in Cornwall. Would their London set even recognise him? His face softens as he considers the young woman with the warrior soul and the wild gypsy spirit who came crashing into his life that fateful day Byron jumped out of the woods. When she'd put on the boater with its pretty red and white ribbon and Robyn remarked how lovely she was, he couldn't deny it. And Cass – still unaware of whom she truly is and the power she possesses – was so appreciative of his gift that she'd momentarily rendered him speechless.

One eyebrow lifts wryly.

He must not allow himself to think of her too fondly. However lightly Amanda may take their marriage vows, he honours fidelity. His wife is who she is. They *are* a good match. And yet...

The countryside is suddenly plunged into darkness and Luke gazes up at dark clouds that briefly obliterate the moon.

'All things will pass,' he says quietly to himself.

Placing the half-empty glass on his desk, he turns away from the window.

40

Even though it's late in the evening, the warmth of the day still lingers and a suggestion of wind whispers through the tops of the trees. As I clear away the remains of supper, I hear the Great Dane gnawing on a bone in the utility room. Luke tackles the washing-up at the kitchen sink. We've spent the day walking the cliffs, seeking out hidden coves and collecting seaweed from which he had rustled up a superb meal, befitting of any Michelin-star restaurant.

As always, it's good spending time with Luke. Despite Ginny's warning, I find I'm in his company for increasing amounts of time, often wrestling with my conscience and wondering what Amanda would say if she knew. But she has nothing to fear. We are just good friends. Where's the harm in that? And anyway, it's easy to forget these unsettling thoughts because on a day-to-day basis she is removed and at a distance. However, she makes her presence felt whenever she phones her husband, and I'm forced to remember the part she plays in his life.

Following Luke through to the sitting room, I make myself comfortable in one of the plump armchairs while he switches on the television, selecting the late evening regional news. It's later than I think. I should make tracks soon.

A sudden violent gust of wind rattles the sash windows. It whistles around the house with an unearthly sound, investigating the many hidden nooks and crannies, and exploring the most inaccessible areas under the eaves of the thatched roof. Outside, the old ship's bell gives a muffled clang.

'Where's that wind come from? It wasn't forecast.'

'Cornish weather can be changeable and sneak up without warning,' Luke replies. 'It's like being out at sea.'

On the screen, a newsreader reports that despite an extensive search, ten-year-old local schoolgirl, Nicola Benney, is still missing. An image appears of a fresh-faced girl with brown eyes, a freckled snub nose and long brown hair.

'Nicola was last seen with her West Highland terrier near the Bush Inn, Morwenstow, late Wednesday afternoon,' the newscaster continues in a West Country burr. 'If anyone has any information that could be helpful in finding Nicola, please contact the police on…' He gives out a telephone number.

What can have happened? Two days is a long time to go without any sightings, and search parties have scoured the area. Yesterday, the local primary school organised a group to conduct their own search, which Ginny and the farmhands joined. Zac and Rhea had wanted to take part in looking for their schoolmate, but Ginny told them they were too young. I remained at the manor to oversee the children.

Where is Zac's classmate? Her parents must be frantic with worry.

I frown. 'It's one hell of a terrain to search, but we didn't notice anything unusual today.'

'The weather was clear, so we'd have noticed anything untoward.'

Another squall batters the windows and I shiver.

'I guess I should go.' I rise to my feet. 'Thanks for a great day, Luke, and another wonderful meal, but you really should allow me to make one for you. You spoil me.'

'I like spoiling an appreciative diner.'

I laugh.

'But if you insist, the kitchen is all yours.'

'It's a deal. Next time, I'll cook.'

I walk out into the hallway and Luke follows. As he opens the front door the wind almost snatches it from his hands.

'I can't believe the change in the weather. I should have brought a jacket.'

'I'll walk with you.' Luke extracts a large umbrella from a ceramic stand in the porch.

'You don't need to,' I protest. 'There's no point in us both getting blown away.'

'Well, at least take one of these.' He hands me a waterproof jacket from the coat rack. 'And take a torch.' Stretching up, he takes one down from the shelf above.

Gratefully, I put on the jacket. It's one of his and it swamps me.

'Looks good on you,' he says, his eyes twinkling.

'Well, at least I'll have some chance of staying dry!'

I step out into the increasingly wild night. It's unusually dark. Whipped by a frenzied wind, the trees around the house sway violently and driving rain stings my face.

'Great!'

Pulling up the hood, I turn to say goodbye but a light on the far horizon catches my eye. Weak at first, for a moment it grows brighter and then vanishes.

'That must be the search party.' I point in the direction of the cliffs. 'Surely, they're not searching at this hour and in this weather?'

Luke turns towards the distant headland. 'Can't see anything.'

A shout on the wind.

'Listen! What's that?'

We strain our ears, but the noise of the storm drowns out any other sounds.

'Look.' I point again in the direction of the intermittent flash of light.

Luke shakes his head. 'Still can't see anything.'

'I'm going to investigate.'

'What? In this weather! Cass, the search party knows what it's doing.'

'But what if it's not them? What if it's Nicola lying injured and desperately signalling for help?'

He considers me for a moment. 'Let me grab another torch.'

Changing his shoes for boots, Luke shrugs on a waterproof jacket and takes down another torch from the shelf. Then, guided by torchlight, we lean into the wind and rain and set out across the lawn towards the edge of the trees. As we enter the dark interior and descend into the wooded valley, a clap of thunder directly overhead makes me jump. Hunching deeply into Luke's jacket, I scramble after him and follow the flickering torchlight along slippery, narrow paths. By the time we reach the stream it has swollen to a torrent and it's hard to discern whether it's the wind or water creating more noise.

Luke glances back and shouts, 'You OK, Cass?'

I nod and motion him to continue.

We follow the watercourse until reaching the ford crossing Zac and I negotiated with Caspian and Dylan. White water rages around the five stepping stones that now barely poke their heads above its surface.

'We'll have to cross here,' says Luke. 'The current will be too strong further down.'

Confidently, he steps out onto the first rock. As he shifts to the next, I flash my torch onto the vacated stone and step out onto its uneven surface, irrationally curling my toes inside my boots as I try to gain greater grip. For one awful moment I teeter but, before slipping into the maelstrom, I take a deep breath and launch myself onto the second stone. It moves precariously. Steeling myself, I step purposefully onto the third rock and quickly follow Luke's rapidly disappearing figure. Arriving safely on the other side, I flash the torch around but he's nowhere in sight. Maybe I'll pick up his light in the dark. I switch off the torch. It's pitch black and for several minutes I peer blindly into the surrounding woodland. There's no sign of Luke anywhere. As I flick the beam back on I notice a choice of two paths. The left follows the stream, while the other leads steeply upwards through the trees. I take the right path. Perhaps at a higher level I will be able to see any lights in the valley.

On either side the ancient trees sway, and I curse as a branch whips across my face. There's something 'other-worldly' in the woods tonight, and I recall the odd feeling

I had when Zac and I first rode through. My imagination runs amok. Grotesque, leering faces and creepy witch fingers loom out of the trees, and I have the unnerving sensation that many eyes are focused on me, all silently watching the drama unfold. Keeping my head bent low, I concentrate on the steep path ahead. As I climb, my breathing becomes laboured but, eventually, I emerge onto a higher track. Drawing air deeply into my lungs, I flash the torch around. I've lost all sense of direction.

Suddenly there's a shout, and I turn. Through the driving rain, a few hundred yards ahead, I make out a flickering light. Luke can't have realised how far I've dropped behind. I call out to him, but my voice is snatched away on the wind. As my eyes grow accustomed to the dark I become aware of movement to my left. There are many shadowy figures, muffled sounds and whispered shouts in the valley, and I tell myself this must be the search party. And then I hear other noises, further away, and they freeze my blood; splitting timber followed by an ungodly scream and the sound of waves crashing against rocks. But I'm nowhere near the cliff edge... I have most of the valley still to traverse.

Bending into the gale, I continue onwards and will the torch battery not to die. There's still no sign of Luke and little point in attempting to shout. Another clap of thunder and a flash of lightning lights up the scene before me, and I gasp. I'm much nearer to the cliffs than I'd thought. Cautiously, I continue. I have no desire to end up another reason for the search party to be out on this wild night.

A light shines in the distance and I carry on towards it, taking me out along the ridge of the promontory. The wind is now storm-force. Wary of being blown over the steep, slate escarpment, I drop to my knees and creep along on all fours. I can hear someone coming up fast behind me, breathing heavily, and I stifle a scream as I swing the torchlight in the direction of the noise. Thankfully, it picks out Luke's familiar face but my relief is short-lived.

'How come…? I thought you were in front of me.' I turn in the direction of the light I was edging towards.

'I followed the path by the stream. It comes out on the cliff path further down.'

'But that would put you far ahead of me. I took the higher path.'

Luke's confusion matches my own. The next minute, he drops to his knees as a particularly severe gust of wind sweeps over the promontory and threatens to blow us both off.

Way below is a muffled bark.

'Did you hear that?'

Luke nods. Carefully working his way towards the edge, he shines his torch over. As another squall assaults us, I grab the hem of his jacket.

'Hellooo… Anybody there?' Luke calls.

Nothing.

'Nicola!' I shout into the wind.

Another bark; followed by a cry.

As Luke wriggles further over the edge, I hold on tightly. 'Nicola, is that you?'

The reply is faint.

'Stay where you are,' Luke shouts. 'I'm coming.'

He squirms up the escarpment.

'There's a path further back leading down to the cove. I'll follow it and hopefully find where she is.' He takes his mobile from his pocket. 'Contact the police, Cass. Tell them we're on the point and we think Nicola is trapped in the cave facing Hawker's Hut.'

I nod.

Hazel eyes meet mine. Despite the night's wild elements, they are calm... but I notice another emotion hiding just beneath the surface.

'Keep low on the ridge, Cass.'

'I will. You be safe too, Luke.'

He gives a brief nod before setting off on hands and knees toward the main cliff path. For the second time that night, I watch Luke disappear into the dark.

As I make the call to the emergency services and wait for their arrival, I watch the light ahead of me continue to flash; weak at first, growing stronger and then disappearing. As the minutes pass, the rain abates and the wind dies down a little.

It doesn't take long for the coastguard team to arrive. It's quite a spectacle watching the lights of the air ambulance sweep in across the Atlantic, and as it hovers above the promontory I'm caught in its downdraught. Alarmed, I scramble back along the ridge to the coast path and watch anxiously as a figure is winched down from the helicopter towards the base of the cliffs. Minutes later, the cable retracts and then another crew member and a basket stretcher are winched down.

I haven't seen or heard anything of Luke since he vanished into the night. Inching along the path, I peer down at the waves surging against the dark bulk of the cliffs, dramatically illuminated by the helicopter's searchlight. But I can't make out Luke. Some ten minutes later, the stretcher and a paramedic are winched up into the helicopter before the cable descends again to retrieve the second crew member. Once he is safely on board, the air ambulance suddenly turns, its lights sweeping over the sea as it disappears away into the distance. All at once, an eerie quiet descends.

As a pale dawn breaks on the horizon, a policeman approaches me. 'Are you Cassandra Shaw?' I nod. 'Well done locating the girl's whereabouts.'

'Is she OK?'

'She has a broken leg but it could have been far worse. Your man has her dog.'

I look over his shoulder to where Luke stands with a couple of men. On the end of a rope, sitting at his feet, is a perky-looking West Highland terrier.

'The search party's light alerted me.'

The policeman frowns. 'Search party? It was called off at dusk when the Met Office reported bad weather coming in.'

'Over there.' I point towards the end of the promontory.

The policeman's gaze follows my finger. 'There's nothing there.' He turns back to me with a puzzled expression.

In the increasing morning light, I see that it's true. I've been alone on the rocky outcrop for most of the night with only the empty, grey swell of the Atlantic for company.

41

As Luke and I follow the policemen and paramedics along the valley towards Foxcombe Cottage, the West Highland terrier trots happily ahead seemingly none the worse for its recent adventures.

'How did you find Nicola?'

Luke glances across the path at me. 'When we heard her shout I knew we were almost directly above the cave. I suspected she might have sheltered there. Luckily, I was right.'

'Did she say what happened?'

'Little Jock, here, slipped over the ridge. Apparently, she followed. She's lucky to have just sustained a broken leg.'

'Goodness! Just peering over the escarpment is frightening enough.'

'It's wise to be respectful of the landscape and elements at any time, but especially when walking the cliffs on your own.' Luke throws me a tender look. 'Thank you for being here, Cass.'

Does he mean accompanying him in the search for the missing girl, or is he referring to something else?

I give him a smile and check his mobile phone, which I still have in my hand. 'I must call Ginny and let her know what's going on. I'm supposed to be doing the horses in the next half hour.'

As we walk along the track, I can't believe how quiet and still it has become. There's no indication of the wild weather that lashed the landscape throughout the night. The valley sparkles in the early morning sunshine and a pale blue sky promises another clear day ahead. All is good with the world once again...

I ring Ginny and briefly explain Nicola's rescue and that we have the young girl's dog.

'I'll phone her parents immediately and let them know,' Ginny says. 'They will probably come and collect the dog or Zac can walk it home. Don't worry about seeing to the horses this morning, Cassie. You must be exhausted. Just come home and take it easy today.'

'Thanks, Ginny.'

She pauses. 'I'm glad you and Luke came to no harm.'

I end the call and hand the mobile to Luke. 'What I don't understand is, the policeman told me the search was called off at dusk yesterday due to the bad weather coming in, yet the valley was full of people last night.'

'Was it?'

'Well, I didn't actually see anyone, but I was aware of shadowy figures moving through the landscape and muffled shouts. I also heard the sound of splitting timber and a scream.'

It was more than a scream; it was *unearthly*.

'I didn't hear anything other than the noise of the weather. Mind you, you were on the top path. Perhaps the wind was in a different direction.' He frowns. 'I didn't notice any driftwood in the sea. If a vessel was caught out in the storm there'd be flotsam and jetsam washed up.' He gives me a searching look. 'We'll let the police know what you heard in case we've missed something.'

'Yes, let's do that. I'd feel so much better.'

We continue along the track in comfortable silence with Jock scurrying ahead, sniffing the wind and investigating the foliage on both sides of the path. After a further twenty minutes we reach the ford crossing and I stare in disbelief. No longer is the stream a raging white-water torrent. Instead, it trickles, untroubled, around the stepping stones; the quintessential babbling brook.

'It was unusual weather last night, wasn't it?'

'Yes.' Luke holds firmly on to the rope, as the Westie bounds across the rocks. 'It appeared from nowhere.'

I step onto the first stepping stone, expecting it to be as precarious as last night, but the rock is steady. Lightly, I tread from one to the other, and each is solidly set. Once reaching the other side, I fall behind Luke and the terrier as the path narrows and follow them through the woods. When we finally emerge from the trees, Zac and Rhea are waiting for us on the veranda.

'You've found Jock!' cries Rhea, running towards us. 'I'm so happy.'

Bending down, she makes a fuss of the little dog, which immediately rolls onto its back for a tummy rub.

'Nicola's parents want us to look after Jock while they're at the hospital,' Zac announces.

'Have you heard how she is?'

The boy shakes his head. 'Mum told me to tell you the local paper is sending a reporter to interview you and Luke.'

'Our five minutes of fame!' Luke smiles wryly, as he

hands the Westie's lead to Rhea. 'I'll get some coffee on the go. Do you kids want a drink... tea, coffee, orange juice?'

'Orange please,' Rhea says sending the little dog around her in a large circle on the end of the rope. 'Look, Cassie, Jock's lunging just like Biscuit.'

'He's a natural.' I smile. 'But I'm sure he'd like something to eat and drink after his adventures of the last forty-eight hours.'

We all walk across the lawn towards the cottage, which looks welcoming and homely – a safe haven – the thatch gleaming in the early morning sun. As Luke opens the front door, Byron appears in the kitchen doorway and silently observes us as we make our way towards him. The little Westie pulls on the rope and his tail wags furiously as the dogs inquisitively touch noses.

'Well, that friendship seems to have got off to a good start,' Luke comments, as he crosses the kitchen and opens a cupboard door. 'Do you want orange juice as well, Zac?'

'Tea, please.'

'Cass, would you make it while I give Byron and Jock some food?'

'Sure.'

As Rhea helps Luke feed the dogs, I find mugs, throw teabags into a pot and fill the kettle. While waiting for it to come to the boil, I gaze out of the window and smile. Despite the serious nature of last night, it is fun doing things with Luke, and having Zac and Rhea here with us... well, any stranger would think we were one happy family.

There you go again, playing 'happy families' with those that don't belong to you.

David's harsh judgement rings in my ears and the smile

slips from my lips, but a loud rapping sound soon brings me back to my senses.

'I'll get it.' Zac runs down the hallway and opens the front door.

A young woman stands at the threshold. 'Hello. Is Luke Metcalfe at home?'

'Yes he is.'

From the door to the utility room, Luke calls a greeting. 'Hello. How can I help?'

'I'm Debbie Cooper, reporter with the *Cornish & Devon Post*. This is my colleague, Gareth.'

An eager young man with a camera in his hands steps into view. He gives a cheery wave. 'Hi folks!'

'We heard you found the missing schoolgirl last night,' the reporter continues. 'We'd like to interview you, if that's OK?'

Luke joins Zac at the front door. 'It wasn't just me who found her. It was Cass as well. In fact, if it hadn't been for Cass I wouldn't have ventured out in that awful weather.'

The young woman looks down the hallway to me and smiles. 'It sounds like there's quite a story here. Would you mind if I interviewed both of you and Gareth took some photos?'

Luke glances at me. 'Are you happy with that, Cass?'

I shrug. 'I guess so.'

'Come in,' Luke says, standing back from the door. 'The kettle's on.'

For the next hour we are interviewed about our experiences during the previous night. Even Zac and Rhea are questioned about their friendship with Nicola, and then we all decant onto the lawn for photographs with little Jock taking centre stage. Byron, too, is included.

Just as we've waved goodbye to Debbie and Gareth, Ginny turns up with Tegan, so I make another brew and we sit around the kitchen island, chatting. Suddenly the phone rings. I brace myself, expecting it to be Amanda, but when Luke answers it's hard to tell who he's talking to.

'Well, well, well... quite the media circus!' he says, replacing the receiver in its cradle on the wall. 'That was West Country TV. They're on their way over now to do an interview with you and me, Cass, for this evening's news.'

I raise my eyebrows. 'Guess I'd better visit the make-up department before they arrive.'

'No need for that, Cassie,' Ginny says. 'You're beautiful just as you are.'

From the other side of the kitchen, Luke agrees.

As I glance around the room at these wonderful people who have so generously and unquestioningly welcomed me into their lives, gratitude engulfs me. I have *never* experienced this level of inclusion in my life before. Not even with David... yet, still there's that tug at my heartstrings.

42

Amanda stares at the computer screen through strained eyes. She's been at the office since 7.30am searching for patterns and market trends amongst the data. She loves her work and thrives on the challenge of analysing indications through the media and stock market fluctuations, finding investors and quickly developing strategies. The financial rewards can be *enormous*. However, having put in just shy of one hundred hours this week alone she feels exhausted. Thankfully, though, she doesn't have to worry about rushing home to prepare meals for her husband, or giving baths to a rabble of kids or reading bedtime stories. Moving her head from side to side, stretching tense neck muscles, Amanda closes her watery eyes and leans back in the chair. She will rest for a few minutes...

'Sorry to disturb you.'

Opening her eyes, Amanda sees Sasha, her personal assistant, hovering in the doorway.

'Yes,' she snaps.

Sasha steps into the fishbowl office, surrounded on all four sides by glass walls.

'Did you know your husband's in the news?'

'Not another award!' Feigning disinterest, Amanda's attention diverts to the screen.

Somewhere in amongst all this data are investment opportunities that will provide her with a strategy to outperform other funds. She just has to find them. Covering her mouth with one hand, she yawns. Perhaps that final drink with Max last night hadn't been a good idea after all! It was unusual for him to suggest meeting up on a Sunday, but it's important she fosters the relationship. Driven by a keen, competitive desire to do better than other funds, she knows networking and contacts are key to making the most of business opportunities and dealings with investors.

'No. Not an award. He found a missing child.'

She looks up from the screen. 'He did what?'

'I was doing a search on the internet...' Sasha's cheeks colour and she hurries on, '...and it just popped up on my screen.'

Amanda gives her assistant an interrogating look. What exactly was Sasha searching for? Turning back to her screen, she reduces the open window and brings up Google.

'What search terms did you use?'

Turning a deep shade of crimson, Sasha mumbles, 'Hunter Harcourt.'

Amanda's eyebrow arcs in wry amusement but she makes no comment. It never fails to astound her, the number of fangirls her husband collects. Who'd have thought *nature* writing would amass such a loyal and young – but also not so young – female following! She types her husband's pseudonym in the search box and immediately the screen is brimming with reports on the incident.

Award-winning writer rescues missing schoolgirl! shouts the headline.

Amanda clicks on the link.

Hunter Harcourt (38), the well-known naturalist author and environmentalist, saved the day when he discovered missing North Devon schoolgirl Nicola Benney (10), and her West Highland Terrier Jock (3), on cliffs near Morwenstow.

Amanda snorts. It's *so* irritating when journalists state people's ages, as if these are important... and the dog's too. How insane! She continues reading.

The schoolgirl and her canine companion went missing for over 48 hours. Harcourt discovered them during a violent and sudden storm that besieged the area on Friday evening, which saw raging seas and miles of thundering grey Atlantic surf pound the high cliffs of North Cornwall and North Devon.

When asked how he'd found the girl, Harcourt answered in his trademark self-effacing manner: 'The weather was so bad that I wouldn't have ventured out if it hadn't been for my friend, Cassandra Shaw, urging me to accompany her in the search.'

Amanda sits up straight. The reporter has caught her attention now.

So, he was with his *friend* Cassandra Shaw...

Aware that Sasha has walked around her desk to read the screen over her shoulder, Amanda quickly scans the rest of the report.

'The wind was gale-force and we had to crawl along the point. It wouldn't have taken much to blow us over the edge. We shouted as best we could and heard a dog's bark and a faint call. I retraced my steps and carefully descended the cliffs at the location where the point merges with Vicarage Cliff.'

When asked how he knew where to find her, Harcourt replied: 'I knew from our position on the ridge that the cave was immediately below us. I hoped Nicola would be sheltering there. Fortunately, my assumptions were correct.'

'What a hero,' croons Sasha.

A hero indeed! The words lodge in Amanda's throat.

The report concludes with a photograph of Luke, Cassandra, the two older Kinsman children, a West Highland terrier and Byron.

How very cosy...

'Well, this isn't achieving anything.' Abruptly, Amanda closes the page and reopens the previous screen of financial data and percentages. She glances up at her PA. 'Was there anything else, Sasha?'

No.' Sasha frowns. 'I thought you'd like to know.'

'Thank you. Now, I must get on.' Amanda concentrates on the figures on the screen.

Taking the hint, Sasha moves towards the door.

'And close the door behind you,' Amanda says, without looking up.

As she pulls the door to, Sasha glances back at her boss.

Amanda waits until her assistant has walked the full length of the corridor before opening the news page again. For several minutes she stares at the image on the screen and then searches for more details about Luke's recent heroism. There's plenty of information on the internet and she becomes increasingly hot under the collar when she discovers his *friend's* part in the dramatic tale. One of the local papers even misreports Cassandra Shaw as Hunter Harcourt's girlfriend! Amanda splutters in indignation. And then she comes across a link to West Country TV. Clicking on the news page, she watches the interview in full, unable to ignore how comfortable and at ease Luke and 'the hireling' are in each other's company.

'Playtime over, Lukey babe.'

Picking up the phone, she punches in her husband's number. On the sixth ring, he answers.

'Hello, darling.'

'Hello, Mandy. Everything all right?' Luke says in surprise. It's unusual for his wife to phone this early in the day.

'All's fine. I'm ringing to congratulate you on your recent *Superman* performance. Quite the action hero!'

Usually his wife's spikey wit would amuse him, or wash over him at least, but Luke can't prevent his irritation from crackling down the line. 'The girl is safe. That's what's important.'

'Of course.' Swivelling her chair, Amanda stares out of

the plate glass window at the busy London street below.
'I see the exotic creature is still around.'

Did her husband just sigh?

'If you mean Cass, yes, of course she is. She's employed
by the Kinsmans. Where did you think she'd be going?'

'Oh, you know.' Amanda makes sure her voice is *ever
so* light. 'These casual roles suit a certain type of person.
You can never be sure how long these vagrants will stick
around.'

For a long moment neither husband nor wife says a word.

'Well, Luke, as I said, I just phoned to congratulate you
on your heroics and also to check what time you expect to
arrive tomorrow.' Amanda turns back to her desk.

'Late afternoon.'

'And remind me… what day is your book signing?'

Was that another sigh?

'The following day, Amanda,' Luke says in a level voice.
'Wednesday evening.'

'Oh yes, silly me! You'll have to excuse my lapse
of memory, I'm *that* busy.' A movement at the end of
the corridor makes her look up and she watches Sasha
approach, holding aloft a huge bouquet of flowers. 'Must
dash, darling. See you tomorrow evening.'

Amanda replaces the phone and as her assistant reaches
the glass door to her office, she waves her in.

'I think you have an admirer,' Sasha says, passing
over the bouquet.

'Find a vase please, Sasha.'

At once, a sweet, delicate scent fills the office and
Amanda examines the flowers; four varieties of rose, bloom
chrysanthemums, nigella and seasonal foliage. Stapled

to the clear cellophane wrapping is a small white envelope. Laying the bouquet on the desk, she removes the envelope and takes out a card, and as she reads the written sentiments her lips curl into a self-satisfied smile.

For Amanda,
Who makes analysing trends & discussing financial &
stock market fluctuations such a turn-on!
Don't keep me waiting too long...
Max xx

43

As I walk along the track to the cottage, I notice the obvious signs of a change of season. Cooling temperatures and darkening nights as autumn approaches. Gulls hover in fields, now scattered with round hay bales waiting to be brought in, and all along the hedgerows blackberries ripen against leaves turning amber, crimson and gold; heralding shorter days to come. On the cool, easterly breeze I detect a soft, musty, organic scent. Summer has slipped into the time of mists and mellow fruitfulness, and I wonder what the winter will have in store for us all here on the North Cornish coast.

I try to avoid thoughts of Christmas, as I know this year will be different to the previous ten. I've always worked hard over the *season to be merry* – David likes Stone Farm to be 'open house' – but I wonder what the Kinsmans will expect of me. For several weeks, the Porter's Lodge has been booked for the festive period and we've had to turn away many disappointed potential guests.

As I approach the five-bar gate opening onto Foxcombe Cottage's tarmac drive, I frown deeply. Earlier, when Luke phoned to say he was back from London he'd sounded strained, and when he asked me to visit straight away the seriousness to his voice set my nerves jangling.

What can be of such importance to put me so on edge? Is he unwell?

A dull ache settles in the pit of my stomach.

Best not overthink things.

Opening the gate, I follow the winding drive through the trees. As I pass the small orchard, I notice ripe crimson and russet fruit lying fallen on the ground. My nostrils twitch at the distinct, sweet, rich aroma and my mouth waters at the thought of apple and plum crumble, topped off with cinnamon cream.

All is peaceful. There's no indication of the dramatic events that unfolded the previous week, when the unusually severe weather had turned the woods into something wild and strange, capable of confusing the senses and home to shadowy figures and unexplained noises. It's as if the landscape remembers its history and exists out of time. As I focus on the ancient woodland that surrounds the cottage and spills into the valley, I wonder what other dramas it has witnessed over the centuries, which now lie hidden from sight.

In the late morning sunshine, the cottage's stone elevations glow warm and mellow and the thatched roof gleams burnished gold. It won't be long before wood smoke drifts from its chimneys. Immediately, I'm transported back to the day I first spied the house from the cliff path when I'd imagined a weary winter traveller drawn to the smoke rising from its three chimneys. Was that really just over nine weeks ago? Time has taken on a different meaning since arriving in Cornwall. Foxcombe Cottage is such a handsome gentleman's residence, befitting the attractive man who occupies it. I smile, but it slides from my face as the front door opens. Luke stands on the threshold wearing a serious expression and my heart begins to race. What *is* the matter?

'Hi,' I say lightly.

'Hi, Cass.' He gives a small, anxious smile. 'Thanks for coming over at such short notice. I've just made a pot of coffee. Would you like some?'

'Great.'

As I follow him along the hallway towards the kitchen my stomach churns, and I wonder if I'll manage to keep anything down. I glance through the open door to the sitting room and see the Great Dane stretched out on the carpet, basking in a patch of sunlight. I comfort myself. If there is something seriously wrong with Luke, Byron will have picked up on it and show signs of anxiety, but he is obviously unperturbed by his master's grave demeanour.

In the kitchen, I pull out a stool and sit at the island unit, watching in silence as Luke takes another mug down from the cupboard and depresses the plunger of the cafetière. To anyone else he would appear as comfortable in his own skin as always, but I've come to know him well over the past couple of months and I detect careful self-control over both emotion and movement, which sets me on edge even more.

'So, how was London?'

He glances at me and I'm shocked by the uncertainty lurking in his eyes. I brace myself for the worst possible news, but when he speaks he gives me no reason to fret.

'Busy, crowded, grey. I find myself increasingly resentful of having to go to the city. London is not my life. Rugged cliffs, wild places, hidden tracks, flora and fauna are. I'm so thankful to be back.'

He pours coffee into two mugs, adding a dash of milk to each before passing one to me.

'The talk I gave at Foyles went well. It was an appreciative audience and we sold a number of books.' He smiles. 'While I was there I bought a gift for you.'

My eyes open wide.

'I'll just get it.'

I watch as he walks to the study and, taking a sip of coffee, try to calm myself. Why am I such a bundle of nerves? Is my subconscious warning me of something? There is nothing to suggest anything's wrong with Luke.

A few minutes later, Luke re-enters the kitchen holding a package. 'I had a few moments to browse before I was the main attraction and found this. As soon as I saw it I thought of you. I hope you approve.'

He passes the gift to me. Carefully, I peel back the fantasy woodland wrapping paper; so apt for Foxcombe Cottage. Inside is a moss green, leather-bound book with the author's name and title embossed in gold: *Celebrating Celtic Goddesses.*

Covetously, I stroke the cover and glance up at him with shining eyes. 'Oh, Luke. This is so beautiful.'

He gifts me a smile that would floor a woman at a thousand yards, and my heart flips.

'Thank you. I will treasure it always.' I raise the front cover. Tucked inside is an envelope on which he has written in neat handwriting, *Cassandra Tallulah Shaw.*

Picking it up, I meet his gaze. Anxiously, he watches.

'Should I open it now?'

He's about to answer when my mobile alerts me to an incoming call.

'Sorry.' I stand up and extract the phone from the pocket of my jeans.

'Sandie, love, I'm here… in Cornwall.'

My body *still* jumps to the sound of his voice.

'What! Why?'

David laughs. 'I've come to put things right.'

I hurriedly sit as my legs threaten to give way.

'What do you mean *"put things right"*?'

David laughs again. 'Don't sound so aghast, Sands. It's not something I want to explain over the phone. I'm staying at the Falcon Hotel in Bude. Come over now.'

'Now?'

'Yes, *now!*'

I cringe. David hates it when I'm slow in response; it irritates the hell out of him.

'How long will it take you to get here?' he asks.

I make a quick calculation. I need to freshen up. 'About an hour.'

'See you at twelve-thirty, then. Don't be late! Bye, love.'

I sit in stunned silence for several minutes.

Eventually Luke speaks. 'Is everything all right?'

'I think so.' My heart races. 'That was David. He's here, in Cornwall. He wants to see me.'

Barely able to contain the bubbling hope and rapidly building excitement, I gaze across at Luke. Is that sadness I detect in his eyes? No, I must be imagining it, because the next minute he smiles warmly.

'That's great, Cass. Go and find out what he has to say.'

Rising swiftly to my feet, I scoop up the book and slide the envelope and mobile into the back pocket of my jeans.

'Sorry to cut this visit short,' I say, picking up the mug and taking a large gulp of coffee. 'Thanks for the drink.'

I hurry to the kitchen door, my emotions swirling tumultuously as I'm consumed by thoughts of my imminent meeting with David. But then I turn back. Luke hasn't moved. It's obvious he called me to the cottage to present the book, but that doesn't explain the seriousness to his voice when he'd asked me to visit.

'Was there something you wanted to say to me, Luke?'

He holds my gaze for a long moment and then shakes his head. 'No, Cass.'

Oddly unsettled, I smile briefly and turn away.

As I pull into the parking bay in front of the Falcon Hotel, I glance at my watch. Sixty minutes... to the second.

After leaving Luke sitting in the kitchen at the cottage, I'd jogged up the track to the manor house and freshened up in record time. I'd changed my shirt for a more feminine top, brushed my hair, applied a thin coat of mascara and added a slick of lipstick. I decided against blusher; my heightened emotions provided all necessary colour. Taking a step back from the mirror, I'd critically judged myself through David's eyes. Thinner than when he last saw me, but that was too bad. I couldn't do anything about that.

Now, opening the driver's door, I step out and draw air deep into my lungs in an attempt to gain some composure. Glancing along the row of parked cars in front of the hotel, I notice a bright red Ferrari. I know it will be his, but walking past on my way to the entrance I check the number plate: ASH 1. This must be the latest toy. I climb the steps to the hotel, faint with nerves as I anticipate David greeting me in the lobby. But the foyer is empty. Walking across a highly polished marble floor, beneath an impressive chandelier and past an ornate grandfather clock, I approach the reception desk and smile pleasantly at the smartly dressed receptionist.

'I'm meeting David Ashcroft. Would you call his room please?'

As she gives me a quick once-over it all comes flooding back. I am *always* judged by other women when associated with David.

'Mr Ashcroft is in the Coachman's Bar.'

'Thanks.' I walk back towards the entrance vestibule and stop at an open door.

I see David immediately, sitting at the bar reading a newspaper. He glances up as I enter. Unhurriedly, he neatly folds the paper and puts it to one side before rising to his feet.

'Sandie! There you are.' Smiling expansively, he opens his arms wide.

Heads turn.

As usual, his charisma fills the room. Once again, I'm overcome by his larger-than-life presence.

'Let's have a look at you then,' he says in a loud voice.

Self-consciously, I walk towards him. As I approach, he takes my hands and twirls me around like a spinning top. Embarrassment consumes me. Desperately, I avoid eye contact with the other people in the bar.

'Thin, but we'll soon take care of that.'

KATE RYDER

Giving me a wolfish grin, he leads me to a table in a window alcove near the entrance.

If he'd reserved a table near the door, why did he force me to walk to him?

My humiliation increases as I realise the extent of his blatant manipulation. The reason he didn't come to me as I entered the bar was because he wanted to make an impression on all the other diners by parading me the full length of the room. Is he really so shallow?

'I would have treated you to something in the hotel restaurant but it's only open in the evenings. How quaint! But never mind, I've booked a room for the whole weekend so there'll be plenty of time for you to show me the sights.'

I work at weekends. He hasn't taken that into consideration. I open my mouth to say so, but then close it again.

'So, Sands, choose anything you want from the menu. I intend to put some flesh on those skinny bones of yours.'

'I like being this weight,' I say feebly.

He laughs, his eyes dancing. 'Maybe so, but men like to have something to grab hold of.'

I'm so nervous I doubt I'll be able to eat at all. But, to please David, I order a Caesar salad and force down a few mouthfuls. I watch as he tucks into a rump steak. Without asking what I'd like, he orders an expensive bottle of red wine and, despite my protests, instructs the waiter to fill my glass.

'Tuck in,' he says, between mouthfuls.

I can't eat. Instead, I take a sip of wine, acutely aware that we are the centre of attention. Everyone's eyes are on us, with ears cocked in our direction. This is how it is with

David. Wherever he goes people notice him. It's hard not to. His movie-star looks grow more impressive with age and he exudes wealth and confidence.

'I saw your car outside.'

'I traded in the Merc.' He glances around. 'So, this is where you've been hiding. It's very… how shall I put it…' he leans forward and whispers, '*provincial*.'

'I like it.'

He eyes me for a moment. 'Do you remember, Sands, when we first met, you said up until then you'd spent most of your time concealed away in your bedroom.'

I flush crimson.

'It always surprised me that someone who was such a looker was so meek and mild.' He saws off a large piece of steak and spears it with his fork. 'However, over the years you've come out of your shell.' His clear brown eyes bore into mine. 'You know you can't return to that earlier version, however much you'd like to. You've come too far.'

He puts a forkful of steak into his mouth and chews.

I put down my glass. 'I don't know what you mean, David. I am not trying to recreate a previous time.'

He smiles. 'Good. You see, I have plans for you and me, love.'

I frown. It's difficult to remember who I am in his company. He always takes over.

'What plans?'

He cuts off another piece of steak and I wait patiently. At last he swallows. But then I have to wait a while longer as he raises the glass to his lips and takes a large mouthful of wine.

'You've been very clever keeping me at bay.' He waggles

a finger at me, as if I'm a wayward child. 'But I can tell you, your strategy has worked.' He lowers his voice. 'I'm desperate for you.'

'Even more than for Jen?' The words are out of my mouth before I have a chance to prevent them.

His eyes narrow as he surveys me. Suddenly, he explodes into laughter. Again, heads turn in our direction.

'Oh, Sandie, Sandie, Sandie! You can't still be sore about her?'

My hands ball into fists beneath the table.

'As I've already explained to you, she is no threat. She simply fulfils a need.'

'Yes, OK,' I say, sounding horribly sullen. 'You don't need to remind me.'

He stares at me and then smiles; that old wicked smile of his that is *so* disarming.

'She's good in the sack, Sands, that's all. She's not a candidate for "life partner".'

My eyes open wide. If he's here to discuss us getting back together, how does he think telling me Jen's *good in the sack* makes me feel? My emotions are in turmoil. I know the pretty picture we present. I'm reminded of it so many times by the envious stares I receive from other women and the conspiratorial smirks men share with David when they think I'm not looking.

'Cassie?'

I turn at the sound of her voice. Robyn walks confidently towards our table, dressed in a smart, navy blue skirt suit.

'I thought it was you.' She kisses me on the cheek.

'Hi, Robyn.' I'm so thankful she's materialised. Her presence is a soothing balm to my troubled feelings.

'I'm here to meet a client but he has yet to arrive.' She glances curiously across the table at David. 'Hello.'

'This is David. He's...'

How do I describe him? What is he to me?

As I hesitate, David springs to his feet and holds out his hand. 'David Ashcroft, Ashcroft Enterprises.'

'Robyn Crawford, Chalmers and Crawford,' she responds, accepting his handshake.

I notice the amused gleam in her eye.

'And what is Chalmers and Crawford?' David asks, still holding on to her.

I feel so small and inferior sitting here. Should I join them and rise to my feet?

'A firm of solicitors,' Robyn says, removing her fingers from his grasp. 'And what enterprises are you involved in exactly?'

'Join us.' Charm personified, David pulls out a chair.

Robyn surveys the room. 'Well, just for a moment.' She smiles at me and sits down. 'So, David Ashcroft, do tell...'

David makes no effort to mask his interest in her. 'Innovative inventions.'

'Interesting. Anything mainstream?'

Their conversation bats backwards and forwards across the table while I sit in silence, my head moving from side to side as I follow their banter; merely a spectator at a tennis match. Suddenly Robyn glances towards the door and waves.

'Ah, my appointment has arrived.' She rises to her feet. 'So, Cassie, we'll see you and Luke next Saturday?'

'Yes. We'll be there.'

'Good.' She smiles warmly and squeezes my shoulder

before looking across at David. 'Nice to meet you, David Ashcroft. Good luck with your *innovative inventions*.'

David is on his feet. 'Wonderful to meet you, Robyn Crawford.' He speaks in his sexiest voice and bequeaths her one of his heart-stopping smiles. 'If I'm ever in need of a solicitor I know where to come.'

She nods once and turns away.

As she walks towards the man standing in the doorway, David's eyes keenly follow, and it's only when Robyn disappears into the hotel lobby that he sits down and directs his attention to me once more.

'Didn't know solicitors could look like supermodels.'

I give a small laugh. 'Yes, Robyn is gorgeous.'

'Certainly is!' His eyes narrow as he focuses on me. 'So who's this Luke?'

'A friend.' Infuriatingly, I blush.

'A friend?'

'Yes.' My voice is defiant. 'A friend.'

'Hmm…' He observes me a while longer. 'Drink up, Sands.'

He drains his glass, calls over to the waiter and orders a bottle of Louis Roederer champagne to be sent up to his room. Then, rising to his feet, he holds out his hand to me.

44

Nervously, I glance around the deluxe room. It's beautifully appointed with a king-size bed and a comfortable seating area with a coffee table overlooking the Bude Canal.

'Come here, Sands.'

Opening his arms wide, David gives me a mega-watt smile. It's a smile that's used to winning, and like a dutiful child I walk into his embrace. Immediately I am swamped. His hands slide down my body and encompass my buttocks as his mouth greedily finds mine. Forcing my lips apart with his tongue, ravenously he explores. I can hardly breathe at the onslaught but I'm aware enough to register that this passionate embrace does nothing for me. My body – and mind – up until then, primed and on high-alert, suddenly withdraws from the game.

'God, I've missed you,' he whispers hoarsely in my ear. 'I'm desperate.'

As if to reiterate the point, he presses his body firmly against mine so that I can feel the full extent of his arousal.

A sudden loud knocking at the door elicits a groan.

'Timing!'

Adjusting his chinos, he strides across the room and opens

the door. A young waiter stands in the corridor holding a champagne bucket and two glasses.

'Put it on the table.'

As the waiter does as instructed, he glances at me inquisitively.

'Do you want me to pour, sir?'

'No thank you. That's all.'

Once we are alone again, David approaches the seating area and lifts the bottle out of the ice. Peering at the label, he makes an appreciative sound at the back of his throat.

'Time to celebrate, Sands.'

He pops the cork, pours champagne into the flutes, hands one to me and replaces the bottle back in the bucket.

'Here's to us.' Raising his glass, he gulps a large mouthful. 'Hmm… a fine fruit aroma, tinged with a hint of biscuit.' He gazes appreciatively at the clear bubbles in the pale golden liquid.

I take a sip. The champagne slips down easily.

'So, Sands, what do you say?'

'To what?'

Irritation flickers in his eyes, but his smile remains intact.

'To you coming home.'

I remain silent. He's yet to say anything that will make me reconsider my position. I gaze out of the window. Directly across from the room, on the opposite side of the canal, is the bistro where Luke held his talk and book signing. How long ago that seems now. It's as if these few weeks in Cornwall are the only meaningful life I've known.

'Well?' David sits and comfortably spreads his legs wide.

'I can't come back as we left it.' I sit, making sure I keep some distance between us.

His gaze is steady. 'I've been thinking about that. As you know, I've never wanted a family.'

I nod slowly.

'But...' I watch him gather himself '...to save *us*, I've considered the idea.'

My eyes open wide and he laughs.

'Yes, Sandie. You've won. The house is like a morgue without you and I've missed you and your funny ways.' He takes a deep, shuddering, steadying breath. 'I consent to you having a child.'

For so many years I've yearned for his agreement, but now that he offers it I'm not so sure.

'What, no smile?' David pulls a face. 'Hell, Sands, what more do you want? I'm offering my balls on a plate!'

I flinch. Only a little over two months have passed since I first came to Cornwall, yet his *speak* is alien to me.

'I don't want your permission to have children,' I say in a pathetically reedy voice. 'You have to want them too.'

'Children?' Drawing his legs together, as if to protect his precious balls, he sits up and gives me a long hard look.

I can tell he's weighing up the pros and cons.

'Yes, David. A family. Something many people have once they've been together for a while.'

He turns and peers out the window, and I watch as he grapples with inner turmoil. Rubbing a hand over his face, as if lessening the seriousness of the conversation, he glances back at me.

'OK, Sands. I will give you a child or two so you can play at happy families.'

My jaw drops. I can't believe I've convinced him to agree to something I've craved for so long. But, curiously, it's an anti-climax.

David rises to his feet and strides across the room to the en-suite. He doesn't bother to close the door. For several minutes all is silent.

'Is everything OK?'

'Jeez, Sands, what have you done to me? I'm rock hard!'

Again, I flinch. *Too much information.*

A few minutes later I hear him taking a long pee. *So familiar!* And so *not* romantic…

As I gaze out across the canal to the bistro, I think of Luke. The two men are so different. He has none of David's bluster and confidence, but so much more integrity and authenticity. Luke possesses an armour of quiet strength. Does Amanda appreciate that? I can't help but think she'd be better suited to someone like David, what with their shared interest in money and the need to display their standing in society. A frown creases my brow. What *is* wrong with Luke? Is he ill? I shouldn't be sitting here in the Falcon Hotel. I should have stayed to find out what's bothering him.

As I hear David turn on the taps and move around the bathroom, I suddenly remember Luke's envelope. Withdrawing it from my pocket, I place it on the table. Will its contents explain his serious mood? What will I learn? With trepidation, I pick it up and extract the note.

For Cass
I whisper to you in the space between stars.
My thoughts hold you until the time of your awakening
into the world of form.
Fortunate one, may you understand that your life is
blessed.
May you open your heart and receive what life
is offering you.
Luke, x

I realise I'm holding my breath and, forcing myself to breathe, I blink rapidly as I savour his words again. From the other side of the room David clears his throat. I glance up.

'What are you doing?' I say in a shocked whisper.

He stands with hands on hips, naked. It's obvious he's increased the hours in the gym – or maybe the extra exercise with Jen has helped – because his body is more ripped than I remember.

He grins. 'If I'm going to give you my seed there's no time like the present.'

I gasp. This is *so* not what I want. I want Luke's intelligent, thoughtful company... even if it is only offered in friendship.

'I've made a stupid mistake, love.' David strides confidently towards me, everything swinging freely.

'I've made a stupid mistake, too.' Quickly rising to my feet, I scoop up Luke's note and envelope and slip them back in my pocket.

I turn to David. How foolish he looks.

His grin widens.

'No, David. What I mean is...' I take a steadying breath '...my mistake was coming here today.'

The grin falters.

'I'm sorry, but I have to go.' I hurry towards the door.

'Sands?' He sounds dumbfounded. 'Are you turning down my offer?'

'I am. Save your *seed* for Jen... or somebody else.'

Disbelief replaces the grin.

'Oh, and by the way, my name isn't Sands, Sandie or Sandra. It's Cass.'

His jaw drops and as his trademark confidence deserts him, his hands fly to cover himself.

'But I love you, Sands... *Cass*.'

The name doesn't sound right on his lips.

'No, David, you don't. If you loved me you'd never have let me leave Stone Farm in the first place. You certainly wouldn't have taken up with the cleaner while we were still together, and probably countless others I don't know about.'

I stare at the man with the movie-star looks who suddenly seems reduced in stature. I'm not angry or sad. In fact, I don't feel anything. No longer does he have any power over me.

I wait for David to fight his corner or offer some explanation, but he remains mute.

'Goodbye, David.' I turn to leave, but then stop. There's just one last thing to clear up. 'By the way, that day of the car accident, how *did* you manage to arrive on the scene so soon after it happened?'

Colour drains from his face but he doesn't say a word.

'Well?'

He clears his throat. 'I'm sure you don't want to revisit that time.'

'Go on.'

He swallows hard. 'As you know, it was terrible weather and visibility was exceedingly poor. I was on my way back from a meeting at the office and on the mobile to John. I didn't see the car until it was too late.'

'What do you mean *until it was too late*?' My voice is little more than a whisper.

He knows he can't fob me off this time and his eyes bulge with the effort of being truthful.

'As I pulled out of the T-junction I was distracted by something John said. It was only then that I saw the vehicle and slammed on the brakes. Your father over-compensated and swerved, which made his car plane across the road and hit the kerb.'

Incredulously, I stare at him as everything slots into place. I'd always known there was something odd about the incident. I should have trusted my instincts.

'So, you caused the death of my parents.' My voice is as hard as steel.

'No, Sands... Cass.'

Holding out his hands entreatingly, he takes a step towards me. But seeing the look on my face, he stops and swiftly covers himself again. 'It was an accident, I swear.'

Suddenly his cavalier attitude and many bouts of unexplained irritation with me over the years make sense.

'So your pursuit of me was out of guilt.'

A sheepish expression sweeps across his face. 'At first,

maybe, but I quickly grew to love you. I mean, how could anyone not? Just look at you… you're sexy as hell!'

'Put some clothes on, David.' My eyes flicker over his body for one last time. 'You look ridiculous.'

His jaw hits the floor. Calmly, I turn away.

45

Luke's Land Rover is parked in the turning circle at the side of the cottage and relief floods through me. Pulling on the handbrake, I jump out of the car and run to the house. I have no idea what I'm going to say but I need to find out what is wrong with him. As usual, the front door is unlocked.

'Luke, are you here?'

Silence.

'Luke!'

Thick, impenetrable stillness.

It's dark in the hallway. I switch on the light and peer into each room, expecting Byron to materialise in the kitchen doorway. But he doesn't. Standing at the kitchen island unit, I stare at the abandoned cafetière and mugs, their contents hardly touched. I'd rushed off without finishing my coffee but why didn't Luke drink his? A terrible thought occurs and I hurry back down the hallway, hesitating only briefly on the bottom step. I've never ventured upstairs before. Is Luke so gravely ill that he now lies, unable to move, in a bedroom on the floor above while I search downstairs? I'll never forgive myself if I don't check.

Feeling like an interloper, I tiptoe up the stairs and switch on the landing light. All the doors along the passageway are closed. Which is his bedroom? It's most likely to be sea-facing, overlooking that magnificent view down to the cliffs, but what if he's only managed to drag himself into the nearest room? Fearing what I may find, I open each door in turn. There are five bedrooms in total. This is a family home, one that should resound to the noise of happy children and laughter, but that will never be. Amanda isn't the mothering type. As I close the door on a beautifully appointed bathroom, I turn and gaze back towards the top of the stairs. Luke isn't here. I should feel relieved at not having found him lying prostrate and in pain – or worse – but I can't shake off the thought that I'm on the point of losing something very precious.

Descending the stairs, I fish out my mobile and punch in his number. I don't have to wait long before I hear his phone responding from the study and as I enter, I see it sitting on the desk. As usual, a peaceful and tranquil atmosphere fills the room. Swiftly, I cross to the window and gaze out over the garden and scan the valley to the cliffs. In the fast-fading light the sea is indigo. Where *is* Luke? It's only when I turn away from the window that I notice the closed diary on his desk. Cautiously – and a little guiltily – I open the cover. What will I discover? Will there be hospital appointments with immutable results noted alongside? As I turn the pages, my heart races and my breathing shallows.

Under each date are jotted a few brief notes – mainly literary appointments with industry people, talks and book signings. But when I arrive at the week just gone, the boxes are full to overflowing. Such is my panic that I find it difficult to focus and I hastily read the entries, preparing myself for the worst possible news. It's the entry on the day of the Foyles' book signing that floors me.

> *Tonight we called time on our marriage. It has run its course. It wasn't an easy decision, but I don't think either of us was the least bit surprised – it's been a long time coming. Although we've enjoyed a good relationship, we are both mature enough to acknowledge it's one that belongs to a younger version of ourselves. We have agreed to remain friends, but somehow I doubt a friendship will sustain. I will arrange a formal valuation of the Chelsea townhouse where Amanda will continue to live (she has agreed to buy me out of my share). I will reside permanently at Foxcombe Cottage – what a relief that is to me!*
>
> *Having now drawn a line under that part of my life I must look to the future, and there is only one person I desire in it. I fervently hope she wants it too. I have squandered too much time already and will waste no more. I will ask Cass as soon as I return to Cornwall.*

A tingling sensation shoots through my body and a shiver runs up the full length of my spine. Swallowing the lump in my throat and blinking away tears, I read the entry again. *This* is why Luke sounded so serious. He isn't suffering from some incurable disease. He's on the point of taking a leap of faith and showing his hand, committing to something uncertain. But I didn't give him the chance. I'd abandoned him at the first worthless whiff of a future with David.

I should have known. I should have felt it in my bones…

'You stupid fool!' I cry into the quiet of the room. 'How could you be so obtuse?'

Quickly exiting the study, I walk out of the cottage and across the grassy terrace towards the trees. Cupping my hands around my mouth, I shout out Luke's name.

No response.

The afternoon is fast slipping away, and in the encroaching dusk, long shadows cast their strange shapes across the lawn. As I peer into the woodland's gloomy interior, at the ancient gnarled trees with their mass of twisted branches, I imagine I see a pinprick of light in the far distance and catch my breath. *Déjà vu* – this is my recurring dream! The hairs on the back of my neck bristle as I watch the light dart through the trees towards me, before finally coming to rest at the edge of the woods. It beckons me to enter but, unlike in my dream, I am no longer fearful of the unknown. In fact, I welcome it.

All at once, I realise these trees are the forest, only I'd failed to recognise it. This woodland is much sparser, whereas in my dream it is thick, stretching as far as the eye can see; *a spill of ink across the wild, rugged landscape.* I smile at the light, as if to an old friend, but I know that I don't have to respond and enter the forest. I have already undertaken that testing journey. As this realisation crystallises, the small ball of light suddenly dims and vanishes.

Walking back to the thatched veranda, I sit on the bench beneath the old ship's bell. I have no idea how long I remain sitting; time is irrelevant. I *have* to speak to Luke.

As darkness descends, swirling around the cottage and cloaking her in its protection, I detect a scent of ocean on the wind. Raising my eyes to the heavens, I watch as dark cirrus clouds scud across the night sky to reveal a wash of twinkling stars and planets, and I know that a halo of light will soon surround the moon. Suddenly, I understand. The essence of the man in my dream belongs to Luke.

Glancing at the brass bell above me, I rise to my feet, catch hold of the rope and swing the clapper forcefully against its metal sides. A deep, resonant clang resounds out across the valley. Several nearby rooks indignantly take flight from their roosts and, somewhere far off an owl screeches.

'Luke! Where are you?' I shout.

Silence.

I swing the clapper again. Is that a distant bark on the breeze?

I ring the bell again and again, its urgent toll filling the cool night air. Fighting mounting despair, I slump down on the bench.

Light from the cottage windows spills out across the grass terraces, reaching as far as the woodland, and, feverishly, my eyes search the dark mass of trees creeping across the landscape. Suddenly, there's movement to my right and the Great Dane appears. Curiously it observes me.

As renewed hope fills my soul, I rise to my feet.

'Byron, here!'

The dog turns, as if to look at someone – or something – deeper in the forest before bounding across the lawn towards me.

'Good boy, Byron.' I stroke his large, velvety head. 'Where's your master?'

Is that a flicker of torchlight in the near distance? As I watch the beam grow stronger, my heart hammers painfully against my ribcage and, after what seems an age, Luke emerges from out of the gloom. He stops and assesses me through intelligent eyes.

'Cass! I thought I'd lost you.' His voice is full of relief and gratitude.

I shake my head. 'I've been waiting for you.'

He gives a slow, warm smile. 'Not as long as I've been waiting for you.'

As I recognise Luke's true beauty and all that he is, my breath hitches in my throat. Close by, I hear a whispered, contented sigh, followed by the delicious sensation of silk softly trailing across my body.

The night is still and yet an air current picks up, swirling into a beautiful maelstrom of peacock colours threaded with chestnut. Transfixed, I watch as the whirlwind gathers force, twisting and turning across the lawn, and two shadowy figures take form. Anna and her gamekeeper dance in each other's arms, and I recall Ginny's comment that Daniels *carried himself well*. She was right. Gazing enraptured into each other's eyes, the couple spin across the grass, as elegant as ballroom dancers. There is no sadness here. They are together at last.

As the figures lose form, spinning over the terraces into the valley below, the landscape ripples beneath the richly coloured vortex. Leaving the land, it sends a shimmer across the ocean as two shooting stars appear in the night sky, travelling together into eternity. Instinctively, I know that whatever strangeness has inhabited these woods all these years will be no more.

High above, a halo of light encircles the moon – its inner edge tinged red, the outer an altogether bluer hue – and as I look towards the woodland fringe all becomes crystal clear. There is no doubt. *Everything* that went before has been leading to this very day. At last, the planets have truly aligned.

Hugging unadulterated joy close to my heart, I run lightly across the lawn towards him.

'Cass.' Luke's voice is soft and tender.

'Luke,' I whisper, as I step from my world into his.

Acknowledgements

There have been many influences in the creation of this book, not least, the substantial thatched cottage located in a magnificent, natural setting on the North Cornish coast where I had the good fortune to holiday many years ago. It left a deep impression on me and over the intervening years I have returned to it many times in my imagination. I hope I have done it justice in the fictionalised Foxcombe Cottage (the actual property is known by a different name and in private ownership).

Foxcombe Manor is loosely based on Tonacombe Manor, which dates from the reign of Elizabeth I and has inspired several literary creations other than my own. Its ghostly sightings are well-documented, but I have embellished or fictionalised these accounts of paranormal events for those that occur at Foxcombe Manor. 'Supernatural in Cornwall' by Michael Williams also proved helpful in this regard. I have, however, remained true to known historical facts concerning Reverend Robert Stephen Hawker, of Morwenstow. What an absolute joy it was to discover more about this well-known, eccentric character.

From the first word I had a clear picture of the heroine, Cassandra Shaw, whose passion for horses and affinity with nature were provided by my own memories of living near and riding across the South Downs. However, had I been aware of the full extent of documented unusual happenings and paranormal goings-on at Chanctonbury Ring, I may not have ridden so eagerly in and around that particular copse of beech trees!

To gain a feel for the hero, I read many books on the natural world. It wasn't a chore. In particular, Robert MacFarlane's and Dan Richard's '*Holloway*', with evocative illustrations by the artist Stanley Donwood, proved key to fleshing-out the character of Luke Metcalfe (aka Hunter Harcourt). Also helpful was a wonderful little pocket book, '*Seaweed Foraging in Cornwall and the Isle of Scilly*,' by Rachel Lambert. For those of you interested in discovering what our coastlines have to offer, I thoroughly recommend it.

Writing a novel can be all-consuming and I rarely have the capacity to read anything else during this intense period. However, as luck would have it, I came across '*Legends of the Grail: Stories of Celtic Goddesses*' by Ayn Cates Sullivan, PhD. How fortunate, because Danu's Goddess Blessing sent shivers down my spine when I realised I'd discovered Luke's declaration of love. I immediately contacted the author, who very generously allowed me to reproduce the blessing in full.

Big thanks to Liane Wilding, of Three Ravens Natural Boarding, whose own buckskin Arab cross Warmblood not only transformed into Cassie's horse, Caspian, but also provided the name for Ginny Kinsman's thoroughbred mare. Also, thanks must go to Lisa Trowse, of Mindful Nature Photography, whose many glorious images on social media of the wildlife activity occurring in her garden during lockdown shaped Cassie's early experiences with nature.

As always, thank you to my editor, Laura Palmer, for providing excellent constructive criticism, which helped to hone the tale; Helena Newton who, once again, provided skilful copy editing – I'm thrilled she enjoyed the *intriguing magic realism aspects, local history and literary allusions woven into the story*; Amber Daalhuizen who, despite a power cut, achieved a timely proofread; and to the rest of Team Aria for bringing my words to the market.

Last, but not least, a heartfelt thanks to my beta readers, Sally Tunley, Claire Hainsworth and Helena Ancil for their insights and suggestions. Often writers become word- and plot-blind due to countless revisions and it's always beneficial for 'fresh eyes' to assess one's work. Also, I hope Sally and Claire enjoyed revisiting that wonderful thatched cottage on the North Cornish cliffs, because they, too, experienced the magic of 'Foxcombe Cottage' on that memorable holiday way back in the mists of time...

About the Author

O riginally from the Home Counties, Kate now resides in the diverse and inspirational county of Cornwall, which provides a glorious backdrop for much of her writing. Her career has encompassed travel, property and publishing and she currently divides her time between selling fabulous country piles that she can't afford and writing romantic suspense. Together with her ever-supportive husband, a gorgeous Arab horse and a newly acquired 'rescue' cat called Ollie, Kate lives in the beautiful Tamar Valley in a 200-year-old cottage that she (and said husband) painstakingly restored and which proved the inspiration for her third book with Aria.

Hello from Aria

We hope you enjoyed this book! If you did let us know, we'd love to hear from you.

We are Aria, a dynamic digital-first fiction imprint from award-winning independent publishers Head of Zeus. At heart, we're committed to publishing fantastic commercial fiction – from romance and sagas to crime, thrillers and historical fiction. Visit us online and discover a community of like-minded fiction fans!

We're also on the look out for tomorrow's superstar authors. So, if you're a budding writer looking for a publisher, we'd love to hear from you. You can submit your book online at ariafiction.com/we-want-read-your-book

You can find us at:
Email: aria@headofzeus.com
Website: www.ariafiction.com
Submissions: www.ariafiction.com/we-want-read-your-book

    @ariafiction
    @Aria_Fiction
    @ariafiction